Vurt

Vurt

Jeff Noon

CROWN PUBLISHERS, INC.
NEW YORK

Published by Crown Publishers, Inc., 201 East 50th Street, New York, New York 10022. Member of the Crown Publishing Group.

Random House, Inc. New York, Toronto, London, Sydney, Auckland

Originally published in Great Britain by Ringpull Press in 1993

CROWN is a trademark of Crown Publishers, Inc.

Manufactured in USA

Library of Congress Cataloging-in-Publication Data
Noon, Jeff.
Vurt / Jeff Noon.—1st ed.
p.   cm.
1. Brothers and sisters—England—Manchester—Fiction.
2. Manchester (England)—Fiction.   3. Virtual reality—Fiction.   I. Title.
PR6064.O45V87   1995
823'.914—dc20   94-25544
                                                                          CIP

ISBN 0-517-59991-0

10   9   8   7   6   5   4   3   2   1

First American Edition

For Nick

—totally feathered up, living on the dub side

Vurt

A young boy puts a feather into his mouth . . .

DAY 1

*'Sometimes it feels like the whole
world is smeared with Vaz.'*

S T A S H   R I D E R S

Mandy came out of the all-night Vurt-U-Want, clutching a bag of goodies.

Close by was a genuine dog, flesh and blood mix; the kind you don't see much any more. A real collector's item. It was tethered to the post of a street sign. The sign read NO GO. Slumped under the sign was a robo-crusty. He had a thick headful of droidlocks and a dirty handwritten card—'hungry n homeless. please help.' Mandy, all twitching steps and head-jerks, scurried past him. The crusty raised his sad little message ever so slightly and the thin pet dog whined.

Through the van's window I saw Mandy mouth something at them; 'Fuck off, crusties. Get a life.' Something like that.

I was watching all this in the halo of the night lights. We stuck to the dark hours in those days. The Thing was on board and that was a major crime; possession of live drugs, a five year stretch guaranteed.

We were waiting in the van for the new girl. Beetle was up front, ladies' leather gloves pulled tight onto his fingers, smeared with Vaz. He likes to feel a little bit greased when he rides. I was in the back, perched on the left side wheel housing, Bridget on the other, sleeping. Some thin wisps of smoke were rising from her skin. The Thing-from-Outer-Space lay between us, writhing on the tartan rug. He was leaking oil and wax all over the place, lying in a pool of his own juices.

I caught a movement in the air above the parking space.

Oh shit!

Shadowcop! Broadcasting from the store wall, working his mechanisms; flickering lights in smoke. And then the flash of orange; an inpho beam shining out from the shadowcop's eyes. It caught Mandy in its flare-path, gathering knowledge. She ducked down from the beam, banging, hard-core, on the van doors.

The dog was howling at the cop, scared by the lights.

I opened the doors a thin-girl measure. Mandy slipped through.

The dog went for the cop's legs, twin fangs closing on nothing but mist. That dog was confused!

Mandy handed me the bag.

'You got it?' I asked, dragging her inside.

A tangerine flare from outside, a burning light.

'Got some Beauties,' her answer, as she stepped over the Thing, into the van.

'You got the one?'

Mandy just looked at me.

Something was howling outside. I glanced back and saw the poor dog on fire, the shadowcop moving towards us, reloading.

He let loose a tight inpho, beaming onto our number-plate, which was just a series of random numbers anyway. *You won't find that in your banks.*

The Vurt-U-Want doors crashed open and a young man came stumbling through, looking scared.

'It's Seb,' whispered Mandy.

Two cops followed him out of the doors. Real-life versions. Fleshcops. They chased Seb over towards the wire fence that skimmed one edge of the car park. I turned around to the Beetle. 'It's a bust!' I shouted. 'Let's go, Bee! Out of here!'

And we were. Reversing first, away from the bollards. 'Watch it!' This from Mandy, nervous as fuck, as the van jerked backwards. She was thrown to the floor, landing on the Thing-from-Outer-Space. I was clinging to the straps. Brid was rudely pitched from sleep, pupils in shock from the sudden awakening. The Thing had six tentacles wrapped around Mandy. The girl was screaming.

The van leapt up onto a pavement. I thought the Beetle was trying to dodge the beams, maybe he was, but all we felt was the sickening thud and a yowling scream as the left back wheel put the collector's item out of its misery.

The crusty was crying over his dog and pushing his fists through the shadowcop's smoke as we scorched the forecourt. The van made a wild circle, and I saw the whole thing sliding by—the shadowcop, the crusty, the dead dog, until Beetle got it under control. Mandy was struggling with the Thing-from-Outer-Space, calling it all the names. Over the Beetle's shoulder I could see the wire fence coming up close. Seb was dropping down on the other side, down to the tramlines. The two fleshcops were struggling with the fence. Beetle turned on the headlights, catching them full-beam. He gunned the Stashmobile towards them, total, shouting out, 'Awoohhh!!! Kill the cops! Kill the cops!' The cops fell off the fence. Their faces in the headlights were a joy to behold; fleshcops, scared to fuck. They were running now, away from the van's bulk, but Beetle had it; he swung the wheel around like a true star, last moment, taking the Stashmobile all around the parking space, heading for the gateway. The debris of a thousand trips was banging and clattering all over the floor as we took a vicious U-turn onto Albany Road and then left onto Wilbraham Road. One last glimpse over the Vurt-U-Want wall and I could see the shadowcop beaming messages into the air. The robocrusty was a pile of fused plastic and flesh. A cop siren wailed through the darkness.

'They're onto us, Bee!' I cried. 'Hit the jam!'

Beetle took the brow at speed. Oh boy, were we flying! Stash Riders! Riding the feathers back to the pad. The point of impact squelched Mandy deeper into the Thing's embrace.

Mandy screaming at the Thing, 'Get the fuck off me!'

Keeping firm hold of the strap, I dropped the goody bag, and reached down with the free hand, jabbing at the Thing's belly flesh, tickling him. The one weak spot. How he loved that! His laughter was dredged up from deep inside, from thousands of miles. He was writhing around and Mandy was able to slide free. 'Fuck that! Jesus!' She was shaking from the fight.

Through the back windows I saw a cop car's lights flashing. Its siren was loud, piercing. The Beetle took the corner onto Alexandra Road without slowing. Brid was clinging to the straps, desperate for sleep, her skin full of shadows. The Thing-from-Outer-Space was crying out for a fix. Mandy had a tight hold of herself, and I had the goody bag back in my free hand. The Beetle had the wheel.

Everybody has to grab hold of something.

Alexandra Park was a dark jungle shimmering the right side windows. We were skirting Bottletown by now and no doubt the park was full of demons; pimps, pros, and dealers—real, Vurt, or robo.

'Cop car's closing, Beetle!' I shouted.

'Hang on, folks,' he replied, cool as ever, twisting the van into a tight right, onto Claremont Road.

'They're still with us,' I told him, watching the cop lights following.

Beetle burned all the way down, over the Princess Road, into the Rusholme maze. Cops were following, but they were up against three killer factors: Beetle had lover's knowledge of these streets, all moving engine parts were greased with Vaz, Beetle was hooked on speed. We hung on tight as he took a vicious series of lefts and rights. It was a tough job, hanging on, but we didn't mind. 'Do it, Bee!' cried Mandy, loving the adventure. Old-style terraces passed by, each side of us. On one of the walls someone had scrawled the words—Das Uberdog. And underneath that—pure is poor. Even I didn't know where we were. That's the Beetle for you. Total knowledge, fuelled by Jam and Vaz. Now he was driving us down a back alley, scraping paint off both sides of the Stashmobile. That's okay. The van could live with that. A quick glance through the back windows; there go the cops, speeding on by, towards some dumbfuck nowhere. Bye, bye, suckers! We came out of the alley, and there we were, the Moss Lane East. Beetle took another right, heading us back home.

'Slow down some, Bee,' I said.

'Fuck slowness!' he replied, burning the world with his wheels.

'We're like eggs back here, Beetle,' said Mandy. And the guy slowed us down, some. Well there you go; some things will slow the Beetle down; the chance of a new woman, for instance. Bridget must have had the same feeling; she was looking daggers at the new girl, smoke rising from her skin, as she tried her best to tune into the Beetle's head. I guess she wasn't getting too far.

No matter.

We were in some kind of easy travelling by now, so I picked up the goody bag, emptying the contents out on to the tartan rug. Five blue Vurt feathers floated down. I caught a few as they drifted, reading the printed labels.

'Thermo Fish!' I said. 'Done it.'

'How was I to know?' said Mandy.

I read another. 'Honey Suckers! Oh my shit! Where is it!?'

'Next time, Scribble,' Mandy said, 'you go shopping.'

'Where's English Voodoo? You promised me. I thought you had contacts?'

'That's what he had.'

I read the other three. 'Done it. Done it. Not done it, but it sounds boring anyway.' I'd let the feathers go in disgust. Now they were floating around inside the van.

Mandy's eyes were darting from feather to feather, as she spoke; 'These are very beautiful.'

'And the rest . . .' I said.

'What's that mean?'

'No messing. The whole bit. English Voodoo. Deliver.'

A blue feather had landed on the stomach of the Thing-from-Outer-Space. One of his tentacles reached out for it. His spiky fingers took a hold, and a hole opened up in his flesh, a greasy orifice. He turned the feather in his feelers and then stroked it in, direct, to the hole. He started to change. I wasn't sure which feather he'd loaded, but from the way he was moving his feelers I guess he was swimming with the Thermo Fish.

I sure know that wave.

The Beetle glanced back at the noise of the waves, shouting; 'He's going in alone! No one goes in alone!'

The Beetle had this obsession about doing Vurt alone. That you'd need help in there, friends in there. What he really meant was—you need me in there.

'Cool it, Bee,' I said. 'Just drive.' Just to spite me he put on a sudden spurt but I was holding tight to the straps. No problems.

I turned back to Mandy; 'Give!'

'You want?' said Mandy.

'I want. You found the Voodoo?'

We turned right onto the Wilmslow Road, as Mandy pulled a stash from the inner reaches of her denim jacket. It was a black feather. Totally illegal. 'No. But I found this . . .'

'What is it?'

'Seb called it Skull Shit. You think he got away?'

'Who gives a fuck! This is all you got?'

'Said it was red-hot. You don't like?'

'Sure. I like. It's just not what I want.'

'So make do.'

'Mandy!' I was losing it. 'I don't think you realise . . .'

Her red hair was catching fire from each passing streetlamp; I had to pull myself away from the flames.

That new girl was getting to me.

Behind the back of Vurt-U-Want, when the time was right, so Mandy said, you could buy a bootleg remix. The mainman was Seb. The supplier, so Mandy said. He worked the legit counter, with a nice little side-sweep in black market dreams. So Mandy said. So we'd sent the new girl after English Voodoo. Girl had come back with five cheap Blues and a vicious Black. Added all together—a thousand miles away from the Voodoo. Girl had failed.

The van took a sudden swerve and we were all thrown to the wall. The black feather slipped from Mandy's grip. The Thing made a swipe for it, but he was so wave-deep, pressed against the van side, his feelers were numb and he missed out.

I scooped the outlaw flight up into my palms. The van took another swing, no doubt dodging some dumbfuck pedheads. The Beetle was shouting through his window; 'Fucking walkers! Get a car!' He was driving like an insect; not thinking, just reacting. The guy was high. Cortex Jammers. You know how a fly flies? At the top speed always, and yet dodging obstacles instantaneously?

That was how the Beetle drove. They say don't jam and drive, but we had total belief in the master. He was jammed right out of fear, and that was beautiful.

I twisted the black feather around to read the label. It was handwritten, which always meant a good time.

'Skull Shit . . .'

'It's good?' asked Mandy.

'Is it good!? Oh come on!'

'You don't want?' she said.

'I've done it already.'

'No good?'

'Sure. It's fine. It's dandy.'

'Seb told me it was sweet.'

'Sure it's sweet,' I said. 'It's just not the Voodoo.'

The Beetle jam-reacted to the title. 'Did she get it, Scribble?'

'She did fuck.'

'Well bully!' spat Mandy.

'Yeah. Well fucking bully!' I told her.

'Hey, you two. Keep it quiet,' Bridget said, in that smoky voice of hers, the shadowgirl. 'Some of us are trying to get some sleep.' Bridget was Beetle's lover, and I guess she was just putting the new girl in her place.

'Sleep is for the dead,' replied Mandy. One of her slogans.

'Almost home,' announced the Beetle.

We were riding through Rusholme, straight down the curry chute. Mandy hand-cranked a window. She managed a half-inch gap before the mechanism failed, clogged up with rust. But through the tiny gap a rich complex of powder smells was making my tongue wet; coriander, cumin, cinnamon, cardamom—each of them genetically fine-tuned to perfection.

'Christ!' Mandy told the gang, 'I could kill a curry! When did we last eat?'

The Beetle answered; 'Thursday.'

'What day is it now?' slurred Bridget, from the half-lit world of Shadow.

'It's the weekend, sometime,' I said. 'At least I think it is.'

The Thing-from-Outer-Space was by now a blur of feelers and I could almost see the Thermo Fish swimming his veins. It was making me envious.

'Can anyone tell me why we're carrying this alien shit around?' asked Mandy. 'Why don't we just sell him? Or eat him?' The van went silent. 'I mean, why are we chasing around after feathers? We've got the Thing right here. We don't need feathers!'

'The Thing comes with us,' I told her. 'Nobody touches him!'

'You just want to make the swap,' Mandy replied.

'You got a problem with that, Mandy?' I asked.

'Let's just get home.' Her voice defiant. 'Let's take some stuff.'

'We will do.' I felt for her all of a sudden. She was new to us, two days old in the gang and full of the will to please.

It's just that she had a hard act to follow.

'I know I did bad in the Vurt-U-Want. I didn't know what to look for.'

'I told you, didn't I? Precisely?'

'Let's stay up all night playing Vurts,' she said. 'Let's make a meal from scraps in the fridge. Let's not go to bed.'

'We'll do all that,' I told her. *Anything to hold back the pain.*

We took a hard right turn into Platt Lane, and then another into the garage space behind the flat. The van scalded to a sudden halt. 'We're home,' announced the Beetle. Didn't we know it? Only the Thing was coping, his body full of wave-knowledge, Vurt-knowledge. He just sort of flowed into the doors and then away, loving it.

And then the voice . . .

'Scribble . . . Scribble . . . Scribble . . .'

Words floating upwards, from nowhere, calling my name.

'Scribble...'

Desdemona's voice...

I looked around to see who was playing the fool.

Oh shit. Nobody should use that voice. And I got a sudden flash then, of Desdemona falling away from me, through into a yellow blaze...

'Who said that?' I demanded.

'Said what, Scribble?' asked Mandy.

'My name! Who the fuck said it?'

A silence fell over the van.

'It was in... it was in Desdemona's voice...'

'Do we have to keep thinking about her?' asked Mandy.

'Yes.'

Yes we do. Keep thinking about Desdemona. Don't ever let her go. Not until I find her again. And then keep her forever.

I listened to the van settling its rust deposits.

The Riders were looking at me. Even the Beetle was twisted around, his eyes full of jam; 'Nobody said anything, Scribb.' But then I got it again, that voice.

'Scribble... Scribble...'

And I got where it was coming from; the Thing. A gash had opened in his flesh, a set of black gums peeled back from crumbling teeth, and a tongue of lard moving there, between them.

'Scribble...'

But only I could hear. Why was it only me, and why was he using that voice? That beautiful voice...

Beetle broke the mood; 'Let's do it! Inside!'

I heard an owl calling, from the Platt Fields. Real, Vurt, or robo—who can tell the difference any more?

No matter.

It had a longing to it.

G A M E   C A T

This week's safe selection, my kittlings. Status: blue and legal.

THERMO FISH. You went swimming in the Seas of Pitch. But now you're back on Earth and you're feeling slightly queasy. It can only get worse. Because the Thermo Fish of Pitch have invaded your system. Your blood stream is a river home for them. They love those passages. You're feeling the heat inside, the biting heat. One thing to do; buy yourself some nano-hooks, some pitchworm bait, go fishing for a week. You know the Game Cat doesn't lie.

HONEY SUCKERS are out to get you. They want you for supper. Six legs, four wings, two antennae and a demon sting. They'll cover your body with bites and turn you into a swarm. Only quork juice will save you. It turns the Honies to pulp. You better find some, and soon, because those bugs are coming. Trouble is, quorks live on the planet Jangle. The Cat says squirt those suckers!

F L E S H
T E C H N I Q U E S

We had to drag the Thing-from-Outer-Space out of the van, his fat sack of a body clinging to the tartan rug, glued by the juices.

Beetle opened the van's doors. 'Come on, lazy fucks,' he shouted, reaching into the back to gather the dropped feathers from the van floor. One of them, the black, he slipped into his baccy box. 'I feel like tripping out somewhere.' He was walking fast towards the house.

The pad was on the top floor of the Rusholme Gardens. Sure, it was in Rusholme but no trace of a garden. Just an old-style block of flats on the corner of Wilmslow and Platt.

The doorcam reacted to Beetle's image in a loving way, opening its gates in a slow, seductive swing. Brid was back in shadow mode, sleep-walking to the step-light, so that left me and Mandy holding the can. The can was the Thing and he was like Vaz between our fingers. Oh boy, Thing was hot; totally adventurous. Respect to that.

'Let's move it, Big Thing,' I said.

The Desdemona calls had stopped. Now he was rambling in his own language. Xa Xa Xa! Xhasy Xhasy! Stuff like that. Maybe he was travelling the Vurt-waves, looking for a new home. Maybe I'm some kind of romantic fool, especially when the Manchester rain starts to fall in memory and I'm scribbling this down, chasing the moments. Bridget used to say that the rain around there was special, that something had gone wrong with the city's climate. That you always thought it was just about to start raining, but it always was, anyway. All I know is that looking back I *swear* I can feel it falling on me, on my skin. That rain means everything to me, all of the past, all that has been lost. I can see big spots of rain on the gravel. Over the road the black trees of Platt Fields Park are whispering and swaying, receiving the gift of water gratefully. The moon is a thin knife, a curved blade. Miles from there, and years and years later, I can still feel that slow struggle towards the flat door.

Thing-from-Outer-Space wasn't really from Outer Space. Mandy just called him that, and we'd all latched onto it. Well then, what would you call a shapeless blob that didn't speak any known language and that had come into your world by a bad accident? Tough one, huh?

'Stop dropping him!' hissed Mandy, her voice heavy from the exertion. The rain had plastered her red hair flat to her brow.

'Does it look like I'm dropping him?'

'His head's on the floor!'

'Is that his head? I thought it was his tail.'

Mandy was getting angry at me, as though I should enjoy carrying aliens over wet gravel, in the dark, in the rain. As though I should know all the various techniques of carrying aliens.

'Keep a hold of him!' she screamed.

'Keep a hold of what? He's all slippery.'

Just then a shadowcop flickered into life, broadcasting from the Platt Fields' aerial. He moved like a fog, the starry lights of his mechanisms going on and off, on and off, as he drifted through the trees. I told Mandy to get a move on.

'Look who's talking about speed,' she replied.

We had to bend the Thing into a strange shape to get him through the house doors, a kind of Mobius knot variant. The Thing didn't mind; his body was super-fluid anyway, from the embrace of Vurt. A quick glance over the shoulder told me that the shadowcop was out of the park and heading towards the flats. I slammed the door on the sight. Silence. Pause. A catch of breath. The look of despair in Mandy's eyes, naked eyes under the hall lights, her arms straining to hold the weight of alien meat. 'Shit!' I said. 'We forgot the rug.' The Thing was naked in our hands.

'How did we get here?' Mandy asked.

'What?'

'Why is it always like this?'

'Never mind that. Keep going.'

Above us, on the next landing, Brid was drifting with the shadows, trailing smoke. 'Follow her,' I said.

It was like carrying a bad dream up a flight of greasy collapsing stairs.

Sometimes it feels like the whole world is smeared with Vaz.

'Are you after the Beetle?' I asked, halfway up the first flight.

'Beetle? Don't be daft.'

'Oh good. Because Bridget would kill you.'

'Seb told me something.'

'Oh yeah?' I managed, between panting breaths.

'There's a new delivery, tomorrow.'

'Of what?'

'New stuff. Good stuff, he said. Bootlegs. Well black.'

'Voodoo's not black. I told you that.'

'Yes, English Voodoo. Seb—'

'He's got it!? Mandy!'

'Not yet. Coming in tomorrow—'

'Mandy! This is—'

'Watch out! The Thing! He's . . .'

I was dropping the alien. My hands were too sweaty. I was losing the world. A feather was floating in my mind. A beautiful multicoloured specimen. I almost had it! Just reach out!

'Scribble!' Mandy's voice calling me back down. 'What's wrong with you?'

'I need it, Mandy! No messing. We've got to find Seb again.'

'Not him. He gave me the contact name. Said that Icarus was getting a new delivery.'

'Icarus?'

'Icarus Wing. That's his source. Seb's supplier. You know him?'

I'd never heard of him. 'Mandy, why didn't you say this before?'

'Would have done. Just the cops . . . and all that . . . the shadow-cop . . . the dog. Scribble, I got confused. I . . . I'm sorry . . .'

I looked at her then, her greasy scarlet hair a mess from the rain, a last smudge of paint on her bottom lip. Oh sure, no great beauty under the harsh light of a stairwell, face creased from the carrying of that lump of alien flesh, but my heart was calling out a song, a kind of love song, I guess. Christ knows, it had been a long time without singing.

'Do you think Seb will be alright?' she asked.

'Find him, Mandy. Ask him about English Voodoo—'

'I don't think he'll be working that Vurt-U-Want counter any more.'

'Don't you know where he lives?'

'No. He's very secretive . . . Scribb!' Mandy's eyes in shock mode.

'What? What is it?'

'Over there! The corner—'

We'd reached the first landing by now. There was a store
cupboard set into the wall. It was marked NO GO. In the dark
space between it and the wall lay a coil of rope, a violet and green
rope. It moved. Sudden like.

'It's a snake!' screamed Mandy. *Oh fuck!* Just then the lights
went out.

Bastard landlord had them on a strict timer and the next switch
was some two feet away, down the landing. Two feet's a long
way to go when you're carrying an alien and it's dark and there's
a dreamsnake on the loose.

'Don't panic!' I said to her, in the dark.

'Turn on the fucking light!'

'Don't move!'

Mandy dropped the Thing. I still had my hands under one end,
and I felt the weight jerk as the bulk hit the floor. Mandy was
running to the next switch. Snakes can see in the dark, but we
can't. *So hit that switch, new girl!* I was sweating with the fear and
the Thing was starting to slip from my fingers. The lights came
back on but it wasn't Mandy who'd hit the switch. The woman
from 210 had come out to see the noise and she'd got to the
switch first. This is what she saw: Mandy, frozen, two inches from
the control, me holding on for dear life to a pulsating mess of
feelers and grease, a whip-fast coil of violet and green slithering
to the nearest shadow.

I felt a nagging pain in my left leg, just where I'd been bitten.
But that was over four years ago. *So why the pain?* Memory can
be a right bitch sometimes.

The woman just stared at us for two seconds and then started
to scream; 'Arghhhh!!!!!!!!!!!!!' It was a knife-hot screeching, high
and loud. The noise shot down the corridors, threatening a mass
stepping-out.

Mandy hit the woman.

I'd never seen her violence until then. Only thought about it.

The woman was knocked into silence. I could imagine all of the occupants quaking in their beds from the scream, and then its sudden termination. Hopefully they would stay scared.

'What is it?' the woman said at last.

Mandy looked at me. I looked at Mandy, then at the Thing in my weakening hands, then at the woman.

'It's a prop,' I said.

She looked at me.

'We're part of an avant garde theatre company. We're called Drip Feed Theatre. *Say what!* We're doing a new piece entitled English Voodoo . . .'

'That's right,' said Mandy, coming out of shock.

'We're very experimental and wild. We've had this . . . uh . . . this . . . thing . . . made for us by a mad artist. He made it out of old tyres and a ton of animal fat. We're just taking delivery.

'Do you like it?' chipped in Mandy.

The woman just kept on looking, maybe building up to another screaming session.

'We live in 315,' I said. 'Say, do you want to come up? We're having some friends round. We're going to rehearse the play. Fancy it?'

'Oh my God, how gross!' the woman said, before slipping back inside of her flat, slamming the door.

Mandy and I smiled.

We smiled. And something passed between us.

Don't ask what.

'Has the snake gone?' Mandy asked.

Dreamsnakes came out of a bad feather called Takshaka. Any time something small and worthless was lost to the Vurt, one of these snakes crept through in exchange. Those snakes were taking over, I swear. You couldn't move for them.

'It's gone. Hit the switch one more time. Let's finish this.'

* * *

So we climbed the stairs together. Two humans, one alien strung heavy between them, and we managed to get to the second landing before the lights went out again. We clattered down the corridor, Mandy going for the switch with one hand, the other desperately trying to hold onto the slippery flesh. No luck. *There's never any luck!* The Thing hit the floor like a sack of meat pulp. The darkness was thick, and full of breathings.

'Do the lights, new girl.'

'I can't—'

'Do it.'

'I can't find it.'

'Get out of the way—'

Just then her fingers found the switch.

The light came on for an instant, then was gone, with a flat pop of burn-out. Bulb gone. In the brief flare we both saw the rapid flicking of violet and green.

'Snake!' I was screaming. 'Move it! Move it!'

We hauled the Thing up and dragged him along, as best we could, which wasn't that good, and more or less manhandled that meat towards the haven of flat 315. I smashed into the door, expecting hard response, but the way was open, well open, as we fell through, all three of us; male, female, alien. Mandy kicked the door shut with a neat back-heel and we collapsed into one shivering heap on the hall carpet.

The snake's head was trapped in the door and the Beetle walked through from the kitchen, carrying a breadknife.

He cut that fucker off.

G A M E   C A T

This week's black selection:

SKULL SHIT is one heavy fuck. Don't try it alone, kittlings. This Vurt is going to blast you. You'll be travelling the paths of your own mind, and that's some maze in there. There's a beast at the centre and it's angry. Only the chosen know what the beast looks like, because only the chosen get that far.

The Cat's been there, of course, and lived to write the review, but I wouldn't wish the sight on my children (if I had any). Unless they're ultra-brats, in which case . . . feed them this. Skull Shit aka The Synapse Murders, Head Fuck, Temple Vomit, Id Slayer. Call it what you like, do what you like; remember the rule: Be careful. Be very, very careful. Not for the weak.

Note: possession of this beauty can land you a two year stretch. That's a load of game-time to be missing, so stay cool. Keep it close. This Cat has warned you.

(S O M E   S E R I O U S)
S K U L L   S H I T

Brid was slumped on the settee, slow-gazing at a two-week-old copy of the Game Cat. Beetle was standing by the window, leafing through the feather stash. He had the snake head pinned to his jacket lapel. I had the right side of my face laid out on the dining table, my left eye fixed on a small lump of apple jam. I was getting my gear back together. That was a hard ride. The Thing-from-Outer-Space was lying on the floor, waving for a fix, his grease dripping onto Bridget's Turkish rug. Mandy was in the kitchen, eating bread and honey.

Yeah, sure! And the King was in his counting house, counting out his money. *No doubt.* Except that we'd just trashed a week's dripfeed on five lousy Blues and a single done-it-already Black. Sure, the Beetle could sell some low-level Vurt to a robo-crusty. Or maybe I could persuade Brid to sing some smoky songs in one of the locals, me on keyboards and decks, but the shadowcops were everywhere. Most pubs had one, broadcasting from above the Vurtbox, shining inpho all over undesirables. Those inphobeams could match a face up to the Cop Banks in half a nanosec.

Everybody was afraid of the shadowcops. There was this rumour going around that they could beam right into your brains, reading your thoughts there, just like a shadowgirl could do. Not true. They were just roboshads; taking in only what their beams could see, which was only the everyday surfaces. Don't believe the hype; shadowcops ain't got soul.

DEAR SIR, WE HAVE REASON TO BELIEVE THAT YOU ARE CURRENTLY RECEIVING BASIC NEEDS ALLOWANCE. *Who the fuck doesn't take dripfeed these days?* WE HOPE YOU ARE NOT RECEIVING PAYMENT FOR TONIGHT'S PERFORMANCE. I would look over to the bar, seeking assistance from the landlady. She would be hiding her face in a jar of Fetish. THIS WOULD BE IN DIRECT VIOLATION OF DECREE 729. PLEASE DISCLOSE.

Of course, officer. Straight away. *I think not.*

That apple jam sure looked tasty. Boy, we were hungry!

Mandy came back out of the kitchen, clutching a doorstopper sandwich. She plumped herself down on a scatter cushion. We were all there, all five of us, the Stash Riders, in some form of life or other. The Beetle turned to face us, the five blue feathers clutched in one hand. He took each Blue into his other hand, saying their names out loud, each in turn, and then let them fall to the carpet. 'Thermo Fish. Crack Flowers. Venus Dust. Thunderwings. Honey Suckers . . .' We watched the feathers drift. Beetle turned directly to Mandy; 'Cheap Blues,' he said. 'We don't do cheap Blues—'

'I had to buy something,' cried Mandy. 'You can't just go in the shop, ask for black feathers! Seb would've laughed—'

'You got the hots for this shop guy?' Beetle asked. Mandy just

turned away. The Beetle opened his baccy box, took out the black
feather. He moved towards us, waving that Vurt like a dream
ticket. 'So. For tonight's entertainment . . . Skull Shit.' His lips
were smiling. It was a wicked smile.

Mandy turned back to face him; 'Christ, if I'd known it was
going to be like this—'

'You want this, don't you, Scribble?' The Beetle asked, totally
cutting her out.

'It's not the Voodoo, Bee,' I said.

'I don't believe you guys!' Mandy butting in.

'No, it's not the Voodoo,' the Beetle drawled. 'But it's all we've
got. And the Beetle needs succour. Let's take some feather!'

Mandy opened her mouth immediately, like she had something
to prove. The Beetle pushed the feather into her mouth, until he
could stroke it against the back of her throat. New girl took it all
the way, like a Pornovurt star, and her eyes started to glaze. 'See
how she takes it?' said the Beetle. 'Smooth and easy. That's my
baby.' Beetle pulled the feather out, and then turned to Bridget.

Brid was lying on the couch, face covered by the copy of Game
Cat. 'Can I miss this one?' she asked, in that smoky voice. 'I'm
not up to it, Bee. I'd like to just settle down with Co-operation
Street.'

Co-op Street was a real low-level blue Soapvurt. You bought
it every Monday, Wednesday, and Friday. It took you to a small
Northern terrace, gave you a house to live in, gave you a home
and a husband or a wife, and you got to interact with all the
famous characters as their epic stories unfolded. Seemed like the
whole world was hooked up to it. Except for the Dodos of
course; those few poor flightless birds, who could take feathers
down to the stomach, and still not feel a flutter. Officially they
were known as the Vurtually Immune, but the kids called them
Dodos, and it stuck. I had met one years ago and the look of
despair in his eyes would never leave me.

'Nobody misses nothing,' Beetle said, scrunching the paper from Brid's face, and then forcing the feather into her mouth. *Shit! That was face rape!* But I was too weak to do anything. Next he turned to the Thing, feeding the feather into the nearest orifice. The Thing was rolling all over the carpet; I swear I could almost hear him cheering. Then he turned to me.

'Scribble . . .' The Beetle's voice calling to me, over the years.

'I'm not into it, Bee,' I said. 'I just want to find Voodoo—'

'Nobody misses out,' he replied.

'Desdemona . . .'

'We'll find her.'

'There's some Voodoo coming in, tomorrow . . . Mandy told me. Let's wait—'

'Fuck waiting! Take it!'

He forced my mouth wide open; the fingers of one hand squeezing my cheeks, the other hand pushing the feather home, deep, to the back of the throat. I could feel it there, tickling, making me want to gag. And then the Vurt kicked in. And then I was gone. I felt the opening advurts roll, and then the credits. The pad went morphic and my last thoughts were; *Why are we doing this? Skull Shit? It's so low-level, it's even got advurts in it. We should be going higher, searching for lost love.* Instead we were just playing, just playing at—

Screaming down tunnels of brain flesh, putting thoughts together, building words and cries, cries from the heart. Electric impulses, leading me on, the room wallpapered in reds and pinks, blood all flowing down from the ceiling. Brid hiding behind the settee. The Beetle taking Mandy from behind on the Turkish rug. A Thing-from-Outer-Space floating in the air, gently landing on the dining table. Me walking through a swamp of flesh towards the kitchen door, in search of breakfast cereal. Stepping over Beetle and Mandy, finding the kitchen door locked and barred, looking just

like a wall of beef. Blood pulsing from the keyhole. Brid coming
out from behind the settee, clutching a breadknife. The Thing
finding a lump of jam on the table top. Licking at it. I wanted that
jam for myself. Jam turning into spunk, apple spunk. Thing licking
at it. Me turning to the lovemakers. Brid taking slices out of the
Thing's backside, trying to feed them to me. Me turning my face
away from the pink flesh. Didn't know why. Flower clock reading
twenty petals to eleven. Beetle shooting apple cum. It splattered
over my poster of Interactive Madonna at Woodstock Seven.
Mandy coming with him. Brid turning the blade into Beetle's neck.
Blood flowing from Beetle's neck. Me licking up the blood. Tasted
like apple jam. Tasted like Vurt. Just like a dream. Tasted like a
dream. That means . . . *oh shit!*

Sudden scream.

*Shit! I was getting Haunted! That means . . . that means we're in the
Vurt!*

Now it was the alien making love to Mandy. And the Beetle
was on the table covered, head to toe, in that apple jam. Acid
jam. Jam was burning him. He was shrieking. I was just watching.
Brid was turning the blade inside her wrist. And it was getting to
me. Like this is all too much. It can't be real. Those kind of feelings.
The Haunting! There's another life somewhere. *This isn't the only
one!*

'This isn't real, Bee!' I think I was shouting. The Beetle just
looking at me, his lips covered with apple jam, that smirk on his
face—

'Beetle! Listen to me! We're in the Vurt! I'm getting the
Haunting!

The Haunting was the feeling you got sometimes, in the Vurt;
the real world calling you home. *There's more to life than this.* This
is just a game.

The Beetle just kept on tasting the jam, rolling it on his tongue.

He reached out to stroke Mandy's arm, as she plunged the knife into her veins. The blood was spraying over Interactive Madonna, mixing with the spunk already plastered there.

I guess that dead star was really interacting now.

And then Mandy had Desdemona's face, and it was Desdemona doing the screaming. The blood pouring out of her beautiful mouth. It was too much for me. I had to get out of there.

Sudden jerk! Backwards!

Ghost grabbing me, under the armpits, jerking me into reality and then the real world breaking open. A locked door being axed open. Me screaming backwards, into the clock-face. Two fingers of time grabbing me, the hour and the minute hands . . .

The chair receiving my body like a corpse. Blood seeping back into the closing wounds on the wall. The room a scream of pain. A glass vase, containing flowers picked by Brid, in shatters, broken by the jerk. A voice calling from the mirror on the wall . . .

'Who the fuck!'

Beetle's voice.

'Who the fuck? Who the fuck jerked out?'

No answers.

Beetle was wide-screening us all, his eyes still covered with layers of flesh, of game-flesh. He had a raging full-on and he was waving it like a flag.

'Who the fuck! Any answers?'

Nothing.

Brid on the settee, Game Cat torn into shreds. Mandy on the floor, beside the scatter cushion. Two vicious gashes had torn it apart. Feathers floating.

'I was having a good time in there!' the Beetle said.

I was trapped in the chair. Through a haze of feathers and flesh, the desperate shapes of Vurt still clinging on to life, I could just about make out the Thing-from-Outer-Space. He was screaming and shaking, watching the cushion feathers fall, waving his feelers in a mad dance, thinking them Vurt feathers. He stuffed a dozen or so into various holes that had opened up in his flesh. Then spat them all out. Man, he was suffering, and I could see the holes in his flesh where the knife had cut. The Thing was always affected badly by Vurt. But the wounds were healing over, regenerating. This was the Thing's special skill; total flesh replacement. But still he was suffering. Everything goes wrong. *Eventually, everything goes wrong.* I still couldn't move, just listening to his keening. The Thing just wanted to be home and peaceful. What the fuck were we going to do with him?

'Who the fuck pulled out?'

'Not me, Bee,' I managed. Lying. Scared.

'I was having a good fucking time! Nobody takes me out like that! Nobody!'

Silence then. Each of us looking at him. The last glaze of Vurt falling from him, from all of us and the room was suddenly cold, cold and lonely, and full of aftershock.

Pulling out was bad. Real bad. It was a built in-option with low-level theatres but nobody liked doing it. It was like admitting defeat. Like you weren't strong, not up to it. Who dared admit that? Even worse, you pulled all the other players out with you. And that was painful. That was like being skinned.

'It was me.' Brid's lonely voice. 'I was scared, Bee.'

'The fuck you were!'

'Bee!'

'That's the point. Tell me. Isn't that the point?'

'That's the point, Beetle,' answered Mandy.

'Scribble?'

'That's the point, Bee. That's the point of Skull Shit. It gets you scared.'

I was ashamed . . .

Beetle hit Brid right across the lips.

She was crying in the corner now and if I could've just got out of that chair, well then, maybe I would have done some good deed for a change. Maybe I would have killed the bastard.

. . . ashamed at my weakness.

Maybe everything. End up with nothing.

The Beetle gathered up every Vurt feather he could find and rammed the whole bunch down the Thing's throat.

At least one of us would have a good night.

Beetle left us then, slamming his bedroom door behind him. Me, the shadow, the new girl, the alien. And everything going wrong and the far off call of the owl.

If they can remix Madonna after she's dead, why can't they remix the night?

Who can answer that one?

G A M E C A T

Awake, you know that dreams exist. Inside a dream you think the dream *is* reality. Inside a dream you have no knowledge of the waking world.

It is the same with Vurt. In the real world we know that Vurt exists. Inside the Vurt we think that Vurt *is* reality. You have no knowledge of the real world.

THE HAUNTING. This is the bitch incarnate. Once that ghost has got hold of you, you just gotta go with her. Back to life, back to the boredom. That's how you feel, right? Except that the Haunting isn't a bad thing. What? What's that the Cat's saying? Haunting isn't bad? Man, the Cat's losing it! Listen up, kittlings.

Only a chosen few get the Haunting. They are the edge riders. Those strange people who can't make their minds up; just what am I? This is their question. Vurt or real? The Haunted are of both worlds; they flicker between the two, like fire flies. What are they? Insect or flame? Both! Believe it. The Haunted are special. They just don't know it yet. The Cat's advice to them; resist the temptation; don't jerk out. Jerking out is giving in. Giving up. Giving up on your true vocation.

The Haunting is calling you; come up, come up! Let me take you higher. The Vurt wants you.

The Cat wants you.

S L E E P L E S S

I was. I was sleepless. Locked in my room, writing all this up in the ledger of those days. Living up to my name. Scribbling. Trying to make sense of it all, and trying hard to find a way out.

And now I'm looking back and thinking. And the thinking makes me weary. It's the loss of things that kills us. And of the four humans in that pad that night, only two of us are still living and that's a bad dream come true. That shouldn't happen any more. Vurt should have taken all of our bad dreams and turned them into theatre, brilliant theatre.

I was scribbling late into the ledger, listening with half a mind to the creaking bed through the wall. Beetle making love to Brid, to the sleeping Brid. Despite the arguments, I knew this would happen, knowing the score.

And then a soft knock on my bedroom door. I opened it a

crack and there was Brid, anyway, standing there, and the noises of love still coming from the next room.

'Scribble?' she said, her eyes heavy lidded, voice clogged by smoke.

'I'm working, Brid,' was all I could manage, still listening to the noises.

'Beetle's with Mandy,' she said.

'Sounds like it.' I was trying my best to be uncaring, it's just that the shadows in her eyes made me melt.

'Can I come in?' she asked and I let her walk past me into the room. She dropped onto the bed and then started to curl up like a flower's petals when the sun has gone. I went back to my table to carry on with the writing.

Brid was breathing sweetly now, lost in sleep.

I was putting it all down in words, a small desklamp hiding me in a shadow. The glow of my ledger burning softly as I banked up the words, the stories.

'What are you writing, Scribb?' I thought she was asleep and when I looked at her she was comatose and happy, eyes shut, curled up in her own shape. I couldn't see her lips move and then I realised, Brid was dream-talking, putting thoughts into my mind, which is the gift of the Shadows.

Shadows are the thought-readers. They are born with the powers of telepathy and their mind can by-pass the vocal cords, putting words into your brain, and stealing the secrets that you thought were yours alone. Shadowcops are the same, but mixed up with robo, rather than flesh, so they're not as strong; they can't go deep down, into the soul. Still pretty scary though, especially when you're out on a spree. The human Shadow works best when asleep, so that's how you find them, usually, dreaming their dreams of knowledge.

'Don't let it worry you, Scribble,' Bridget thought.

'I'm not.'

'I was just wondering...you're always writing. What's it all about?'

'Everything,' I answered, out loud.

'You don't have to talk,' she said, except that the words just formed themselves into my mind. I looked at her again, her sleeping face, and I knew what she meant.

'This is weird,' I thought. Just thought!

'What do you mean, everything?'

'Everything that happens.'

'Between us?'

'Sure. The Stash Riders.'

The Beetle called us this, and it stuck. He was making life into a kind of adventure, I guess. Just like a kid, but what's so wrong with that? That's the score with Cortex Jammers; they just want to be kids again.

'It's our story,' I thought.

'That's nice,' she answered.

And then a deep silence. Just the sound of her breathing in my head and the soft petals falling off my alarm clock as it shed the minutes away until morning.

I was back to writing but nothing came out, nothing good, so I stopped, took a cigarette, a Napalm filter, and watched the smoke drift for a while. And petals falling from the clock. Stuff like that. All quiet now from the next room.

Brid's voice coming into my mind again; 'Is it all right if I sleep here, Scribb?'

'You've got a bed of your own.'

'Not tonight, Scribb. Not tonight.'

I took another few hard drags whilst forming the words in my mind.

'That's all right, Scribb. It's a pleasure.'

Shit! Some real dirty thoughts about Brid had flickered across my mind. When the shadowgirl was this deep, I had no secrets left.

'That's right, Scribb. No secrets.'

'Give me a chance, Brid!' I said. Out loud, not thinking.

Brid's voice in my head again; 'It just comes in pictures. Pictures and shapes.'

'I'd rather just talk.'

'Sure. You don't mind me sleeping here?'

Why should I? She looked real beautiful in sleep, and the world was waiting for me to climb right on in there, curling up, losing myself in all that drifting smoke.

'Thank you,' she thought.

Like I said; no secrets.

'I just wanted to thank you,' I told her sleeping face. 'For taking the rap for me. You know, with the Beetle, in the Skull Shit.'

'We all jerk out sometimes.'

'You took the blame, Brid.'

'I guess I like you.'

'More than Beetle?'

'Don't ask. You'll get hurt.'

'I saw Desdemona in there. In the Vurt.'

'I guessed that.'

'She was in such pain. I couldn't stop pulling out. But I couldn't admit it, not to the Bee.'

'You like that man too much, Scribble.'

'So do you.'

'You're thinking about her again.' She meant Desdemona. Bridget's words floating into my mind, like a mist over the pale shape of Desdemona; 'Can't you forget her, Scribble?'

'We've got to find her, Brid!'

'We will, Scribble,' said Brid's voice. 'You want to sleep next to me?'

It wasn't a question. Because she knew the answer anyway. And the mist closing it all up, in drifts of blue, and me falling through it into the land of Bridget, which is called the land of Shadows, the land of sleep.

I woke up early, my arms around the shadowgirl; an innocent gesture, for an innocent night. The ledger was still glowing, throwing a blue shade over our shapes. I turned it off and went into the living room.

The Thing-from-Outer-Space was asleep on the rug, with his mouthful of feathers and a grin on his peaceful face. 'How you doing, Big Thing?' I asked.

'Xhasy! Xha xha. Xhasy. Xha!'

Looking for a way home. Something like that, I guess.

'You got anything else from Des, Big Thing?'

'Xhasy. Xhasy. Xha!'

No.

I watched him for a while, imagining the dreams he was on, and then walked into the kitchen for breakfast. The house was mine at this hour and I made good use of it, spreading apple jam on toast and watching the day begin.

I ate the sweet stuff at the scarred table, all the time keeping a close watch on the door to Beetle's room. They were making noises again and I couldn't stop my mind wandering, right on in there, seeing all that pleasure being given and taken, all those jars of Boudoir Vaz being used. Protector, lubricator, contraceptive, inflamer; all in the same jar. The noises were getting to me. It brought back Desdemona, her beautiful body all over mine. Her hands and her lips. The dragon tattoo. Her face coming close to mine, the feel of her skin, the shine in her eyes.

But that was just a memory. And memory was not enough. I wanted her back, for real. In my arms.

I looked over at the Thing again.

Something bad was coming into my mind.

I got up out of the chair and walked over to his sleeping form. Boy, that Thing was ugly! I reached down to tickle his stomach. He sighed contentedly, from the depths of Vurt sleep. There was a loose flap of skin, still not yet fully re-formed from the battles of Skull Shit. It broke off easily in my fingers. The Thing didn't even stir. I brought the greasy lump up to my lips.

Eating Vurt flesh was the direct route to the theatre. It was a potent cocktail of meat and dreams. Highly dangerous. Highly desirable. The Game Cat had talked about it once, in the maga-zine. I was looking down at more than a King's ransom of live drugs, street value. We could sell the Thing, and get ourselves right out of here, somewhere good. All except for Desdemona; without the Thing she was lost for ever. But maybe this would lead back to her. Maybe I could take some flesh, just a little bit, see where it lead? The Cat had said that it just took you back to where the Vurt creature came from. I didn't know where the Thing came from. But maybe from there I could find a door through to Desdemona. Maybe. Game Cat had warned against it, saying it was a sucker's trip, that it led to wild, uncontrollable games, mutant theatre.

The Cat had said no. That was good enough for me. And the Beetle would be real mad if he found me going in alone. He would beat me. The Cat and the Beetle said no, and that was good enough for me.

Anyway maybe the Thing came from a yellow feather. They are the highest feathers; you can't jerk out of them, you can only win the game. Or die. I really didn't want to chance that.

I licked at the Vurt flesh, and then took a small bite . . .

* * *

I'm being smothered by flesh. I can't breathe any more. There is no space in the world, only flesh. It has a sweet aroma, as it presses up against my face. I can't do anything, I can't even struggle, the flesh is that powerful. The sweet smell stirs a memory in me. There is no way out now. this is my life; to be slowly smothered by thick sweet-smelling lard! I can't even scream. When I try to, the flesh just comes into my mouth, filling me with its aroma. My world is clogged. I know that smell from somewhere. I am drowning in the flesh. These are my last seconds alive. The sweet stench is overpowering me. I know that smell! I have smelt it all my life. This is my life. No! Before then. I have smelt that stench before now. In some other . . .

Christ!

I'm getting the Haunting!

The flesh enveloping me. All of my openings filled with the meat. I'm being killed by Vurt flesh.

Vurt! I'm in a Vurt. Which one? Let me do a jerkout!

The flesh of the Thing wrapping me in fat. I've got no breath left. These are my last seconds . . .

The Thing! Christ! Hope it's not a Yellow.

Jerkout!

I'm lying across the Thing, right in front of the fire. The Thing has got its tentacles around me, squeezing. I can hardly breathe. Let me tell you; hardly is enough. At least it's stale, unhealthy Stash Rider pad air that I'm breathing. That is enough. That is beautiful. I slide out of the Thing's sleepy embraces, falling onto the pad floor.

The carpet is most welcome, a real haven of bliss.

Above me the ceiling dances with pictures. Desdemona had painted them there; images of dragons and snakes, all writhing around a sharpened blade. That was her mind. And I was part of it.

Let us concentrate on the days to come, all the good things to come. Stash Riders finding English Voodoo, for instance. Riders getting the Thing back to his home planet. Swapping him over, for Desdemona. Riders getting out of this junk palace, getting a good life. Bridget finding a better love than the Beetle. The Beetle finding something, something to cling to.

All the things that we had to get done.

And the petals falling from the clock.

Just then the telephone rang. It sounded harsh and ill against the murmurings of love, and I could tell it had bad news to give, because that phone had been cut off, unpaid, some six months ago. No way could it be ringing! I jumped up from the floor, and reached it on what seemed like the last ring—

'Scribble!'

The voice.

'Desdemona!'

'Scribble . . .'

'Is that you, Desdemona?'

'Scribble. Help me.'

Oh Jesus, Desdemona . . .

'Help me, Scribble.'

'Where are you?'

'Find me! It hurts. The razor . . .'

'Where are you, Des?'

'A curious . . .' Her voice was drifting off, into the Vurt spaces.

'Curious? Curious what? Des?'

No answer. Just the waves of static coming through, wave against wave, yellow on yellow; I could hear the colours!

'Talk to me, Des! For fuck's sake!'

'Find a door . . . a curious house . . .'

'What?'

The voice just a whisper. 'Find a door . . .'

'Where? Where to?' I was shouting now.

'Get to me, Scribble . . . get to me . . .'

The way through was dying in my hands.

'Des! Talk to me! Talk to me . . .'

Silence.

Oh Desdemona. Sister, oh sister. Where are you going?

I had my ear pressed up hard against the phone, but there was nothing. Nothing there. Just a bad buzz on the line. And the silence in the room.

And the petals falling, falling, from the face of the clock, making a carpet of flowers, where I would lay myself down, forgetting all my troubles.

All my troubles . . .

G A M E   C A T

It has been calculated, by the calculators, that one night can hold SIX DREAMS only. There is a colour for each, a feather for each. BLUE is the colour of safe desires, legal dreaming. BLACK is the colour of bootleg Vurt, feathers of tenderness and pain, one sliver beyond the law. PINK is the colour of Pornovurts, doorways to bliss. CREAM is the colour of a used-up feather, one that has been drained of dreams. Only blue, black, and pink feathers go cream. The makers build this property in to the flights, just to make sure you come back for more. You only get one trip per journey. SILVER is the colour of the operators; those who work the feathers—making them, filming them, doing the remixes, opening doors. They are the toolkit feathers, and the Game Cat has a collection worth dying for. YELLOW is the colour of death, and should be avoided at all costs. They are not for the weak. Yellows have no jerkout facilities. Be careful. Be very, very careful. If you die in a yellow dream, you die in real life. The only way out is to finish the game.

DAY 2

'Good dreams of bad things.'

WEARING DANGEROUS SMILES

I was watching the world through tears.

Mandy and the Beetle had emerged, two o'clock in the afternoon, from a damp bed, and were now taking late breakfast at the table. Mandy's cheeks were glowing like an ad. You know the kind of thing—SEX IS GOOD FOR YOU—DO IT EVERY DAY. THIS HAS BEEN A GOVERNMENT INFORMATION MESSAGE. Beetle was his usual self; hair gelled slick-back with Vaz, his Peter England shirt hot-pressed to the limit. He was shaved to the edge, and the tangy aroma of Showbiz arose from his skin like the smell of celebrities at a first night party. Both of them looked fruity from the afterglow of sex, and I just couldn't take it, couldn't take the fresh love. The Beetle was cleaning his gun at the table, smearing Vaz into the chambers. I guess he was doing it to impress the new girl. It worked.

'Is that real, Bee?' she asked. 'Neat!'

Oh like, wow.

The Beetle's gun was a joke really. He'd bought it off some old acquaintance, a real bargain, he'd said, and that—what with the city turning the way it was—you could never be too careful. Of course he'd never fired it, never had need to, and after two weeks of carrying it everywhere, he'd slipped it into some hideaway, and that was that. Now it was out again, getting the full Vaz treatment, all for the sake of some tough new street girl.

I wouldn't mind, but Mandy was my discovery. I'd found her hanging around the Bloodvurt stalls in the underground market, her eyes full of buzz and spark as she stroked the feathers, trying some on, just to the lips, falling under spells of violence and pain. And me falling under the spell of her. So I'd asked her to join, become a Stash Rider. She made fun of the name, but still, I could see the need in her eyes. Maybe I was just trying to replace Des the easy way. Maybe. *Maybe we all get a little desperate at times. Maybe there are no easy ways.*

'You heard about Icarus, Bee?' I said, keeping it cool.

He didn't even bother replying, too busy drawing in lungfuls of first-thing Haze. Its pungent odour was giving me half-glimpses of the dream and the things that I saw there made me shiver. 'Icarus Wing? Didn't Mandy tell you about him?' I glanced over at Mandy. She was shovelling spoonfuls of JFK flakes into the gap between her smeared lips, her eyes dead to my need. 'She told me that Icarus Wing was bringing in some Voodoo today.' Still no response from the Beetle. 'You know this Icarus guy, Bee?'

'No.' His voice coming slow and easy, from the Haze.

'No?'

'Never heard of him.'

'You know everybody, Bee! Everybody!'

'What are you saying?' His voice growing sharper.

'You're holding out on me? I—'

'Fuck you, Scribble!'

'Bee—'

'You don't know who's helping you? Is that your problem? Is it?'

His eyes were cold and steely, through the smoke of his joint.

'You two have a good night?' Don't know why I said it. Just came out. They looked at each other. They *smiled* at each other. 'You think Bridget's going to like that?' I asked, knowing full well that Brid would take a nail file to Mandy's eyes. God knows what she'd do to Beetle. Maybe she'd pour all her smoke into his head, working his brain up, into a frenzy. They called it a Shadow-fuck. It was like doing Skull Shit, with the lights on.

'Bridget will have to live with it,' The Beetle said.

'Where is the shadowgirl, anyway?' Mandy asked. She made the word shadow sound like some kind of bad disease.

'She slept in my room'

'Whoo, whoo, whoo!' shouted Mandy, full of rude life.

'Nice one, Stephen!'

'It's not like that, Bee.'

'Stephen? Is that Scribble's real name?' laughed Mandy. 'Aw, how cute!'

'That's the way with Stevie baby, Mandy,' the Beetle said, knowing full well he was getting to me. 'It's never like that. Not with women.'

'Piss off, Bee.' My best reply. 'And the name's Scribble.'

'He's very sensitive this morning,' Mandy said.

'Maybe we *should* sell some bits off the Thing,' the Beetle said. This was just to get me going even more. I wasn't having it.

'No way, Beetle. No fucking way!'

'Just bits off him. The Stash Rider wallet is empty. I can't wait till the next dripfeed. Come on, Scribble! Just an arm, or a leg. A chunk off that fat stomach.'

'We need him! All of him!' I had hold of Beetle's arm. My voice was straining; 'You know why, Bee! Desdemona . . . she . . .'

'Big Thing'll grow them back, anyway. What's the loss?'

'I'm getting desperate, Bee . . . I . . . I think Des is reaching out. She . . .'

'What is it, Scribble?' asked Mandy, around a last mouthful of flakes.

I looked from her, and then back to Beetle. How much could I tell them? Should I tell them about the telephone? Christ! Beetle thought I was crazy anyway; he was certain that Desdemona was dead by now. The phone call would just finish off the tale of Scribble's madness. *Shit! Maybe I was mad! Maybe Desdemona was just living on, inside of me?* No, no. Don't even think that!

'She's alive, Beetle.' I did my best to keep the voice calm. 'I know it.'

A warm light came to the Beetle's eyes. 'Sure thing, Scribb. She's alive. We'll find her. Right, Mandy?'

'You bet.'

They were just being good to me. I could live with that.

'Shall we go see Tristan? Would that suit you, Scribble?' asked the Beetle.

'Tristan?'

'An old friend of mine. He's a spot-on guy. Sold me this gun. Knows all the stuff I've forgotten. And then some.'

'He'll have English Voodoo?'

'He doesn't do Vurt any more. He might know where to find some.'

'He might know about Icarus Wing?' I was getting some kind of hope back. At least we were moving. I just wanted to keep moving, keep the faith going. 'You reckon, Bee?'

'We could try,' the Beetle smiled. That old Beetle smile. 'And we can check out this Seb friend of Mandy's first. Does that plan grab you, Scribb?'

I was falling for him again; the Beetle was in command and the world was looking rosier.

Something always has to spoil the day.

That bad something was somebody knocking on the door. Not the bell, ringing from far away, from the ground floor. No . . . this was a close-up attack. And the noise was powder to the Beetle's trigger. There was something human out there. No one did that any more. The flat was rigged up to the in-house system, and only bona fide inhabitants could find a way past the doorcam. By-passing that system was a beauty, and only a cop could have managed it. A way-up cop.

Beetle activated into Jam mode, moving like a land speed record. First thing he did was slip the gun into his pocket, then turning to us, he whispered; 'Get that fucker out of here!'

That fucker was the Thing-from-Outer-Space, who was still deep in feather-dreams next to the fire. Mandy and I took each end of him, like veterans, and bundled him into the store cupboard. I got back to hear the Beetle talking to some presence through a one-inch gap in the door. 'Certainly, Officer,' he was saying. 'No problem. Please come in. Feel free.'

The Beetle sounded super-confident, and no doubt had cleaned the floor of all incriminating evidence, but how did they find us? Maybe the Vurt-U-Want cop had flashed a better than usual message. Maybe the Platt Fields' cop had seen the alien in our arms.

A real life cop walked into the living room. Not the shadow kind. This cop was flesh and blood; collector's item. She had a curly perm. Yeah, that collectable.

'What's happening?' she asked.

There was a moment of silence. Over by the door stood the shecop's partner, some mealy mouthed fleshcop from hell.

'Nothing much,' replied the Beetle.

The two cops were wearing dangerous smiles.

'Nice pad,' said the boss. 'I'd like to look around.'

'Any time. You got a warrant?'

'Do I need one? Mr . . . ?'

'Beetle. And I have this thing about privacy.'

'We have reason to believe that you are harbouring an alien presence.'

'A what?'

'A Vurt being. A live drug.'

'Really?'

'You know that's totally illicit?'

'Is it?' Beetle was playing it cool.

'Just checking,' said the cop woman, eyes all over the unused Blues and the played-out Creams that littered the floor.

'Nothing but the best,' the Beetle told her. 'Strictly legal.'

'Of course,' she said. 'Nothing but.'

'What's your name?' asked Mandy, from nowhere.

The cop woman looked directly into Mandy's eyes. 'I don't need to tell you that.'

Mandy gave her the bad eye, the best Bloodvurt kind. I'd seen that look before; it made you fearful. The cop took it like a feather's glance. No sweat. Cop was cool.

'Well, it has been pleasant,' said Beetle.

The shecop was looking all around the room, searching for clues. 'I'm just warning you. Don't go upsetting the neighbours.'

There you go. Nosey bitch from the next floor down.

'We'll do our best,' the Beetle told the cop.

'Listen good, kid. I'm not easily satisfied.'

'Well I can see that.'

'You got a job?'

'Not as such.'

'I have this thing about dripfeeders; they really get on my case.'

'We can't all be in sugar.'

There were some intense moments passing by, as Beetle tried his best sex charms on the woman. She was having none of it. She just stared right back, her eyes full up of hard metal. Beetle meets his match!

It was the dumbo partner that broke the spell; 'Let's split, Murdoch. Just a bunch of wasted kids.'

Murdoch didn't look back at him. She just jabbed a long finger at Beetle, like a weapon. 'I'm coming back for you. You got that?'

'I've got it,' replied the Bee, cool as fuck.

The door went shuck behind them, closing with a comfort fix. Beetle was out of the cool in an instant; he popped two Jammers and went straight for me and Mandy.

'What's this about the neighbour shit?' he demanded. His face was full up of anger. One long streak of hair had escaped from the grip of Vaz, and was swinging around against his powdered face like a black plant creeper. 'Well what the fuck's going on?' he shouted, and Mandy and I couldn't even look at each other any more.

'It was my fault,' Mandy said.

'Tell me about it,' said Beetle.

'We got caught on the landing, carrying the Thing,' I added.

'Oh, brilliant.'

'Some woman on the second floor,' said Mandy.

'Didn't you cover it?'

Mandy looked nervous. Her eyes turned to mine.

'You know that we didn't, Bee,' I offered, praying to the God of Vurt to take me right out of that room and up to the theatre of heaven, where the angels play.

No such luck.

The Beetle hit me. Across the face. Felt like a hammer. The real kind, mind. Hardened steel, with a hard wood handle.

I took my hand away from my nose, and there was blood on the fingers and the palm.

That guy is gonna suffer one day.

And he would. But not at my hand.

JAM MODE

We were in Jam mode, screaming down the back roads, all rattling around in the van. Me, the Thing, Brid and Mandy. Beetle at the wheel, jammed up to the nines. The scenes of south Manchester sped past the black windows like a bad foreign movie. The Beetle had popped so many Jammers, fear was just a bad memory. The man was on a demon trip, and he was taking us with him.

Brid was wide awake for once. It had been my job to wake her. Which was like waking up a stone, some dead lump of inanimate matter. Man, she had screamed at me, and then, whilst the half-dead world came rushing back, she had called for Beetle's blood, promising slow tortures.

I'd had to slap her.

She slapped me back.

Which hurt.

Which hurt the both of us.

Then I'd half-kicked her down the stairs, into the van. And then back for the Thing-from-Outer-Space. He was just coming round from the night of feathers. I'd give him about an hour or so, and then he'd be screaming out for more memories of the homeland. Christ! Who'd want to live there? It was Mandy and I, of course, left with the task of carrying the Thing. This time we covered him in a blanket, and the journey down the stairs went like a dream, until Twinkle showed up.

'Is that you, Mister Scribble?' her tinkling voice asked.

'Get lost, kid!' was my response.

'Mister Scribble, that's not fair,' she answered back.

Twinkle was a blue-eyed sweet kid of ten, with a patchwork bob of hair, as blonde as the day was doomed. I loved her dearly except that she was a total pain, and a bit of a nutflake.

'What's under the blanket, Mister Scribble?'

'Kid, fuck off,' said Mandy.

But the kid was hot: 'It's that alien from space, isn't it?' she asked.

Twinkle lived on the first floor, the child of a three parent family; man, woman, hermaphrodite.

'It's just Bridget under here,' I offered. 'We can't wake her up.'

'No way. I saw you kicking Brid down just before. You've got an illegal alien.'

'No we haven't,' said Mandy.

'I've seen him before. I've seen you carrying him around. The whole place knows.'

'Listen, Twinkle . . .'

'Leave her, Scribb,' said Mandy. 'Let's get it loaded up.'

'I wouldn't mind an alien of my own,' Twinkle continued. And then, the dreaded question; 'Can I be in your gang? Can I, Mister Scribble? Can I be a junior Stash Rider?'

She was always after this. 'No you bloody can't!' I answered. 'Now get out of here!'

Twinkle looked at me for a couple of seconds, and then took a slow, toe-scuffing walk back down the corridor, towards the door of her flat.

First off the Beetle drove us over to Chorlton, where we checked out the Vurt-U-Want for signs of Seb. The manager, a paper-thin young wisp of a girl, told us that Sebastian hadn't turned up for work that morning, and that, as of now, he was off the payroll anyway, for bringing the cops down on them, and that Vurt-U-Want was a peace-loving company, and that kind of employee just didn't fit in with their current business vision. She gave us his address from the employee file, and we drove the van out there, West Didsbury, only to find that Seb wasn't in, and that he hadn't be home since last night. The pale and spotted youth that answered the door told us that he didn't have a clue where Seb was.

Now we were heading down the Princess Road, towards Bottletown and Tristan, away from the bad dream of Murdoch and the cops. It wasn't that bad, maybe, not to my mind; just a dumb cop out on a limb, looking for the easy pickings. Beetle thought otherwise. 'That Murdoch bitch will be back, no kidding,' he called from the front seat. 'She's got that look, that hunger. Believe me. You ever been down the Bottle, Mandy?'

'No.'

'You'll love it. It's real scary—'

'Beetle, you're a twat,' Bridget announced.

'That's life,' he answered.

'I heard you last night.'

'And here's me trying to keep it quiet. It would have been worse, otherwise.'

Brid threw Mandy a bullet stare.

'That girl can sing. Real good,' said Beetle.

I thought Brid was going to tear Mandy's eyes out then, except that the van was snaking like a rocket in a bad patch of space, and the Bee was driving like a maniac. He made a deliberate swerve towards some old pedhead with a walking frame. That old woman screamed. Beetle missed her by a jammy whisker and then made an ultra-left onto Princess Road.

'Jesus Christ, Bee!' snarled Brid, from the floor.

We all got back in place and Mandy hid her face behind the latest copy of Game Cat. She was on some kind of crash course in home study, no doubt trying to get within loving distance of Beetle. *No chance, baby. He's a closed up shop. Find that out, and soon.* Some things you just can't say in the back of a crowded-up box of rust on wheels, speeding down towards Bottletown.

'I'm looking at you,' said Brid, her dark eyes brooding on Mandy.

Mandy ignored her, face hid behind the mag. 'We going down the Bottle, Bee?' she asked.

'That's right, babes. Straight down the Bottle.'

'We're going to visit Tristan?'

'We are.'

'After English Voodoo?' Mandy was playing on all the information she had over Bridget.

'That's right, babes.'

'I found out about Icarus Wing,' said Mandy, proud as a pimp.

'This is my van, bitch.' The Brid spat, once, and then carried on; 'Get the fuck out!'

'Pardon me,' replied Mandy, lowering the Game Cat, 'but the vehicle is moving at quite a pace.'

'I know what you're thinking.'

Mandy looked nervous, just for a moment. Her eyes flicked over to the Beetle, and back to Brid. Brid had her best smoky stare on. 'It's good you know, then,' said Mandy, braving the stare. 'Beetle feels the same.' The Beetle said nothing. *New girl had everything to learn about the man.* 'Maybe now you'll leave us alone.' A groove of pain appeared across Mandy's brow. That's how it started. Beads of sweat running down her face. Her mouth tightened. 'Beetle!' Her voice was feeling it too. *Christ! Brid was doing the shadow-fuck!* Mandy was holding her hands to her head, her face creased up with the pain. 'Beetle!!! What's she doing?! Help me!!!!'

'Brid!' I shouted. 'Leave her alone!' Did no good.

'Beetle!!!' Beetle didn't even look round to see the action. Maybe he knew just how far Bridget would go, before deciding that the message was home. Maybe.

'Get the fuck off! Fucking shadowbitch!!!'

Bridget was smiling. 'You know what they say, new girl. Pure is poor—'

Mandy went for her, claws out, tripping over the Thing, who was still too feather-drunk to care. The two women ended up in a mess on the floor, and the Thing was joining in anyway, tentacles waving; no doubt adding it to the whatever Vurt dream he was still revelling in.

And I was just watching the mess, thinking, why is life like this? *Why the fuck is life like this?*

Beetle poured the van into the Moss Lane East.

Brid and Mandy rolled off the Thing, and into a corner clinch. I couldn't say a thing, but the Beetle was on hand; 'Quit the fucking. We're here.'

Indeed we were. Beetle swung the van into a parking space marked NO GO. Jammer didn't care any more. The van jolted to a vicious halt, sending Mandy and Brid back into the embraces of the Thing. The six tentacles wrapped themselves around Bridget. It was a loving embrace. Mandy scrambled away from the mess, breathing hard. 'Fuck that! Fuck it! I just don't need that! Okay!'

The Beetle turned back to look at the women. 'My bed is warm and wide,' he said, 'and life is short. Is that clear?'

'Clear,' said Mandy.

Brid said nothing. Her eyes were closing to the pain. She was moving deeper into the Thing's enveloping body, gathering comfort from the deep shadows there.

Beetle twisted further round, to look me sideways in the eye. 'Let's go, Scribble.' Then he saw something in my eyes. 'You scared?'

'No.'

'You should be. Pures don't go down the Bottle.'

'I'm waiting. Let's go.'

'No options. Know what I mean, Scribb?'

Sure. *Sometimes you just get no options.* Even when you're as pure as the rain, and your life is just a wet kiss on glass. And the Thing was speaking to me. 'Xhasy! Xha, xha! Xhasy, xha!' *Don't leave me here, alone.* Something like that.

'We can't take the Thing,' I said. 'Too dangerous. We need him too much. One of us will have to stay.'

'That's right, Scribb. That's why you're staying here?'

'Beetle!'

'No options.'

'It's my trip, Bee. I know what we're after.'

'And I know this place. Your battle's to come, Scribb.'

Mandy opened the back doors. 'Let's do it, Bee!'

Beetle turned back to Bridget. She was lying in the arms of the alien. 'You got anything to say to me, Brid?' His voice had some kind of feeling in it. Tenderness. Just a trace. Bridget lifting her sleepy head slightly, from the arms of the Thing.

'It's your game, Beetle.' her voice was shadow-deep. And then

I got it. She wasn't talking, she was just thinking! I'd picked up the path between them.

The Beetle answered in a whisper. 'That's right. My game.'

Beetle got out of the van, and went round to the back doors, where Mandy was waiting for him. He leaned into the van, to talk to me. 'You look after things this side,' he said. Then he lowered his voice some. 'I'm doing this for you, Scribble. Remember?'

'I remember.'

'And for Desdemona . . .'

I remember.

G A M E   C A T

EXCHANGE MECHANISMS. Sometimes we lose precious things. Friends and colleagues, fellow travellers in the Vurt, sometimes we lose them; even lovers we sometimes lose. And get bad things in exchange; aliens, objects, snakes, and sometimes even death. Things we don't want. This is part of the deal, part of the game deal; all things, in all worlds, must be kept in balance. Kittlings often ask, who decides on the swappings? Now then, some say it's all accidental; that some poor Vurt thing finds himself too close to a door, at too crucial a time, just when something real is being lost. Whoosh! Swap time! Others say that some kind of overseer is working the MECHANISMS OF EXCHANGE, deciding the fate of innocents. The Cat can only tease at this, because of the big secrets involved, and because of the levels between you, the reader, and me, the Game Cat. Hey, listen; I've struggled to get where I am today; why should I give you the easy route? Get working, kittlings! Reach up higher. Work the Vurt.

Just remember Hobart's rule; $R = V \pm H$, where H is Hobart's constant. In the common tongue; any given worth of reality can only be swapped for the equivalent worth of Vurtuality, plus or minus 0.267125 of the original worth. Yes my kittlings, it's not about weight or volume or surface area. It's about worth. How much the lost ones count, in the grand scheme of things. You can only swap back those that add up to something, within Hobart's constant. Like for like, give or take 0.267125.

We have prostrated ourselves at the feet of goddess Vurt, and we must accept the sacrifice. You'll want them back of course, your lost and lonely ones. You'll cry out for them, all through the dark and empty nights. Swapback can be made, but the way is full of knives, glued-up doors, pathways of glass. Only the strong can make it happen. Listen up. Be careful. Be very, very careful. You have been warned.

This comes from the heart.

DOWN THE BOTTLE

The Beetle and Mandy, walking on a path of glass.

The noise of a window cracking in the afternoon.

A spectrum of colours radiating out from the sun, as it flared above the high-rises. The light refracting through moisture suspended in the air.

The shimmering air.

A million pieces of the sun shining on the walkways.

Beetle and Mandy disappearing into the rainbow mirage.

I followed them as best I could, moving up to the front seat for a better look. From every direction the crystal sharp segments of smashed up wine bottles, and beer bottles, and gin bottles, caught and magnified every stray beam of Manchester light. The whole of Bottletown, from the shopping centre to the fortress flats, shone and glittered like a broken mirror of the brightest star. Such is beauty, in the midst of the city of tears. In Bottletown even our tears flicker like jewels.

I knew that the Beetle had the gift of seeing beauty in ugliness. It's just that I'm more used to ugliness than he is, seeing it every day in cruel mirrors, and in the mirrors of women's eyes.

Bottletown had only been around for ten years or so. Some kind of urban dream. Pretty soon the wholesome families moved out and the young and the listless moved in, and then the blacks and the robo-crusties and the shadowgoths and the students. Pretty soon the students moved out, sick to the back of mummy and daddy's car with too much burglary, too much mugging. Then the blacks moved out, leaving the place to the non-pure—hybrids only need apply. About a year later the council opened a pair of bottle banks on the outskirts of the town, one for white glass, one for green. The nice people from the outlying districts would come there, just to the edge of dirtiness, in order to drop their evidence of excessive alcohol intake. The council stopped emptying the bottle banks, and anybody walking there had to sink into a bed of pain, just to get near the good times.

When the banks were full, and overflowing, still they came, breaking bottles on the pavements and the stairs and the landings. This is how the world fills up. Shard by shard, jag by jag, until the whole place is some kind of glitter palace, sharp and painful to the touch.

On one of the nearby walls someone had scrawled the words, pure is poor, but I was watching Beetle and Mandy rise above all that, walking the stairwells one by one, heading for the fourth floor. They would vanish from sight, and then come back into view, as they reached each landing. It was a rhythmic picture, and I was lulled by it. I saw them for a moment, just before they entered the fourth staircase, then they were gone, and my eyes jerked up to the next landing, waiting for them.

Waiting.

Waiting.

Waiting for them to reappear.

Minutes passed with no sign. And then Mandy was running along the fourth corridor, some stranger chasing her.

I was out of the van in seconds. Glass cutting into my feet, through my trainers, as I raced towards the ground floor entrance. Lift wasn't working, so what's new? I took the stairs three at a time. I could already hear Mandy's cries, even from down there, that low, and I didn't have a weapon, no gun, no knife, just these two weak arms, these legs, pounding the stairs.

Second landing.

Racing upwards.

Towards the noise.

Falling onto the third landing, out of breath, sweat pouring off me. *Get up! Get up, dumbfuck! Keep going!*

Next stairs. I could hear the Beetle's voice now, calling out in defiance, and all the light draining from the day, as my eyes filled with sweat and the blood made a fast pulse all through my veins. I was running through the feelings, struggling to find courage, and my left ankle was throbbing with a piercing ache. *Don't start on me now, old wound.*

There was a fight going on, just beyond the stairwell, and I managed to pull myself back, holding onto fear.

Crack! My body hitting the liftshaft, pressing itself into the shadows there.

I glanced around the corner, taking it all in. The Beetle was down. He was down on the floor, his arms clutched around his head. Three men were laying into him with kicks to the head, the chest, and the back. The men had that death warmed-up look so popular with the younger robogoth; all plastic bones shining proudly through tight, pale skins. A woman was overseeing the attack. She had the smoke coming off her, dark swirls of mist rising from her skin, just like Bridget when she was roused. Shadowgoth! Mandy's voice was echoing down the walkway, all the curses of the young and strong. Then she came into my field of vision, being dragged along by another two robogoths. She was digging her nails into their flesh. Did no good; that roboflesh was long dead to feeling. One too many live bootleg Vurts of the Shadow Cure, I guess. The woman had black webs over her eyes and she was chanting a black litany—Pure is poor! Kill the pure! Mandy screamed in pain as the goths flung her against a wall, and held her tight there. The shadowgoth came up close to Mandy's face. I guess Mandy was cruising for another shadow-fuck because the first thing she did was spit a big glob of sputum straight into the shadowgoth's face.

The Beetle and Mandy were out there, still fighting, and all I could do was cling to the shadows of a dead liftshaft, holding back the urge to run, to jerk out, except that this wasn't theatre, this wasn't a feather trip. Real life, like Yellow feathers, has no jerk-out facility. This is why the two are so alike.

Even in shadows, no place to hide.

A slithering noise at my feet.

Shadowgoth wasn't reacting to the spit that clung to her cheeks. 'I'm getting a tingle,' she said. For one second I thought she was referring to herself, to her feelings of power, but then I got the story.

Shadowgoth had heard me thinking!

Christ! Girl must have a heavy shadow, to think around corners, into the darkness.

That slithering at my feet again, and my ankle calling to me, from the years gone by, with a hard knot of pain.

'I'm getting the tingle of another pure one, my brothers,' Shadowgoth said. 'Pure is coming!'

I watched them from my depths, turning towards the darkness where I buried myself. Their robo-eyes were glinting with red lights, and the shadowgoth had eyes of smoke, which were looking into my soul, seeing the fear there. The slithering was so loud now, I just had to glance down. *Dreamsnake!* Violet and green whisperings. Snake seeking out my wound!

It must have been the panic and the fear that sent me spinning, into a vision of myself catching spikes between my teeth, spitting them loose, snapped in two, taking up a long-handled hammer against the mighty weight of the Nailgunners. Shit! I felt good! Done this low-level Blue some years previous, but here it was again, in my brain, and totally featherless! Vurt was called Spike Attack and usually I ended up dead from the spikes, one in each eye, but now I felt good! Well good, and I wanted to take on the world, especially some thin-bodied smokegirl and her rusting robo-nerds.

I stepped out of the shadows, kicking at the snake the same time. It landed some four feet off, directly under the feet of one of the robogoths. He jumped back from the snake, losing his balance. Goth was falling. He looked a bad mess, on the floor.

This was me, Scribble, hero of Spike Attack, coming to the rescue.

Some kind of fool.

The snake was withering from the Spiked-up strength of my kick, but somewhere between there and my reaching the fray, the Vurt dropped away and I felt a distant pain somewhere, far off, and then realised it was my cheekbone. A fist like iron had smashed into it, and then another, to the left eye, and I was down, and thinking. *This isn't me! I'm not like this! Last time I had a fight, I was thirteen years old. It was my dad doing the beating and I got hammered.* I had my arms wrapped like a mother around my head. I stole a look through my fingers and thumbs, only to see the shadowgoth standing over me. She aimed a vicious beauty at my teeth. Jesus, that hurt! This was some heavy kind of real life, and it hurt like a knife blow, even more so because the glass shards were breaking my skin as I pressed myself into the floor, seeking relief.

Found none.

The girl's monkey boot swung back for another attack and I was thinking. *All I want to do is be in Vurt. Be in Vurt forever. Life's too much for me. I can't stand the pain.*

That boot never made it.

There was a sharp cry of pain, and then a hard crack. And it wasn't me! It was nothing to do with me! I rolled over into a sitting-up position. Through a haze of blood I saw Mandy pulling the goth girl back, away from my tender features. Two of the robogoths were nursing painful wounds. *Man, I loved that girl just then, and I wished her total happiness and forever more.* The Beetle had grabbed hold of a stray ankle. He was twisting it all around, until you could hear the plastic bones cracking. I was on my feet again, and the battle was turning.

Shadowgoth pulled out a knife.

The blade of a knife catching fragments of colours, as it moved back and forth in the hands of a woman, over a walkway of broken glass.

Mandy moved back from the knife.

Beetle lifted the leg of the robogoth up, with a fierce jerk, so that the sad fucker fell back, against a hard brick wall. Shadowgoth swung the knife around to face him. Beetle just laughed at her. She thrust forwards, the blade glittering. It entered Beetle's flesh, the left side of his stomach. He fell back, his mouth open, his eyes wide and staring. He clutched at the wound with his hands. Mandy went for the Shadow. That new girl was proving herself. The blade came back round, in a circle of colours. Mandy made a perfect move backwards, away from the slice, except that a robogoth was waiting for her. He wrapped his arms around her body, pulling her back. The shadowgoth moved in, holding the knife tight against Mandy's throat. The Beetle was slumped against the wall and I was the only one left to save the day.

'Hey fuckers!' I shouted, or tried to. My voice was weak from the struggle. 'You better leave my friends alone!'

Oh wow! I guess you can say anything, if the blood is stirred enough.

The shadowgoth laughed. Her robo partners were back in action by now. They gathered in a circle around us. Shadowgoth turned her face towards me, blinked, just the once, and then I felt her finger in there, inside my mind, pulling me apart. Shadowfuck!

All I wanted was a shadowcop to flicker into life, except that this was the Bottle, a no-go cop zone.

'The game's over, little man,' the shadowgoth said.

Oh fuck. Game's over.

Just then a door opened. Some two flats down. And a man stepped through. His hair was a long, thick net of grease, leading straight back into the doorway.

Guy was beautiful.

He had a dog on a long lead. The dog reached out with a vicious set of jaws, took a loud snap, came up with that errant dreamsnake in its jaws. The dog swallowed it in a quick gulp.

The goths looked back at the white guy with the jungle hair, and the dog from hell.

'Tristan! My man!' The Beetle calling from where he lay.

'The fun's over,' said the jungle hair.

He had a shotgun, cocked and ready. And a dog.

Cocked and ready.

No contest.

HERBAL HAZE

The room was thick with Haze. And a jungle of hair.

We were all safe and sound inside of number 407, the home of Tristan. His girlfriend, Suze, was bathing our wounds with some herbal concoction. It smelt like the ripest fruit, but tasted like wine, and it touched our cuts with a sweet hand. Tyrannosaurus Rex were singing on Tristan's system, all about the light of the magical moon, and I could hear dogs howling through the walls.

A line of dreamsnake skins were pinned over the fireplace.

Tristan had lodged his shotgun against the doorjamb, just in case. Now he was mixing up a lethal brew in a stoneware pot. Suze dropped some seeds in there as well. It gave off a dense pall of smoke and the smell was wondrous to the senses.

'Who the fuck was that goth woman?' asked the Beetle.

'Take a good sniff of that, my beauties,' announced Tristan. So we breathed deeply of it, as the gunmetal blue mist filled the room. And straight away I was into paradise land, touched by angels, caressed by spirits.

'Who was she?' the Beetle asked once more.

'Can't you handle it, Beetle?' Tristan said. 'The Beetle getting beaten by a woman?' And maybe that was it; the hardcore man was smarting. Suze had lifted his shirt up, free of his jeans. She was applying the sweet lotion to his cut.

'Tell me! Who was she? I need to know.'

'They call her the Nimbus,' Suze said.

'Nimbus is one top-level shadowgirl,' added Tristan.

'She's just a mist, Trist,' Suze replied.

'Nowhere near as lovely as you, my lover,' Tristan said, running his fingers through the smoke that was rising in thick waves from the herb jars. And that was true. It wasn't anything obvious, Suze's beauty, but it was getting to me. Her look was cool, serene, like she'd lived through some bad things, but was now on the other side. It was the eyes that got you; they had a soft golden glow to them. What with the eyes, and all that hair, this woman was affecting me. Maybe this smoke was getting to me. Through the Haze I saw that Mandy was flat out on the floor, wrapped up in the dog. His paws were all over her.

'That's one big robodog, Tristan,' The Beetle said.

'Karli? She's just a puppy,' he replied.

A puppy. That was the biggest dog I'd ever seen!

Suze was speaking. I kind of caught it through the mist. 'That's a nice trophy, Beetle.' She was admiring the snakehead attached to Bee's lapel. 'We don't have no trouble with snakes around here. Not with the dogs.'

'Yeah! That dog did good,' The Beetle said.

'What brings you around, Beetle?' asked Tristan.

'What else, Tristie. Drugs.'

'What kind? Got some nice Mexican Haze in. You're breathing it right now.'

'I'm looking for some good Vurt, my man.'

'Now you know, that's not really my trip. Not these days. I'm into natural things now. Vurt isn't natural.'

'We're looking for English Voodoo.'

Tristan went quiet then. He tugged for a few seconds at his hair. Suze felt the tug and responded in the same way, tugging back on the plaits that joined them. They were twinned crusties, sharing the same haircut. Six feet of thick entwined hair stretched between them, and you couldn't see where one ended, and the other began. Over the years their hair had knotted, and knotted hard, until separation was an unthinkable torture. They would walk the world together, never less than six feet apart. *Now there's love for you.*

'You want English Voodoo?' asked Tristan.

'You know where to find some?' Beetle said.

'No. Not at all.'

'You telling the truth?'

'I got rid. Pretty quick. I don't like that stuff. It's not natural.'

'But you had some?' I asked, shaking from the knowledge.

'I told you, the once. I don't do Vurt any more. Period. And may I suggest, young kid . . .' Tristan stared directly at me. 'That you keep off that stuff yourself. It's a killer.'

'You heard of Icarus Wing?' I asked.

'What's that? Some new killer feather? Man, they just can't leave it alone.'

'No. It's a man. A man's name. He's a feather seller.'

'Like I said, I don't work those areas any more.'

Suze had gone silent. She was adding some new herbs to the pot. A fresh brew of Haze floated into the room.

'For old time's sake, Tristie,' asked the Beetle.

'It means that much, yeah?' Tristan replied.

'We lost someone. To the Vurt.'

Tristan went quiet again. And when he did speak, this was all he could come up with; 'That's a bummer, Bee.'

'You really not got any Voodoo, Tristan?' asked the Beetle.

Tristan's reply was the softest whisper; 'Years ago. Years ago.'

'Just wondered.'

'Wonder not, Bee. English Voodoo fucks. It leads to bad things.'

This was too much for me. 'Someone good,' I said. 'Desdemona.'

'Who's Desdemona?' asked Suze.

'Scribble's sister,' replied Beetle. 'We lost her. To the Voodoo.'

'Uh uh, I get it,' said Tristan. 'Swapback time. It doesn't work, Beetle. I've never known it work.'

'Scribble's on a mission trip,' the Beetle told them. 'And we're all getting dragged along. He's set on finding her. He'd give his all. Wouldn't you, Scribb?'

Tristan and Suze looked towards each other. I saw their hair as a river, flowing from each to each.

'Only a fool goes into English Voodoo,' said Suze. She was looking straight at me. The robopuppy had come up close to me, licking my face. I was doing my best to discourage her, but that dog just kept on licking. 'Karli likes you,' Suze added. I was covered in dog spit by now, so I couldn't argue. 'Tell us,' she repeated, and something in her voice got to me, some kind of recognition. Like I'd known her for ages, without ever meeting. *What was that feeling?*

'You'd better tell the story, Scribb,' the Beetle said to me. 'You're better at it than I am.'

So I told them.

It went like this . . .

ON THE WASHING OF DROIDLOCKS

Brother and sister walking it home from a club; vanless, way past the last bus time, no money for an Xcab. We were halfway down the Wilmslow Road when we heard a screaming. A woman screaming, and we took that walk, right into a fist fight.

A guy was clutching a woman, shaking her. She was screaming, over and over, face twisted towards the indifferent traffic.

'Get off me! Stop hitting me! He's hitting me! Get him off me!'

'I think we should stop,' said Desdemona.

'What?'

'I think we should do something.'

Oh wow, like thanks, sister.

'What's going on here?' I said, my voice doing its best to sound cool and hard. Totally failing.

'We just found this woman, man,' said the guy, a black guy. 'We was just driving along.'

His car was parked just forward a small way, one wheel mounted upon the pavement. Another guy, a white one, was hunched up in the driving seat. There was a woman in the back seat, and she was kind of rocking, you know, back and forth like a snake victim.

'She was screaming by the road,' the black guy said. 'Just screaming . . . you know?'

'He's lying,' announced Desdemona, and it wasn't exactly pleasing.

'I am not fucking lying!'

'So what's going on?' I asked, still trembling, just to please the sister.

'I was just trying to help her,' he started, but I think we'd got him riled, because just then the woman found a way out of his arms. She ran straight into the road, into the path of an oncoming car. Car screeched to a halt, wheels slipping. Good driving but not that good. Car hit the woman. More like this, actually; woman hit the car, kind of threw herself at it. She was down, face to the tarmac, for maybe two seconds. Then she sprang up again, banging on other cars as they passed her by, slowly, scared faces peering out.

'Help me! Help me!' she was screaming.

Nobody stopped. *Who the hell stops these days?*

Drivers were looking at me as though I was some villain in this. Felt strange. One of those moments you'll think you'll remember forever, but it just slips away. Until such a day arrives when you've got nothing else to do but list your memories, no where else to live but inside them.

Early morning air was misty and serene, with hours to go until sunshine.

Screaming woman was miles away, seemed like, almost down to the next set of lights. I could hear cars braking over the screams.

The black guy was just standing around, hopping from foot to foot, building his anger up. White guy just sitting in the car, chewing gum.

Desdemona had opened the back door. Now she was reaching in to help the swaying woman.

'I think we need the cops, Scribb,' said Desdemona, from the back seat. 'Girl's in a bad way. She's feathered up on something. I can't move her.'

The cops? I'd never called them before.

'I don't think we need that,' answered the black, moving towards me. His fists were bunched up, and he had that look on him, like the idea that pain was a pleasure to give.

I backed away, towards the car.

'Are these guys hurting you?' I heard Desdemona ask.

No answer from the comatose girl. The other one, down the road some, was screaming anyway for the both of them.

'Des?' I whispered, trying to get her attention. Sister wasn't answering so I made a quick turn, aiming to drag her out of there. But she was too busy to care about me; too busy searching through the woman's handbag.

'What are you doing, sister?' I asked

'Looking for an address. I think these men are using her.'

'Big deal, sis. There's a bad guy out here.'

'Keep him off, Scribb!' the sister said.

Well thanks for that. Like how?

The black guy was up close now, waving his fists around, close enough to do damage to a soft face.

Sound of a cop van in the distance.

Fists faltering.

Sometimes, don't you just love the cops, despite the fact that they have hurt some good friends of yours? Because sometimes, just occasionally, they turn up in the right place, at just the right time. Don't you just love them for that?

Cop siren sounding. And the black stepped back, a small step. Then another.

Then he was running. Out of there!

White guy started the car engine.

Desdemona was half in, half out of the car. 'I've found something!' she shouted. The car started to move off, and Des was thrown out, hard to the pavement.

The siren bursting in my brain, as the cop van pulls up in front of the car, wheels squealing, blocking the escape.

And although my sister's body was on the floor, although she was obviously in pain, and the sun wasn't even awake yet, never mind rising, still I could see her grasping tight hold of something. It was feathery, and it was glinting yellow as it passed through the air, towards her pocket.

What you got there? What you got there, sweet sister? Must be a beauty.

If only I'd known then. If only.

Suze and Tristan are washing their hair, which is each other's hair. Which is their shared hair. As they listened to my story.

Mandy was awake again, sitting on the floor, playing with the big puppy dog. Something about its body made me uneasy; the way the plastic bones shone through the taut flesh stretched over its rib-cage. Suze called the dog Karli.

The Beetle was sucking on a demon bong-pipe, his eyes drifting to other worlds, as the water popped in bubbles of Haze.

I was trapped in the armchair, drugged by the smoke, fascinated by the ritual.

Suze was taking water to the joint locks. Adding herbs to the water, she mixed up a slick lather, which glistened with perfume. Like you could see the smell, you know? She worked this lather into each thick strand of hair, each in turn, from her own roots to Tristan's, until their hair was a stream of suds. It was lovely to look at, and Tristan was smiling through it all. 'You're very privileged to see this,' Suze said, in a whisper.

'It's a good story, Scribble,' Tristan said. 'You want to carry on?'

Their eyes were heavy-lidded from the shampoo pleasure, and it was like watching sex. Drugged-up sex. 'It's very beautiful,' whispered Mandy.

Through the walls I could hear the hound dogs howl.

'Don't worry about them, Scribble,' said Tristan, dreamily.

Desdemona and I, back in the Rusholme Gardens, fingering the feather.

The Beetle and Bridget were out for the night and the morning, travelling in the van, visiting a down south Vurt Fest, gathering contacts and suppliers. The cops had taken some details, pronounced us innocent. We were back home, and it was all ours; the flat, the feather, the love.

'Wonder what it's called?' Desdemona asked, letting the feather's yellow glints shine under the table lamp. The feather was 70% black, 20% pink, 10% yellow. There was a pale space on the shaft where somebody had peeled the label off.

'Plug us in, Des,' I said.

'No way!' she shouted. 'Not on our own.'

She was following the Beetle's rules. Nobody goes in alone. Just in case it gets real bad in there.

'Go on!' I pleaded. 'We've got each other. What can go wrong?'

This I will never forgive.

'Beetle's doing it,' I told her. 'Right this moment. Down South. Oh come on, sister! He's at a Vurt Fest! With Bridget! Of course he's doing it. He's in Vurtland, right now!'

'We've never done a Yellow before, Scribb.'

This was true. Yellows were ultra-rare. Low-lifers just didn't come across them. 'It's not a full Yellow,' I said. 'It's just got some Yellow in it. Look, a tiny amount. It's safe.'

'We don't even know what it is!'

'Let's do it!'

She gazed at the feather for a full minute, saying nothing, just drinking in the rainbow of colours. And then, finally; 'Let's do it, Scribb.' It was a soft voice. And she looked at me with those eyes made out of plums, juicy plums, as I stole the feather from her hands.

Some things just seem bound.

And she opened her mouth, my sister, waiting for the feathering. She was too full up of love to resist, so I stroked her there, deep in the mouth, and then myself, and this is how we lost the sister. Desdemona was taking it, all to heart.

Tristan uncorked a new jar and reached inside, with wide open fingers. And when he pulled his hand back out, it was covered in thick green slime, like hairvaz, but living. Nanosham! Read about it in the Cat, but never seen it before. Those minuscule machines were dribbling from between his fingers.

'Watch this,' he said. And with a broad and sexy sweep, he set those tiny machines working on his and Suze's hair. You could almost hear them feeding on the dirt and grease. Nanosham was a jelly base containing hundreds of baby computers. They turned dirt into data, processing hair clean, giving the people droidlocks; the ultimate crusty accessory.

'My darling,' whispered Tristan to his love. 'This is the sweetest pleasure.'

Suze turned to me, holding out a clutch of the nanoes. 'You want to try some?' she asked. Her eyes knew all my secrets. I felt her there, inside my body, and it was like she was caressing me.

Maybe Suze was a shadowgirl. But no, it wasn't that, it felt different. Felt like she was becoming me.

'Young man's got no hair anyway,' Tristan said.

I couldn't answer. Couldn't even shake my head. All of the air had turned into smoke. Maybe the herb brew was giving me visions. I saw a thick snake of hair writhing between the heads of a man and a woman. And voices drifting through like mist patches, like waves of knowledge. I didn't know where I was . . .

The people were talking all around me, about me, but none of them made sense; all I could feel was Suze's body inside mine, touching all parts of me. I was getting a hard-on! What was this? The voices . . .

'You should.'

'Little boy.'

'Saves on shampoo.'

'He's got no hair.'

'Call that a haircut?'

'It's a crew job.'

Who was saying what? And when? And to whom?

I felt a sudden, clammy hand stroking my short blond hair. *Okay, it's short. Well who gives a fuck! Some of us look like shit with long hair. This the beautiful people will never understand. I'm just trying to look good, you know, my best. Some kind of best.* And I shivered as I felt those fingers stroking my head. *Get the fuck off me!* Until I realised it was my own hand. It was my own hand stroking me; through the fog it had come, in order to stroke.

'Aw! Look at the baby.'

'He's shaking.'

'He's stroking his hair.'

'He's nervous.'

'He just doesn't know any more.'

All those voices calling to me, through the mist . . .

The world was a haze. 'What's she doing to me!' I shouted. 'Stop her!'

And the voices falling to silence and all those eyes on me now, as Tristan told Suze to stop playing with me. Suze said that I had the dream within me, but I was well gone, and the feeling of bliss fading as Suze removed herself from my body.

What was that woman?

'Tell the story, Scribb.' Beetle's voice.

The last drop fell away and I was myself again, with only a lonely space left in my soul, and a story to tell . . .

Last time I saw my sister, for real, she was sitting opposite me, across an apple jam–smeared table, with a feather in her mouth, expecting to fly. It was me, the brother, holding the feather there, turning it all around inside of her mouth. And then moving it to my own mouth, and Desdemona's eyes were glazed already by the Vurt, as I twisted the feather deep, to follow her down. Wherever she was going, I was going too. I really believed that.

We went down together, sister and brother, falling into Vurt, watching the credits roll; WELCOME TO ENGLISH VOODOO. EXPECT TO FEEL PLEASURE. KNOWLEDGE IS SEXY. EXPECT TO FEEL PAIN. KNOWLEDGE IS TORTURE.

Last time I saw my sister, close up, intimate, in the Vurt world, she was falling through a hole in a garden, clutched at by yellow weeds, cut by thorns, screaming my name out loud. A small yellow feather was fluttering at her lips.

I told her not to go through that door. It was a NO GO door. She went anyway.

I told her not to. She went anyway.

'I want to go there, Scribble. I want you to come with me. Will you come?' My sister's last real words to me, before the yellow feather kicked in, and she was falling, screaming my name.

Some of us die, not in the living world, but in the dream world. Amounts to the same thing. Death is always the same. There are some dreams you never wake up from.

Desdemona . . .

The room, in silence.

Later that day. Hours of smoke uncounted, but now the mist was drifting apart, revealing tiny fragments of the real world. These little glimpses stung the eyes like needles. I could no longer tell the tale; its telling was too much for me. I was shaking from the memories; Desdemona was aching in my heart.

Tristan broke the mood. 'You found another feather in there?' he asked. 'Is that what you're saying?'

I just nodded.

Through the tears I saw that Suze was sitting at a small table, consulting the oracle. She was shaking a can of bones around, and then dropping them onto the table. On the baize lay a spread of picture cards. She took note of which cards were touched by which shape of bone, and then threw the bones once more. Karli the robodog was licking my face, like she loved me, or something. Her tongue was long and wet, slick with nanoes. I swear I could feel them cleaning my face for me, cleaning all the salt tears away.

'It was a yellow feather?' Tristan asked.

'Yes. Small and yellow. Totally yellow,' I managed. 'It was beautiful.'

'You want to tell how you found it? Or what happened?'

I didn't. Tristan just nodded. 'I understand,' he said.

Did he?

'I've been there,' he added.

'What?'

'I've been inside English Voodoo.'

'Tell me.' I was desperate for knowledge.

Tristan looked over to where Suze was working the cards and the bones. Then he looked back at me. 'You lost your sister there?' he asked.

'Yes.'

'And got what in return?'

'I don't know what it is. Some kind of Vurt alien. We call him the Thing.'

My mind dragged me back. Me waking up from the English Voodoo feather, covered by the weight of slime. The Thing writhing about on top of me. Me screaming at it, pushing with all my strength to get out from under, tears falling from my eyes, a cry rising in my throat. The sister gone forever, replaced by this lump of stuff.

Tristan nodded. 'The rates of exchange are complex. Nobody really knows how they work. Only that a constant balance has to be kept, between this world and the Vurt world. Both worlds must always contain the same worth.'

'The Thing can't be as worthy as Des. Just can't be . . .'

'In his own world, that Thing is loved just as much. Everything adds up. The Game Cat tells you this. Believe me, the Game Cat knows.'

'What do you know?' I asked.

Tristan looked over at Suze once more before answering. 'Your sister took Curious Yellow.'

Oh Christ!

Even the Beetle was aroused, out of Haze slumber. 'Curious Yellow!' he shouted. 'Holy shit! We're fucked, Scribble, baby!'

'Most probably,' Tristan said. 'Curious Yellow lives inside English Voodoo. It's a meta-feather.'

Curious Yellow was often talked about, never seen, never felt. It was up there in the higher echelons, where the demons and the gods lived. Nobody pure could ever touch it, but Desdemona had touched it, tasted it, and now she was no more of this world, and the chances of getting her back were falling rapidly to zero.

'What is Curious Yellow?' I asked. 'How can I find it?'

'It can't be found, Scribble,' Tristan replied. 'It can only be earned. Or stolen.'

'Desdemona's in there. I know she is!'

'Most probably she's dead.'

His words cut me, but I wasn't giving up; 'No. She talks to me. She's alive! She's in there, somewhere. She's calling to me. What can I do, Tristan?'

'Give up.'

'Is that what you did?' I asked, and I could tell that I'd got to him. He'd lost somebody! He'd been there, in the Voodoo, lost somebody to the Curious. I could see the pain in his eyes, like a mirror.

'There's no hope,' he answered. 'Believe me. I've tried.'

'So you won't help us?' the Beetle asked.

Tristan stared at Beetle. Then he turned away, towards Suze. He was running his hands through their joint hair, almost like he was testing just to see if she was still there, attached, safe. Suze picked up a card from the table, and held it out to me.

'This is your card, Scribble,' she said.

'No. No, it's not.'

'You just don't know it yet.'

The first drifts of darkness showed through the flat's windows, and I was thinking about Bridget and the Thing, and how I should get back there, see how they were doing. And how everything was over, and another night without love.

'Well, cheers, mate,' said the Beetle, with bitterness in his voice.

I guess the guy was looking out for me.

"Karli will see you home," said Tristan.

"You won't get scared without the pooch?" asked Beetle.

Tristan opened a door in the wall and I smelt turds and bad breath, meat and piss.

I looked into a dark place. The walls were covered in scratches and bites. In the shadows were darker shadows. Sleeping shadows, moving and breathing to a slow pulse. A low growling started up as Tristan turned on a sad little light and I saw the dogs there, a fur-lined duo. Great beasts. All plastic bones and synthetics.

'Robohounds,' Tristan whispered. 'Karli's mum and dad. Be careful. They bite.' And I could see something in Tristan then, some trace of something dog-like.

'These are the beauties that keep us safe,' he said.

'Christ!'

'Indeed. Bow down to the dogs.'

TORCHERS

Walking along a gangway, like on a tall ship, concrete ship, miles above the sea of glass. Me, Beetle, Mandy, Tristan, and Suze. Oh yeah, and the dog. Karli. Great slavering fur-metal beast, stretched out taut at the end of Suze's leash. Tristan carrying his gun, just for show really. Who's going to touch him? Because they know what would be coming then. And two robodogs left back in the flat, looking after the homestead. Night coming down. No one talking much, just walking the high-rise, hung up on private things. Each still strung out on wisps of herb, just enough to make the world seem kind of beautiful, even this place. The emptiness inside of me reflected in the glass fragments. So I was a thousand times sad, with each footstep. *Sometimes even broken glass, cracked cement, sad lives; well they seem like the good dreams of bad things.*

And I was thinking well perhaps all is well, and Brid and the

Thing will be glad to greet us and we don't need this old crusty anyway. We were the Stash Riders, and Desdemona was one of us, and we would be back together, just as soon as I got my act together. Shit, man, it was easy! All I had to do was find some English Voodoo feather, go inside, taking the Thing with me. Find some meta-feather in there, some Curious Yellow, the most famous feather in the world, go inside. Find Desdemona in there, swap her back for the Thing, breaking all the known rules of Vurt, find our way back out. Shit, man, it was a piece of cake. Shit cake.

Now we were descending the stairwell.

'Sorry about not being much help,' Tristan was saying to the Beetle.

The Beetle just shrugged.

'I'm just trying to warn you, my friend.' There was an edge of sadness to Tristan's voice, but I wasn't paying much attention.

'You had a good night, though?' Suze asked.

'Great night,' said the Beetle. Maybe he meant it.

We'd reached the bottom of the stairs, and we could smell fire in the air. Dogs were howling all through the Bottletown night.

'What's that?' asked Mandy.

'Some jokers,' answered Suze. 'Don't worry.'

'Happens every night,' added Tristan.

'They love to burn things.'

'They call themselves the Torchers,' said Tristan. 'Crazy tribe.'

'Oh fuck.' That was me.

'It'll be some waste-bin,' said Suze.

But I knew. But I fucking knew it!

We turned the corner of a dead liftshaft, into the car-park, and there was our lovely Stashmobile in a shroud of flames. Burning. Burning.

'Shit!' The Beetle's voice. The van a forest of fire. No one could live through that. No one. Low-level shadowgirl and an alien from Vurt. Gone to the flames.

The five of us, and the dog, all of us transfixed. As the van burned, and the glass told the story a thousand times. Then I was running into the flames, scorching my hands on the door handle.

Oh shit! Oh the Thing and Brid!

And all the hope drifting away from my life, all the hope of an exchanging, the Thing for the sister.

All the hopes of my life . . .

Karli had slipped her leash, she was running around the van, barking at the flames. Beetle had joined me, to help pull open the doors, but instead he was pulling me back, and I was suffering, the smoke bringing tears to my eyes, and the loss, all the losses, bringing tears.

Midnight. A drift of smoke. The van a pile of metal bones, blistered leatherette, melted rubber. My mind burnt. Just sitting there, on a vandalised bench, watching the van's corpse slowly fading. The stench of fire in my head, the glow of embers. A bunch of on-lookers, Bottletown dwellers, come to watch the flames. Some of them were laughing. I was too far gone to care. The night was orange.

Tristan and Suze had rushed back to their flat for an extin-guisher, but their hair had slowed them down, it just wasn't pos-sible. And anyway, it didn't matter. There was nothing to save.

Karli Dog was nuzzling up to me, offering loads of comfort licks. I kept pushing her away, but she just kept on coming back anyway. So I let that long tongue carry on. It did some good, truth be known.

Tristan and Suze had come back with the foam-gun, but it was like pouring water on Hell. That van was going to burn, until everything was cinders. Until flesh was bone.

It just didn't matter anyway.

The Beetle had smeared his driving gloves with a full tube of Vaz. Then he'd gone up close to the dying flames, grabbed the back door handle, wrenched it loose. The door swung open, letting out a thick cloud of smoke. I'd watched the Beetle brave the smoke and the heat, thinking what a good guy he was. Then he turned away from the van, and walked towards me. His face was soot-blackened.

'They're not there, Scribble.' His words.

I'd just looked at him.

'They're not there. It's empty.'

Bottletown kids laughing and dancing in the orange night, and me just sitting on a broken down car-park bench, thinking about the world, and getting licked to fuck by a mixed-up pile of dog flesh and plastic, name of Karli.

Shards of glass under my feet, the colours of dreams.

In Bottletown, even our tears flicker like jewels.

DAY 3

*'We're all out there, some-
where, waiting to happen.'*

BLUE LULLABY

I woke up, inside of a dream. There was wool all around me, a total comfort fix. I was slow-drifting through the heavy layers of murmurs and soft touch, with five lovely angels singing to me, lullabies. And it felt nice.

Like a dream.

Five angels stroking me with azure blue feathers.

One of the angels had blonde hair and a dragon tattoo on her left upper arm. Her name was Desdemona. Another had black hair and black eyes rimmed with black liner and falling eyelids, with smoke rising from her body. Her name was Bridget. The third had six arms, all the better to stroke me with. His name was the Thing. The fourth had teeth like jewels, soft paws, and a long wet tongue of bliss. Her name was Karli Dog. The last of the angels was fat, but wearing it well, with two sets of eyes, one set red, the other white. Its name was the Van.

All five had feathers in their hands, and each a different technique of stroking. Their soft flutterings played all over my skin. I was naked. Unashamed, mind. Not like me at all. But I was just loving the feelings; the voices of the angels, the warm clutch of the dream.

Was this just a dream?

I reached out for the first angel. Desdemona. Blood had started to dribble from tiny punctures in her skin. She had my fingers in her mouth and she was licking at them. Then she bit down on one of them, hard, so that the skin broke, and she was licking at the blood. 'You ever gonna find me, Scribble?' she said. I had no good answers to give my sister except to reach out to embrace her. We fell into a kiss—

'Scribble! Get that fucking feather out of there!'

That was the Beetle's voice, coming into the dream. And somebody forcing my mouth open.

'You know I don't allow that. No one goes in alone!'

My eyes opened. Forced open. Beetle's eyes staring down at me, from close range. His hands messing about inside my mouth, like a fucking dentist. 'Stop biting on it!' he said. Biting on what? He reached deep inside my mouth, pulling on something soft and fluttering that had lodged there. 'Gotcha!' announced the Beetle, pulling a blue feather from deep down inside of my throat. He held it aloft like a treasure, whilst I retched and convulsed, gasping for new breath.

'Sorry,' I gasped out. 'I was dreaming . . . dreaming . . .'

'You weren't dreaming, saddo!' said the Beetle. 'You were going in alone. Nobody does that.'

'Sorry, Bee . . . I . . .'

'Fuck off. Fuck off and die if you want to. Just don't do it on the premises.'

I looked at the blue feather he'd pulled out of my mouth. 'What was I doing?'

'Blue Lullaby. You know that's only for babies.'

I breathed.

I breathed again.

G A M E   C A T

BLUE LULLABY is for when life gets bad. When life deals a
stupid hand. If you should ever find your give-a-fuck factor
has gone down to zero, this is the feather for you. Blue
Lullaby will wrap you up in blankets and cuddles, making the
bad things seem, well you know, kind of good all of a sudden.
It's sweet. But a little warning from the Cat. It works up to
a point, and it's not much of a point. It can cure the tiny
troubles; it fucks out on the big troubles, just makes them
worse. For those who need something stronger may I rec-
ommend TAPEWORMER. Except that the Cat doesn't like
these let's-make-everything-sweet feathers. Life is to be
lived, not to be dreamt about. But when life needs a gentle
hand, Lullaby could be the one. It's a cradlesong. The Cat
says—use the Lullaby, don't abuse the Lullaby. It could turn
nasty on you.
   Status: a lovely sky-blue legal, with warnings.

IT FELT
SO GOOD

I was shaking from the journey, rivered with sweat, tears just adding to the body's liquid content. I didn't know which was sweat, which was tears. That bad. The Beetle was holding my hand. It felt so good. It felt so good, that soft hand, amidst all the wanderings. Karli the robodog was lying at my feet.

'You okay, Scribb?' the Beetle asked, voice all quiet and yearning, like spring flowers, that kind of thing. Most unusual. 'You shouldn't go in alone, Scribb. How many times have I told you? You need the Beetle in there. Isn't that the truth?'

'I was just trying...'

'What's that, Scribb?'

'I was just trying...' I said, exhuming the words. 'I was just trying... I was just trying to find some comfort...'

Beetle holding me tight against his frock-coat, and I could feel his collection of biker badges biting into my wet cheek. 'You poor fucker!' he said to me. 'Brid's gone. Van's gone. Des has gone.' He was waving the now creamed-up feather in front of my face. 'And you think this is gonna bring them back? Huh?'

His voice was hard again, but still with that trace of sadness. Never heard that before. Rain was falling, Manchester rain; we listened to its soft drumbeats against the window. Beetle's eyes were full of the rain, and some drops of it fell down his cheeks, like tears. Except that all the windows were closed, so how could the rain get in? Even the window that never closed was stuffed with an old T-shirt, so how come the rain was rolling down his cheeks like that? Maybe it was tears? Maybe it was tears! Maybe the Beetle had found tears? And that felt good. It felt so good.

Bring me my van of burning desire. How I missed that chariot. And all who ride in her. The Beetle had stolen a cheap car, just to get us home, but it was a pale substitute. The van was a good friend. Now gone. The robodog was licking at my trainers. 'What's the dog doing here?' I asked.

'Suze gave the dog to you. Don't you remember?'

'Where's Mandy?' I asked, suddenly missing her.

'She went out. I think we had an argument.'

I reached into my shirt pocket for a Napalm fag. And pulled out a pasteboard card. *This is your card, said Suze.* How did it get there? Suze must have done a sly pass, whilst I was herb-sleeping. I took a long look at the picture. A young man heading for a drop, hounded by a dog. Real-life model. Collector's item. 'Do you forgive me, Beetle?' I asked, quiet-like, whilst looking at the card.

The flower clock shed a petal; it floated in a zigzag pattern, driven by sighs, down to the carpet.

'I do.'

That voice.

That voice of the Beetle.

Saying that.

Saying I do. I do forgive you. That meant so much. That meant everything. I forgive you for the weakness. I forgive you for the transgression. For doing Blue Lullaby. For going in alone. For trying to find the things that we've lost.

Never heard such words before, not from the Beetle.

'Where are the Thing and Brid?' I asked.

'I don't know. It's getting bad.'

The Beetle, saying that, with such an ache to his voice. I was getting a new picture of the main guy. He was a man without dreams. He dreamt other people's dreams, through the feathers. That was the Beetle's obsession; he had nothing else.

I realised that my eyes had closed.

When I opened them, Beetle was close. He took my body in his hands, wrapping me in his black frock-coat. It felt so good. Like a family, I guess.

I brought the card up close to my face. The young man was walking towards an abyss, a rucksack on his shoulder, the yapping dog pestering his heels. Along the top edge the number zero. Along the bottom the words The Fool. What did Suze mean by this? Karli Dog snuffling around at my feet.

'What now, Beetle?' I asked, not knowing where to go.

'I don't know, Scribble. I just don't know.'

The flat door opened with a soft breath, and Mandy stepped into the room. Her face was flushed with pleasure.

'Where have you been?' asked the Beetle.

'I've found Icarus Wing,' she said.

SNAKE SCISSORS

I was coming in the lips of Venus. She had green hair all around her milky white face, eyes so bright I was nearly blinded, and it was like shooting stars into the mouth of a goddess. And where the semen landed, against the cloth of night, the planets and the stars were formed there. I was making planets with my cock, coming on like God on heat. Took six nights to come the whole universe. On the seventh night I rested. With a giant spliff, some wine, and a Screaming Headache album. And a packet of biscuits. Arrowroot biscuits.

Felt like sitting inside somebody's head.

Which it was.

The final credits rolled. YOU HAVE BEEN DREAMING GOD-HEAD. STARRING CINDERS O'JUNIPER AND TOM JASMINE.

Over this they were playing the national anthem. This is the land that I love, and here I'll stay.

BROUGHT TO YOU BY THE CHIMERA CORPORATION. DIRECTED BY MAEVE BLUNT. PRODUCED BY HERCULES SMITH.

Me and the Beetle, Mandy between us, were sitting on the back row, surrounded by snogging couples, triples, multiples. A splattering of loners, in love with fingers. Karli the robobitch was lying on the floor between my legs.

SCRIPT BY BYRON SHANKS. LIGHTING BY JULES BULB.

People were getting up to leave the shimmy, pulling the pink feathers out of their mouths, dropping them on the parquet. Some were furtive in the leaving, others were full of boisterous laughter. Some were kissing.

SOUND BY CHER PHONER. EDITED BY ICARUS WING.

'Mandy, I love you!' shouted the Beetle. He was hugging her to his chest. Her hands were playing over his lap. I loved her too.

Felt like my cock was on fire.

Mandy had found Icarus. She'd gone back to Seb's flat. Found him in. Forced the knowledge out of him. Don't ask how. The use of hands and mouth. Something like that. No matter. The game was on.

THANK YOU FOR DREAMING WITH CHIMERA. SPONSORED BY VAZINTERNATIONAL. THE UNIVERSAL LUBRICANT. FOR LIFE'S STICKY MOMENTS. NOT TO BE USED FOR ILLEGAL PURPOSES.

Try telling that to the Beetle.

This intense desire for love was in me, fired by the shimmy. I pulled the feather from my lips, watching it go cream in my fingers.

I too wanted to fuck the universe. If not that, then a woman would do. Any woman. Christ! Even a dog would do. That's a good shimmy for you. Makes you into a god. A god of love. Even me.

'Oh Christ!' breathed Mandy, full of want. 'I'm soaking.'

'And I've got a snake in my dick!' said the Beetle. 'Let's get out of here.'

THE CHIMERA CORPORATION. SHARING THE DREAM.

Icarus didn't talk much. Hardly any. He was fat like a pig and he could hardly squeeze into that darkroom with the rest of us tight-packed in there as well. He poured shimmy mist through a viewer, eyes open for good bits.

'You got some good stuff for us?' the Beetle said to him. I could feel the Beetle's arousal, through the talk, and my own, matching him. And Mandy's.

The small room was dripping, lit by a red light. Sex was everywhere.

No response from the shimmyographer. He just kept blowing that spool. His studio was right back of the auditorium, and through the projection ducts I could see the last stragglers leaving their seats. Karli was whining from behind the door, where I'd tied her up to a Grecian pillar. 'That was a hot shimmy, Icarus. It sure got me going.' We left Beetle to do the talking. Mandy was glued to the way that Icarus was mixing the rushes. Speed-driven thrills, yards of dream flesh blurring into orgasm. Ribbons of sex. Wet dreams. Visions of loveliness. Ultra-come.

Like sitting inside somebody's head. Whilst they were mastur-bating.

Me, I had my eye on the glass tank above the mixing desk. A violet and green shape lay curling there, rolling out its tongue like an offering.

Keep that tongue to yourself, snakebreath.

The Beetle was speaking; 'Seb told us you'd got some English Voodoo. That right?'

Icarus pushed the feather further into the deck.

My left ankle started to ache and throb, like it had a hard-on, remembering the twin bite of the fangs.

'Don't know any Seb,' Icarus said.

That's funny, because he knows you.'

'Must have been mistaken.'

'That's a nice specimen you got there,' said the Beetle, nodding towards the tank. 'You see this?' He was stroking the snakehead pinned in his lapel. Icarus didn't even look up from the smoke. 'Caught that fucker myself,' Beetle continued. 'Trapped him in a door. Cut his head off.' He paused for effect, but the editor was busy with the roller; looked like he'd found something. The Beetle turned to me. 'You see that snake in the tank, Scribb?' he asked.

I nodded, not taking my eyes off the slithering bitch.

'That's one big fucker, yeah, Scribb?'

Just watching the tank, my eyes caught on the violet and the green, and the slow undulating body. Must have been all of twelve foot long.

Beetle turned back to Icarus. 'You wouldn't want that big fucker to get loose.'

Icarus looked up at him, just for a second. 'That's my best snake,' he said, and then lowered his face back to the dream mist.

'What you got?' asked Mandy.

Icarus looked over at Mandy. 'Come see,' he said.

Mandy bent low, putting her eyes to the viewer. She looked in there, close up, for maybe a full minute. During that time the dreamsnake did a complete reef-knot of movement. Each slither brought another bead of sweat to my flesh. My left leg was stinging.

'Nothing,' said Mandy, finally. 'Can't see nothing.'

'You need to look close, real close,' Icarus said.

'It's just smoke.'

'You ain't got the juice, girl. Not like me.'

And something real bad came to me then. Icarus was telling us that he had some Vurt in him. Christ knows, must have been a tiny amount; you wouldn't guess it to look at him, but maybe that's how he did this job. But the bad thing was this—maybe I could steal this fat guy and force him into a swapback. Maybe I didn't need the Thing after all, but then he waddled over to the snake cage and I saw just how useless that guy was. He was worthless. No use. Way below Desdemona. Way below Hobart's Constant.

'It's just smoke!' Mandy was saying. 'There's nothing there.'

'I'm turning mist into Vurt. That's my job. Not even that, this time. I'm just cutting bits out. Chopping out the bad bits, making it suitable. I'm making it legal. That's my job. It's not much of a job is it?'

No answer to that. None at all. We all just waited, in the silence, whilst the shimmyographer focused in on the errant scene.

'That is one big snake,' announced the Beetle. 'You really wouldn't want that snake to get loose. Would you?' He made it sound like a threat. A bad threat. The Beetle was good at that.

Icarus wasn't fazed. He reached up and clicked one catch on the tank, then the other. The lid raised up slow and sexy, like a breath exhaling. The dreamsnake unwrapped itself eagerly. I stepped back slightly, just slightly, trying to control myself. My leg hurt was stinging.

'Is there something wrong with the boy?' asked Icarus.

'Ignore him,' said Mandy. 'Tell us what you see.'

The shimmyographer jerked the mist to a frozen standstill. 'There she is!' he announced. 'Offending article. You see, Chimera send these Vurts out to the provinces, but we're just getting the bad cuts. There's stuff still in there. Non legal. I gotta check every second. It's a fucker's job, and I'm doing it. This looks like mist to you. To me it's a dream, somebody's dream, and you can't show everything. It spoils it. People want love. This bit here, the hero's stabbing his father with a kebab skewer. Through the eye.

You just can't show that. Not in a Pornovurt. It's a passion killer. Cut that fucker!'

Icarus reached inside of the tank and grabbed the dreamsnake by the neck. It writhed around like a whiplash crack, but he had it between his fingers, and with the other hand he reached for a small ball hammer. He pushed it into a jar of paste, coating the hammer head with sap.

This was the squeezed-out flowers of the snakeweed, the only known cure for dreamsnake bite. It grew on the plains of Utanka, an obscure high-level Vurt, available only to the cognoscenti. Icarus gently tapped the ball of the hammer on the top of the snake's head. The head proceeded to droop, as the slit eyes glazed over.

We watched as that snake took a vicious bite out of the dream. He lifted it away from the mist, and the two streams of smoke coalesced into a new state, a clean state. 'That's better,' Icarus said. 'Feels clean now.' He stepped closer to me. There were tiny yellow flecks in his eyes, which seemed to glow brighter as he held the snake up to my face. I stumbled back, knocking against a feather bank. Streams of mist were pouring out of it, choking the room.

'What's wrong, young man?' Icarus asked. 'Don't you like snakes?'

'Get it off me!' I screamed.

Icarus waved the snake in front of my nose. 'I'm in control,' he said. 'I'm the boss of snakes.'

'Scribble had an unfortunate incident,' the Beetle told Icarus. 'Some years ago now. Just can't get over it.'

'He was bit by one?'

'Yes.'

'I knew it. You've got the Vurt inside you, boy.'

'Not me—'

'They always deny it at first.'

I'm pure! Tell him I'm pure, Bee!'

'Better had be,' answered the Beetle. 'Can't stand hybrids.'

Icarus was holding me with a bright stare. 'Pure is poor, feath-erboy,' he said, and I swear that I saw the glints of flights in his eyes. 'You're got some juice inside, kid.'

Icarus said that, and I was drawn back. Back through the years, the months, like time was streaked with Vaz.

Something was stirring . . .

I was seventeen years old. There was a red sun that day, I re-member, and the trees were full of starlings. I was lying in the grass of Platt Fields, with a girl named Desdemona. She was my sister, fifteen years old, but I loved her a lot. Too much. More than is good. More than is legal. She was stretched out and hot, and my right hand was stroking her leg, way up, and she was smiling. She moved her head slightly and her lips were touching mine. I had a hard-on. Hard-on for a sister. Five seconds later she was touching the hard-on through my pants, then was up on top of me, her hair a blonde halo against the scarlet sun, and I was caressing the dragon tattoo on her upper arm.

'If father should find us . . .' she said.

Imagine, she said that. She actually said that. Not Vurt or robo; real words from a real mouth. Her twin lips like the two halves of a dream, slightly parted.

Her cunt was pressed against my cock and the world was pretty.

'Don't let's talk about dad,' I answered.

'He scares me, Scribble.'

'I will always look out for you.'

The two of us laughing then, I remember that, before those lips descended to mine, and we were sealed.

Some things you just can't destroy, and this memory is one of them.
She kissed me. A raging full-on contact. The sun was blocked out. My eyes were shut. Her hair fell against my cheeks and lights danced in my eyes. I was in honey. 'I'll love you forever,' the voice whispered, and I can't remember if it was mine, or hers. I felt the pleasure build all the way through me, even down to the ankles, my left ankle especially, for some reason. The pleasure just there was intense, like I'd never felt before. Next thing, Desdemona was screaming, and the pleasure turned into pain. She jumped off me, turning to see the colours flashing. I jerked up, pulled by the fire in my leg, and saw the dreamsnake feeding there, twin fangs clamped shut, around my ankle, and the sun was a blister in my vision.

I opened my eyes to the barking of a robodog. Mandy had Karli by a taut lead, the bitch's muzzle inches from the dreamsnake in Icarus's hand.

'You deliver the goods, Icarus . . .' the Beetle was saying. 'English Voodoo. Or the snake gets it . . .'

G A M E   C A T

Every morning the Game Cat opens his big sack. Oh my
kittlings! All those letters! It's lucky the Cat has such a large
brain, good drugs, and all the time in the universe to spend
on helpful hints. Oh all your problems! How on earth do
you live down there? Real life seems so physical these days;
so very *meaty.* And the one subject that transfixes you,
more than any other? How can I get higher? How can I get
out of this hole? How can I get to live like the Cat? In other
words; let me get my hands on some KNOWLEDGE
FEATHERS. Where can I buy some English Voodoo, some
Talking Bush, some MegaHead? Or any of the other Knowledge Feathers that may, or may not exist? The Cat has said
it a thousand times; you don't buy knowledge, you earn
knowledge. Still the letters flood in. So let it be said, once
and for all: Knowledge Vurt is for the few, not the herd.
They are multicoloured steps on a ladder of dreams. They
are made by the heavenly for their own enjoyment. They

are dangerous to the innocent. That's you, little kittling. Comprendez? They can't be bought. If someone offers to sell you one, believe me, it's a fake, it's a pirate copy. Pirates don't give knowledge, they just steal your money. And bring you grief. Because invariably these cheapo mixes are infested with Vipers. And if you don't know what Vipers are, you shouldn't be within a thousand miles of Knowledge Vurt.

This is your final warning.

AN ENGLISH
GARDEN

Beetle poured his Vaz into another lock, and we drove a cheap bust-up Ford back to base. We were feeling pretty high, what with the afterglow of the sex shimmy, and the Voodoo feather held tight in my fingers. There was laughter and craziness in the car, and every streetlamp brought a dazzle to the Knowledge Feather; it was black, pink, and gold in my hands, and the gold was the most beautiful. We rode into the Rusholme Gardens like warriors. Twinkle was waiting for us. She'd got into the flat somehow, through the tight security, and Beetle wanted to know how.

'I don't know, Bee,' I said.

'You give her a key?'

'Me?'

Twinkle was sitting on the couch, supercool, chewing on a Choc-U-Fat.

'Scribble, get that baby out of here.'

I tried, but failed miserably. The kid wasn't budging. 'She's not moving, Bee,' I said, pulling on her arms. It was like someone had smeared her arse with anti-Vaz.

'I'm in the gang now,' Twinkle said. 'I've swapped with Bridget.'

'Has the kid gone yet?' asked Beetle.

'Not yet. No.'

'What you doing, giving keys away?'

'She's lonely, Bee. Got a terrible homelife—'

Mandy started to laugh. 'Let's do it, Bee!' she said. And then the Beetle was moving to the table, stroking Vaz into the flights of the Voodoo feather. I could see the yellow glints shining and they were opening doors in my mind, onto a yellow haze where my sister was waiting for me. Beetle was popping some Jammers, like he was expecting a hard trip and tickling Mandy's face with the feather, the same time. 'Try this for size,' he said, and he stroked it into Mandy's mouth. 'Oh god, I'm melting,' she said, taking it like a robopro. Then the Beetle moved over towards Twinkle.

'Beetle! It's too high for her!'

'She wants in, Scribble, she gets in.'

'She's underage, Bee—'

'We're all underage,' he replied, and Twinkle's mouth was open, ready to accept the gift. Beetle stroked the young girl. I could see him getting off on it. I'll bet he was getting hard on it, still charged up from the Pink shimmy.

'You ever done this before?' asked Mandy, from the slow depths of Vurt.

'Course I have. Loads of times!' Twinkle answered.

'Well swallow this then,' said The Beetle.

'Go easy, Beetle,' I said. 'Mandy, help me . . .'

But Mandy was gone, riding the feather.

And then the Twinkle was gone, the same trip.

Just me and the Bee left.

'Beetle?'

'What?'

'I think we're doing this badly. Let's slow it down some.'

'Yeah? For why?'

'Voodoo's dangerous. You don't know, Bee. I've been there. It's—'

'Suck on this, baby! We lost Brid and the Thing, just to please you. Now fucking well take it! Let's go find the sister.'

My lips were parted to speak in protest, except that he pushed the feather between them, and I was riding it as well, riding good, down to the wet source, and I could feel the credits rolling, just like all that time ago, with Desdemona at my side, and then I was gone . . .

WELCOME TO ENGLISH VOODOO. EXPECT TO FEEL PLEASURE. KNOWLEDGE IS SEXY. EXPECT TO FEEL PAIN. KNOWLEDGE IS TORTURE.

. . . falling towards the garden.

The garden was serene and beautiful, quintessentially English, just like I remembered, with burbling fountains and a mass of flowers growing wild, overflowing their beds. It was enclosed by a circular wall, but that was miles away, and I wasn't interested in what lay out there. I wanted the garden; its heady perfume was caressing my senses, and a burst of pleasure was choking me, like every drop of blood in my veins had taken a sap-ride to my cock. Felt like exploding some, into the goddess of earth, the witch of dirt. I felt like digging a hole in the soil and just doing it, but something was keeping me back; knowledge of the mission. I was inside the Vurt, and I knew that I was, but I wasn't getting the Haunting! I felt control flood through me, like I'd been seeded with some-thing, some new knowledge. I was in the garden of English Voodoo, looking for the Curious Yellow feather, where Desdemona lay waiting, living in pain. The Beetle and Mandy were walking hand in hand through the flowers, the way that young lovers do. Twinkle was breaking off a flower head, bringing it to her nostrils. She was smiling, feeling the perfume stroking her. Karli Dog was chasing butterflies through the briar patches, getting covered in petals. Shit! Beetle had stroked the robodog too, a feather inside a dog's mouth. No matter. We were all there, having a good time. Knowledge was seeping from the flowers, like the breath of pollen. The Beetle raised his hand, waved at me, lazy-like, and I answered him the same. The world was blissful. I was falling into a haze of peace and it took all that I had just to keep from drifting away. I was looking for the gardeners. The ones Desdemona and I had joined the last time. Or the bird in the trees. But the garden was empty. Just us Stash Riders in there, wandering amongst the flowers.

The garden was empty.

It didn't feel right.

'Beetle!' I called. He turned his slow face to me, smiling. 'There's something wrong,' I said to him. Beetle just smiled.

'Everything's dandy, Scribb,' he answered, with a soft voice. He clutched Mandy closer to him, revelling in her feel.

It didn't feel right, somehow.

A movement in the grass, down at my feet. Maybe it was the yellow bird, searching for food. I looked down.

A violet and green slithering there, amongst the grasses and the stalks.

Dreamsnake!

Even in the garden of bliss, those slimy creatures find a way through.

Stepping back . . .

'Beetle!'

Too late.

The snake rising up from the grass, filling the garden with his whiplash body. Snake-eyes staring at me.

Oh shit!

How did that get in here?

'Beetle!' I shouted. 'There's a Viper in here! Feather's not real. It's a pirate!'

Beetle was too far gone to care. And the snake was laughing at me.

THERE'S SOME VIPER IN YOUR SYSTEM, LITTLE ONE.

'What's happening?' I asked.

Viper was Viral Implant; germs in the Vurt system; ways to make you suffer.

YOU'RE INSIDE A THEATRE. IT'S CALLED ENGLISH VOODOO. IT'S A PIRATE KNOWLEDGE VURT. TOTALLY ILLEGAL. NONE OF THIS IS REAL.

'What?'

'It's worse than real. You're under arrest, kid. That real enough for you?'

I pulled away from that vicious face, looking for the Beetle and Mandy, and Twinkle and Karli. All I saw were four wavering shapes, as they jerked out together, and then I was following them, jerking back, and the garden fading to a patch of weed blackness . . .

The shecop Murdoch was smiling down at me. Her dumbfuck partner was standing two feet off, near the bathroom door, obscuring my Madonna poster. A shadowcop was writhing around the room-space, straight out of the garden, a violet and green undulation. The partner was broadcasting the shadow from a portable unit and the snake was beaming onto us. Never seen one like this before. It was the snake from the garden; he had followed us through into the real world. Snake must have some Vurt in him—robo, shadow, Vurt—all mixed up in a five-foot length of thick smoke, eyes of orange flashing inpho all over us, and a voice of yellow slitherings:

WE HAVE REASON TO BELIEVE THAT THIS IS AN ILLEGAL GAMEPLAY.

'No. I . . . it's . . . it's just . . .'

I was back in my favorite armchair, struggling with the words. I just couldn't find the right ones.

PLEASE EXPLAIN THE VEHICLE IN THE FORECOURT.

I couldn't explain. Couldn't move. Couldn't raise a finger in battle.

PLEASE EXPLAIN THE VIOLATION.

'I . . . I can't.'

My lips were the only moving parts, and then only just. I was mumbling excuses, weak excuses.

Mandy and the Beetle were lying on the settee together, all wrapped up from the garden still. I could see their bodies were still jerking from the dream, but they weren't showing their faces. The young girl, Twinkle, was standing by the fire, her eyes full of life. She had Murdoch in her sights. *Don't try it, kid. She'll just beat you to a pulp.* Karli the robodog was by Twinkle's side, the plastic bones shaking under her fur.

SAID VEHICLE IS NOT REGISTERED IN YOUR NAME.

Twinkle started to move forwards, towards the shecop.

ALSO SUSPECTED PURCHASE AND USE OF VARIOUS OTHER ILLEGAL SUBSTANCES, AS FOLLOWS . . .

'That's enough, Shaka,' said Murdoch.

These things had names!? These smoky wraiths? I never knew that.

THEY ARE ENTITLED TO THEIR RIGHTS, AS STATED UNDER DECREE FIVE.

'Of course they are,' replied Murdoch. 'It's just that I'm taking over.'

Twinkle was two feet away from Murdoch. Beetle and Mandy were still in a close embrace, still shivering but coming down, slowly, ever so slowly.

ALSO SUSPECTED HARBOURING OF A VURT ALIEN. A LIVE DRUG. DECREE FIFTEEN QUITE PLAINLY STATES—

'Okay!' shouted Murdoch. 'This is my score. I'm bringing you down for this. Harbouring, possession, bootlegging. The whole shit. You're getting it.' She pulled a flame gun from her waist band.

The chair was clutching at me, and I could still feel the garden's touch on my fingers.

'Game over. Partner, cuff them.'

The fleshcop started to move, wallowing side to side under his fat middle. Mandy had awoken now, and was rolling over towards the action. Her eyes were fear-shot. The Beetle wasn't moving. Not yet. He was all folded up on the settee, shaking from the jerkout and Vurtlag.

'Out of the way, girl,' said Murdoch, not even looking at Mandy as she said it. Mandy got up off the settee, cool and deadly. Murdoch had the gun pointed straight at the Beetle's head. 'Okay, boss man, this is your alarm call.'

Beetle didn't move.

Me neither. Felt like time was slowing down, and I was just a caught fly in its embrace, wings in honey.

THIS IS NOT THE STANDARD PROCEDURE said the shadowcop.

'You want to file a complaint, Shaka'

NO, MA'AM. I DO NOT.

Karli and Twinkle made a move towards Murdoch, The dog's paws were scratching at the carpet.

'Call them off, little boy. You know it's the end.'

I tried to, but my lips were parched and stuck, and my tongue was dead.

Twinkle and the dog were inches away from the cop.

'Call the fuckers off!' Murdoch screamed, the gun locked between her fingers, aimed with a raging full-on, dead set on the back of Beetle's head.

This is where he is, the hero, when you need him the most. Fast asleep on an old worm-hive settee, bought for a fiver down a Junk-U-Don't-Want.

'I got one cuffed, Murdoch.' It was the partner speaking, his words flabby with heavy breaths. My eyes made a quick glance. There was Mandy, all cuffed up to one of the fatso cop's wrists. He was looking pretty pleased with himself. Most probably he'd never met a girl like Mandy before.

Guy was gonna find out.

The shadowcop was firing inphos all over the room, looking for clues. I'M GETTING SOMETHING, he said.

'What is it?' asked Murdoch.

INSUFFICIENT INPHO AS OF YET.

'Thanks for the inpho, Shaka, but I think you're getting on my nerves, just a little bit.'

UNDERSTOOD. Shaka's eyes were flaring with bright orange, like he was working up to a flame beam.

'Let's keep this under control, people.' Murdoch was putting on a good show, but I could see the sweat on her face. 'That includes you, Shaka! Keep those beams cool. No one gets hurt.' And the shadowsnake's eyes went from hot to cold. You could see the disappointment all the way through his swirling body.

Twinkle and the dog were close to the moment now, except they didn't know what to do, how to handle it. Twinkle was reaching out with one hand, almost as if she was going to say,

'Please don't hurt my friends, Mrs Shecop,' and I wouldn't put it past her. The dog was making a low growl.

'Back off, Twinkle,' I said. My tongue felt like a slug nested in my throat. And she did, the youngster, this being my sad little power over her. Her hand dropped slowly to her dirty dress, where it fiddled and twirled in the folds.

'Back off, Karli.' My voice again. And the dog obeyed, so maybe there was more to Suze than I thought. She'd given me the power over the dog, passed it on, all in secret. Karli moved back slightly but her eyes were still clenched and full of damage.

'Okay. Everybody's happy,' breathed Murdoch, the gun still on a straight run to Beetle's brain. 'Cuff the other one,' she added, nodding her head towards me. The partner came towards my chair, dragging Mandy behind. In his free hand he held a new set of cuffs.

'I'm running out of hands, Murdoch,' he said.

'Just fucking do it!' was her reply. 'To the chair!' So the fat cop made a move towards me, fumbling with the key and the cuffs. This guy was a loser, I know that now, but he still had a few seconds of dominance left in him. He waved the cuffs in front of my slow eyes.

'Take it easy, young man,' he said to me.

I couldn't move my body, but I could move my mouth, having already proved that. 'Take a running fuck, fatso.' I said, not even knowing I had those words within me.

'It's all over, big guy,' Murdoch said to the Beetle's sleeping shape. He moved slightly then, stirring from his deep pit.

'I know it,' he said, his voice full of thick juice from the game. 'I know when I'm beaten.'

That's not like you, Beetle. Where's the fire?

The fat partner had one of my wrists in his free hand, and he was trying gamely to cuff me to the chair. I was struggling against him but the Vurtlag was still heavy in my brain, and I was a slow dream, waiting for the dawn. The cuffs were clunking in a half-bite, missing the hole in the sweat and the fear. The cop was dropping beads of sweat on to my trousers. 'Come on,' he said. 'Do it!' More to the cuffs than to me, I think.

'I thought I told you already,' I told him. 'Go and take a running one.'

He looked at me like I was a bad dream he couldn't wake up from. *Oh good. I'm glad.*

'Come up slowly, Beetle man,' said Murdoch.

'I'm coming up like a slow train,' said the Beetle, turning around on the settee. 'You win, Murdoch. Game over.'

Fat cop had forgotten all about Mandy in his struggles. Shadowcop hadn't though: I DO BELIEVE, SIR, THAT'S SHE'S GOING TO—

Did no good.

Mandy had twisted around behind the cop, and now she had her free arm around his neck, pulling back, until he started to cry out. I felt my mind zooming to focus as the last of the Vurt peeled away, and then my hands were moving fast, faster than snakes, until they reached his free hand, which he was using to prise away Mandy's fingers. My fingers clamped around his knuckles.

'I said leave off, pigshit.'

Murdoch could see the trouble going down so she had moved her gun away from the Beetle slightly, trying to get a new fix. The Beetle rolled over, and then up, until he was sitting on the edge of the couch, and his hand was already inside of his coat.

MURDOCH! I'M GETTING SOMETHING!

But Murdoch had already seen what was happening. She was turning back to the Beetle, but too late, way too late, the Beetle had pulled his hand out again, into the open, and a gun was clenched tight in his fingers. The Beetle's gun. In use at last.

'It's that time of day, Murdoch,' he said.

'Shaka!' Murdoch's call sent the shadowsnake into action. His beams swung in from every corner until they pulled in a tight focus on the Beetle's gun.

FLAME PISTOL. 0.38. FULLY LOADED. SIX BULLETS.

The partner cop was struggling between Mandy and me but we had him tight yet. 'Wooh!' shouted Mandy. 'We're happening!'

'Don't go silly on me,' Murdoch said to Beetle.

'Kill, Karli!' I shouted. 'Destroy!'

Young dog went for it.

Murdoch's gun roared and flashed, but the dog was there first, knocking her off her feet. The shecop was on the floor, Karli on top of her, biting at her face. The bullet lodged in the wall, knocking petals off the clock, and Shaka was beaming everywhere, panic-struck. Twinkle was coming towards me and the fat partner, her tiny fingers bunched into fists. The gun in Beetle's hand waved in the air, and there was a look of pure Jam in his eyes.

The fleshcop made a big push with his bulbous gut, shoving me back into the chair. Then he took off towards the Beetle, pulling Mandy along behind him, still cuffed. She was beating on his back and shouting at him, calling him all the names of the famous fuckers, but he was reaching down to the floor anyway, to where Murdoch's gun lay waiting.

Sometimes we just go too far, partner.

Beetle shot him.

Beetle shot him! *And all these miles and days away, I'm still listening to that shot of flame.*

Murdoch was screaming under the dog Karli, holding those jaws back with fists of pain. Dog was eating at her fingers. And the fleshcop's blood splattered all over the walls and the floor. It made a beautiful mess, like a garden of scarlet wounds, and I was gladdened by the sight of it. My life was just a few seconds adrift in those moments.

'Shaka!' screamed Murdoch, her face bloody from the dog's teeth. 'Shaka, call up! Call up!'

Petals were falling all over, drifting down in waves from the severed clock-face, and Shaka was calling up the station, beaming through the petals. Except that the beams were hot! Petals bursting into flames as the snakehead came whipping around the small room, aiming for a total burn-out. A line of fire along the back of the settee, heading towards Beetle. So Beetle shot the snake. Of course nobody can shoot a Shadow. The Beetle had put a hole in the shadowcop's aerial box. Shaka was a wounded ghost then. And then just a wraith, a thin wraith, fighting for life. His beams went dark. His face was a silent cry and holes were opening up in the body of smoke. He was fading to black, the deep emptiness, which is Shadow-death.

Beetle was glued to the seat, the gun in his hands, both hands clenched, and his eyes wide from the action. Murdoch screaming from under the dog.

'Get the pig off me!' shouted Mandy, her face smeared with the thick blood of the fleshcop. 'Can somebody please undo these cuffs, please.'

I could move then, and I stood up, out of the clutching chair, away from the fear. I moved over to the dead cop. I found the keys on the floor, and set Mandy free. 'Cheers, Scribb,' she said. The cuffs fell to the lino, one ring still around the cop's wrist. Beside his body I saw Murdoch's gun, just lying there. I slipped it into my pocket. 'Karli, that's enough.' The dog moved back slightly.

Beetle had risen up, and he had the flame pistol pressed against Murdoch's temple. Her face was a pleasure to behold, all cracked with fear and blood. Her shecop eyes were clenched tight shut against the moment. I saw a feather down on the floor, next to Murdoch's head. I picked it up. Cheap fake Knowledge Feather, going cream in my hands.

'That's enough, Beetle' I said. 'Job is done.'

We're all just out there, somewhere, waiting to happen.

DAY 21

'Babe, it's going all the way.'

CONTAMINATED WITH BASS

'The djinn is going in! Feel it! Feel it!'

Two hands, separate, but in time with the big rhythm, working the Siamese decks.

'Big djinn going in now! For the Collyhurst disciples. They are in the Limb! They are in the fucking Limb!'

Two hands, two small human hands, working the twin decks, the triple decks, the quadruple decks of the Limbic System house.

'This one's on special import! All the way from Noirpool! Coming on tough-core from the Limbic System, out of the North. This is a white label dream coming at you! Ha ha ha! Dance, suckers, dance!'

Twin hands working the infinite decks, mixing dreams with real time stories, forcing sweat out of hard-packed bodies. I can make a dead man dance. Fuck that. I can make a robot dance, a Shadow dance.

I was looking through the booth glass, watching the submasses moving, groin to groin, or just on their own. Men, women, real or Vurt. Robo or smoke. I'm moving them all, at last, the whole congregation, all of the various shapes of existence, moving to the latest remix from the Interactive Madonna.

'We're all together, at last!' I shouted. And my voice was amplified throughout all of the land, all of the places of Limbic, all of the wide-open spaces, and all of the darkest corners.

'Play that Limbic Splitter, white boy!' called a voice from the dance floor. Voice came through the system like a flare-path, all of a purple sheen, just the voice of a nowhere girl caught tight in a shining moment, but in that moment she was a queen.

'Inky MC is talking to yer, live and direct, from the space between the beats, all the way to the floor. 'This one's for you, lone dancer! Step up lively now! Dance on it!'

She did. And they all did. And the whole house was misting over, side-swaying in step to the house fuel.

'You got them, Ink!' said the Twinkle, from over in the corner where she was eating a Bassburger from a plastic tray. 'You got them going, and good!'

'Hey listen, it's early yet. Watch this!'

'Keep on doing it,' she says, between mouthfuls.

A knock on the booth door then. Uh oh. Another sponger. 'I'm busy,' I cry.

'Come on, Mister DJ, give us a go on the bass,' says the voice from behind the panel. I don't recognise it, but Twinkle opens the door anyway and I see a pale-facer standing there, that look of deep need in his eyes.

'I need some bass, man,' he's saying, eyes full of glazed-up wonder. 'More bass! More bass!'

'I think not,' I answer. He doesn't care.

'Give us some bass! Come on!'

The Twinkle moves in, blocking the door gap. 'The Ink man, he say no,' she tells him.

'Oh come on!'

'Go fuck a sponge cake, loser!' says the Twinkle, slamming the booth door on the sucker.

That girl is growing up too fast and maybe it's all my fault.

Well I don't care any more.

I'm losing the will to care, and I find it beautiful.

Maybe I'm changing for the worst. Maybe for the better.

Because maybe the worst is the best, when you get far enough down.

I slap a Twister on the deck mat and lay the syringe on the run-in groove, lining up the ghost track on the skull-phones, then letting the whole thing kick into bloom with a Manc yell.

'Tune! Tune for the brood! All the people in the block. Limbic dopers! This is from Dingo Tush, latest tune! They're calling it Sampled Under Foot. Know where that comes from! Dingo Tush later, coming on live with the Warewolves. Just for now, here comes the Rain Girl remix. Sampled Under Fuck! Tough-core, babies!!!'

'Can I come to the after-gig party, Ink?' says Twinkle.

'No you cannot. You can just go home, Karli will see you there, and I will meet you later.'

'Aw, Scribb . . .'

'Don't call me that.'

But the noise was coming on loud as I flexed the decks, right up to Ultimax. People are moving, grooving, improving, super-smoothing. From over in a dark corner Karli the robobitch was howling to the music and I plugged her in, direct to the flex, mixing her barking in with beats. Crowd were soaking in it, howling at the full moon lighting patterns. Looked like a fox clan party in the mating season. People were near to rutting, just because of my music, and I was loving it, loving the power, when there's another knock on the door.

'Tell them to get lost, Twinkle. No deals.'

'Get lost!' said the Twinkle. 'No deals!'

'It's me, Scribble,' said the voice from behind the door, and my hands slipped on the decks as I let that voice get to me. Dancers missed a beat, wrong footing, and they were complaining out loud, through the system.

Oh shit! Oh no! Not now!

'Mandy?' said Twinkle.

'Keep her away!' I demanded.

'MC Inky says no,' she tried, towards the shut door.

No use.

'It's me, Scribb. The not-so-new girl.'

And then a silence as I tried to ignore that strong voice. Mandy's voice.

'I've got the Beetle with me,' she added, and I went a little bit weak.

'Scribble?' It was the Beetle calling, his voice so insistent, so kind.

Fuck that! That's all over.

'That's not my name, pal.' I was resisting, trying to resist anyway.

'Beetle wants to see you, Scribb,' Mandy pleaded. 'He's missing your action.'

Moments passed as the voice of Dingo Tush led the crowd towards ecstasy, and Twinkle was looking at me, with that look in her eyes, that sweet look.

'Shall I let them in, Mister Scribb . . . I mean Ink?'

Seven bars of music passed by before I answered.

Booth door opens and that ungodly twosome, that pair of reprobates fall in the DJ box, and I just couldn't help it, my weak heart was full of love for them. A kind of bruised love, truth be known.

'Scribble!' The Beetle drooled.

'Okay, Beetle,' I said. 'The name's Ink MC.'

'Aye. I heard that.' His eyes were triple glazed. 'Long time, my man.'

'Sure.'

I was holding back the feelings, on purpose, just to spite him, just to build my dreams up, just to break even.

Just to break even. Because sometimes you've got to do the best you can, in order to come out smiling, just by a little bit.

'Scribble, baby, you've got your posse with you!'

'I'm busy, Bee,' I answered. And I was, working the decks like a pilgrim, searching for God. That's the god of Limbic. The god of music, hidden inside the beats.

'Twinkle and the Karli Dog,' the Beetle carried on. 'You've got them in tow. That's a nice one. And here's me thinking you were all alone in the world these days.'

'Maybe you don't know me well enough, Bee.' I looked into his eyes and saw a cracked ghost hiding there.

Beetle was like a zombie. One of those zombies you see working the all-night garages, pouring petrol and Vaz into pimpmobiles, eyes full of fumes, blood-knots, and boredom. Never seen the Bee look bored before.

'Maybe you're right all of a sudden,' he replied.

I had to turn away. 'How you sailing, Mandy?'

'Hanging on, Scribble,' she answered. Her hair was as red as the skin of a postbox, and it sure made me tremble.

'Come on, Mandy,' The Beetle slurred. 'Come meet the Scribble once again. He's making a living for himself. He's . . . he's playing the . . . oh shit . . . nevermind . . .'

His voice trailed off into the distance and his vision closed on some thousand-yard stare, some far off wonder, way beyond this realm.

'What's he on, Mandy?'

'Tapewormer.'

Oh dear. Tapewormer. That was a bad feather, Bee. That was a bad move.

'Shit, man!' I said, turning back to him. 'What's happening to you?'

'Hey, Scribble?' he asked. 'How did you manage such a landing? You got contacts?'

'Yeah sure, I got contacts.'

'That's nice!'

'That's right. It's nice,' I answered. 'You look like fuck, Bee.'

'Well I guess so. But it's a good fuck.'

'Anything from the Thing, or Bridget?'

'Yeah sure, everyday . . .'

'What?'

'I'm with them everyday.'

'You found them?'

'Sure I did. They're inside of here, babes,' and he was tapping with an uncut fingernail on the side of his temple. Oh well, that's Tapewormer for you.

'What are you doing here, Mandy?' I asked.

'Said he wanted to find you. Said he wanted to get up close again . . .'

'Damn right, Scribb,' the Beetle said.

'Said he wanted the Stash Riders back together.'

'Stash Riders are dead,' I said. Beetle's mouth opened and closed like a Thermo Fish chewing on some sick blood.

Just then Dingo Tush came on the stage, with his pack of players, the Warewolves. They were a ragged collection of hybrids; robodogs, shadowdogs, girl and boy dogs. They struck up a loud noise, full up on wolf howls and furry beats, and I managed a good fade on the mixer despite the anger flooding my system.

'What we doing, Dogpeople?' shouted Dingo to his crowd.

'Barking for Britain!!!' One voice, one howl.

'Will you look at that turd taster!' announced the Beetle. 'Looks like he's too much Alsatian in him.'

'A whole lot,' I answered, watching the dogman through the glass. He was working the crowd up to a slobber, his fur swinging back and forth to the beat of his dog drummer.

Tune was called Bitch Magnet, and his rap was barking!

'I cannot take that!' snarled the Beetle. 'Dog fucking! I mean, who the hell would find that a pleasure?'

'The brood loves him.'

'Fucking pervs! They're just tart-seed, that lot. Fucking bunch of impurities!'

'Where you living these days?' Mandy asked.

'Can't tell you that.'

'Shit, you can't!' the Beetle said. 'This is the Beetle talking! It was me that dragged you free of the slime. Remember your life, Scribble? Before you met me?'

'The name is MC Inky.'

'You'll always be the Scribble to me. Or maybe Stevie.'

'Then it's over,' I said.

'What's that?'

'Between us.'

'You making a living doing this, Scribb?'

'No. Not really. Just about.'

'I know that story.'

'Keep selling the drugs, Bee. No problems.'

'Plug us in, Scribb.'

'No way.'

'Go on, Ink man. To the bass.'

'You're not getting around me'

'I've got some Vurt.'

'I don't do that any more.'

'Good Vurt.'

'I'm going clean.'

'I've got some Tapewormer.'

'I don't want to know.'

Oh God, keep me strong. Don't let me be tempted.

'Plug me in, Ink baby. To the bass. Me and Mandy. We want it. Right, Mandy?'

Mandy was looking at me, that first look, like when I'd found her, stealing Bloodvurts from the market stall. 'I can't control him any more, Scribb,' she said. Her eyes flicked over to where the Beetle was swaying to some hidden dream, worming the tape back. 'He keeps going in alone. Says I don't belong there, not where he's going. Says I don't deserve to meet the Desdemona. I would've liked to have met your sister, Scribble. She sounds like a cool girl. I don't know what to say. I really miss the group. I miss carrying aliens up the stairs. I miss you, Scribble. That's the truth.'

Moments of silence. Me dumbfounded.

Broken by the Beetle; 'Course you do, Mandy. I mean like, don't we all?'

'You reckon Desdemona misses the Riders?' I asked.

'You still looking for that corpse, Scribb?' the Beetle said, and the anger came through then, into my eyes, causing tears to form there.

'I think you should fuck yourself silly, Bee. And then get out of here.'

'Come on, man! Plug us in. Let's taste the bass! Come on, the Scribb. Deliver. For once! Deliver it!'

Okay, the Beetle. You want it. Come get it. Hope you choke

to death on it. I had the five-pin plug in my hands and I was shaking as I fed it. Straight to the gate. The Beetle was wide open at the mouth, and his gums were bleeding as I rammed the bass flex home. And then I was turning it up, turning the bass right up, way past the legal limits, and I was calling to the crowd the same time.

'Limbic brood! This is for you! Feel it! Feel it! Dingo Tush! Calling to yer! Leave some space for the bass, Dog Star!'

Brood went crazy, pumping it, as the bass kicked in and The Beetle was dancing in the air as the heavy waves pounded his system. Seemed like his body was about to burst. He was calling out my name, calling me to stop the bass from going any deeper.

Babe, it's going all the way!

Know that feeling?

I'll bet.

DAY 22

'My mind was like a stranger,
a cold-hearted stranger
with a gun in his hands.'

S L I T H Y   T O V E

Doorman at the Slithy Tove was a fat white rabbit. He had a blood-flecked head protruding from beer-stained neck fur and a large pocket watch in his big white mittens. The big hand was pointing to twelve, the little hand pointing to three. That's three o'clock in the morning of the night just begun.

Two door whores were trying to blag their way in without a coding symbol. Rabbit was dealing them grief. I flashed my laminated access-all-areas after-gig party passcode, formed to the shape of a small and cute puppy dog half-cut with a human baby, dappled in fur; overleaf, a photo of Dingo Tush, naked but for his (authorised) autograph. Around the edge of the pass ran the slogan—Dingo Tush. Barking for Britain Tour. Presented by Das Uberdog Enterprises.

Rabbit bouncer scanned my pass and then looked up into my

eyes. It was a hard stare. 'I was the Dingo's DJ tonight, partner,' I told him. He was suitably enamoured; he let me pass.

I pushed through the slithy portals, through the hole in the earth, along the shelves of jam, all the way through the corridor of hanging-on liggerettes, straight to the crush.

Must have been five hundred people in there, that small space; friends, lovers, enemies, husbands, wives, second cousins, groupies, agents, roadies, managers, fur dressers, bone-buriers, flea pickers, glitter dogs and litter men, DJ's VJ's, SJ's, mothers, smothers, ex-lovers, record pushers. All the entourage of Dingo Tush, dancing around the handbag Vurt transmitted from the roofbeams, and then more spilling out into the Fetish Garden, under a streetlamp moon, still dancing.

I walked into the crush, and was driven up, and lost, plugged in straight off, with a whiff of Bliss. You just can't get away from it. The love is clinging. Well, when it's breathed in direct, through the air conditioning, I mean, what chance do you have? I took a deep mouthful, felt high as a paper plane. Man, that was good Bliss Wind. I took another gulp, full lungful this time, head was spinning and I loved everybody in the crush all of a sudden. Caressed my way to the bar and ordered a glass of Fetish. The dark spicy afternotes hit my palette, causing sparks, and I was floating, hot. Slithy Tove system was playing The Ace of Bones. Original pressing by Dingo Tush, but this was the hard (hard!) remix, cooked up by Acid Lassie, and it was dancing the crush to a frenzy. I turned around, leaning my back against the bar, just to view the scenes better. I was gazing into a dub mirror. That's the kind where you only get the best bits looking back at you. It was that splendid mix of Bliss and Fetish, dogmusic and crush-dancing; makes you feel like a star in your own system.

I swigged another gulp of Fetish, relished it, breathed deep of the Bliss scent, then turned on, full on, to the crowd and the crush, and just drenched myself in it. Christ, I needed release!

There was a balcony up above, and I had the sudden clear thought that I would like to be up there, looking down on the herd. So I pushed off from the bar, holding my glass tightly, and entered the maelstrom, squeezing through tight gaps between dancers. Some were dressed in black, some in purple, some in vinyl, some in feathers, some in rainbows, some in bare flesh, some in fur, some in smoke and herb, some in tatters, some in splatters. The rest in pin-stripe. All the colours were present. Sweat was dripping off me already, as I entered a small circle of feather sharers, and as I passed they gave me a quick tickle to the throat, just a little one, so I only caught a glimpse of moon-flecked meadows as I flew over them, flapping my thunderwings, chasing the prey. Gang was on Thunderwings, and its sweet feel stayed with me as I moved on, forcing a path towards the stairs. Thunderwings helped me through the crush, and up the stairs. Felt like I was flying those stairs. Up to the balcony, where the world lay waiting.

That was my first Vurt in eighteen days, since the night we took out that fat cop, and it felt like coming home, that tasty. Maybe I was weakening. It didn't seem so bad to be weakening.

Life on the balcony was quieter. Not so tight. There were chairs, and people talking to each other at tables, and food. And food! Hadn't eaten in a week! Seemed like. But first I had to look down, to see that crush from the heights. And as I looked down a last few fragments of Thunderwings made it feel like I was flying over the dancing; dogs and shadows, robo and Vurt, all getting mixed up in Bliss.

There was the Beetle, back down from his bass trip, still shaking some but playing the crowd like a robopro, taking feathers from chance acquaintances. So I looked around for Mandy. Couldn't see no Mandy. But there were Tristan and Suze, holding their mutual hair aloft, as they moved through the brood. Christ! There was that shadowgirl, what was her name? She'd tried to beat us

up in Bottletown. Nimbus! And look, there was Scribble, taking
a feather into his mouth. No! No way! I was here, up on the
balcony, not down there! I wasn't down there! I was fighting for
control, trying hard to place myself.

I watched myself vanish, into the crowd, into the smoke. And
that was better. To be the only one again, to be in one piece
again. I just didn't need that hassle.

There was Mandy now. I'd spotted her. She was pressed up
inside the crush and some chancer was tickling a feather against
her lips, no doubt a Pornovurt, hoping for a turn on. Try a Bloodvurt, my man. More chance of a show then. I guess the guy didn't
pass go, because the next thing he was all bunched up, clutching
his balls, going down in the crush. Not many come up from down
there. Mandy scooped up the feather anyway. Shit! That girl! She'd
be a fine sight to wake up to, all ready for the day's adventure.

Just then a voice spoke to me, from up close, from the left
side, but I was certain nobody was there. So I turned and there
he was . . . this gentleman. No other word for him. The gentleman
was dressed in knowledge and suffering. And a pea-green three-
piece suit of tweed, with leather epaulettes. His face was guarded
by a full beard and moustache, which kind of made up for his
receding hair. What he had left was tied back in some kind of
complex knot that hung over one shoulder, like a mutant topol-
ogy. His eyes were totally yellow, soft and languid. They stirred
the very worst memories. Lips full and red, and when they parted
to speak, well, it seemed like he was speaking direct, direct to
my soul.

'Yes. That girl would be worthwhile,' he said, like he'd glimpsed
all my secrets. His voice was a deep brogue, and it raised memories in me, feelings I couldn't place, like I'd heard it before, but
hadn't paid enough attention to it.

'That's right,' he said, 'You haven't been paying attention to
me.'

I hadn't said anything! Shit! This was just like with Bridget.

'Are you a Sleeper?' I asked.

'Kind of, but nothing like Bridget.'

'What?'

'You're looking for Desdemona. Am I right, Scribble?' He knew my name.

'You know a way—'

'And Bridget, of course. You'd like to find Bridget. Only trouble; you're worried that the Thing is more important to you than Bridget is. Because of the swapback for the sister. And this makes you feel guilty.'

'Who are you?' I demanded.

He took a sip of red wine from his glass.

'Let's get something to eat.' And then he turned away. I turned to follow, but sometime during my turning the gentleman had vanished. I was looking all around, trying to catch a glimpse of him. He just didn't exist any more. And it made an emptiness in my heart, the kind you just don't need to feel.

I turned back to the crush below. Dingo Tush had made an entrance. He was moving through the crowd, receiving the adulation. His fur was fingered and stroked by hundreds of loving hands, and the crush changed its geometry around him. Everybody was lost, except for the centre piece, the Dingo mandog. And over in the darkest corner, far below, a body of smoke was forming. I caught just a glimpse of it, before it smoothed away, into the crush world. But it sure made me jump, and I didn't know why.

I was feeling so empty inside, and food was all I could turn to. The table was sagging under the weight of dishes. It was a spread of joy; my mouth was dripping. There were the tiny wings of larks, stewed in pig's blood. There were the ink sacs of squids, leaking onto a bed of palms. There were the eggs of the wren, griddled over charcoal, with a saffron marinade. And there were the encrusted eyes of virgin lambs, smothered in dark filaments of horse bread, deep fried in shadow oil. Overseeing the feast was the Slithy Tove head-chef, with his long Vazzed-back hair and his sunken cheeks flecked with stubble. And something about his eyes, some bad need in there.

'Tuck in, Crewcut,' he said to me. 'Relish it.'

'I will,' I replied, filling my mouth with the succulence. 'Hey, this is good!'

'Just tell 'em that Barnie made it. Barnie the Chef. Remember that?'

'Will do,' I said, between mouthfuls.

And then Beetle was beside me, building a plateful.

'Nice grub, Scribb?' he asked.

'Sure it is,' I said. 'Barnie the Chef made it.'

Barnie the chef gave me a smile.

'Seen much of Murdoch these days, Scribble?' the Beetle asked.

'I'm keeping low.'

'Oh sure. Playing to a full house of dog turds at the Limbic club. That's real low, baby.'

'I've got to make a living, Bee.'

'Hey, we did that bitch cop good, didn't we?'

'Yeah.'

'You should've let me finish her.'

'They'd send somebody else.'

'I know that. But the pleasure would've been intense. Hey, by the way, Scribb, cheers for the bass ride. That was some fucker-trip! Oh boy!'

'Beetle?'

'What?'

'Don't throw Mandy away.'

'What?'

He was losing it again.

'She's your ticket.'

'Yeah ... well ... I'm moving on from that girl. She's gone cold on me. She won't take the feathers any more. Not the ones I want her to take.'

'I'm worried about you, Beetle.'

He looked at me then, just for a moment, but it was wonderful. One of those old hard-core Beetle stares. Then the feathers set back in, took control, and the triple glaze descended, slithering over his vision.

'You're taking it too much, Bee,' I said. 'Too much Wormer.'

I thought he was going to bawl me out, but he was too busy looking over my shoulder. That hard Beetle light came back into his eyes. 'Tristan! My man! And Suze in tow!' he shouted, greeting the pair as they ascended.

'Beetle ... listen to me ...'

But the guy was gone, pushing aside a frail young diner, walking a jagged line towards the hair-locked couple. I watched as he embraced Suze, and then Tristan, stroking their locks with his long, Vaz-covered fingers. The crusty couple were stroking him back, in turn, and all I could do was watch; totally missing the scene. Suze smiled at me; it was a deep smile, way deep, and again I felt her going inside of me, caressing the whole body with one look. What did that woman have, that no other woman had, apart from Desdemona? The world was spinning around. Fetish and the Bliss, and the dancing; all of them getting to me. I turned away from the love, took a turning step backwards, away from Beetle, into empty space. The Gentleman was waiting for me there, with his three-piece pea-green suit and his wisdom.

'Don't let him get to you, Scribble,' he said.

'Tell me your name?' I asked.

'You know who I am.'

'Yes,' I told him. 'I know you.' *But from where?*

'That's enough for now,' he answered, reading my thoughts.

'Is the Thing still alive?' I asked.

'Still alive. So is Bridget.'

And again, something about his voice got to me.

'How come you know all this?'

'Because I'm watching the world go by.'

'Where is the Thing?'

'I think you should work that out for yourself.'

'Tell me!'

He was looking at me. Yellow eyes. That look of deep recognition you only get once in a while. His gaze was golden and all the bad memories, the losses, they started to drift away. I was falling, seriously falling for this man. But I didn't know why, except it was like falling for a long lost friend, that you'd never met before. He started to speak, but then his eyes flickered away, to the right, over my shoulder.

I turned around, and there were the Beetle and Tristan, hugging each other.

Except that Tristan had no time for Beetle, no time at all. Instead he was staring, deep and pointed, straight into the eyes of the Gentleman. No one else could see him. I realised that then. Only me and Tristan. We were joined by this, but how to fathom it?

'What's happening?' I asked, and his eyes turned back to mine, full of pain and suffering.

'It's like this, Scribble,' he said. 'You've got the poison. It's inside you.'

'The snake bite?' I asked.

'I don't know how you got it. Some have got it. Most haven't. Those that do, they should use it. You're not using it.'

'I'm confused.'

'So was I. Your age. One day you find it. One day you realise. The world slips into place. You'll get there.'

'Like how?' I demanded, only to see the Gentleman doing that slipping away trick again.

'Scribble! Come here!' Beetle's voice breaking into my trance. 'Scribble. Let's chat.' He'd given up on Tristan, and homed in on me once more. His eyes were dancing behind the drugged-up glaze. 'Scribble, something to tell you.' His voice was way deep, still dragging some remnants of the bass injection. 'Listen to me!' he shouted, clutching my arms tight.

'Well say it.'

'Scribble ... I ... I want to ... just to ...'

The Beetle looked around then, all nervous and fearful, and this was rare enough to cause me to stare back hard at him. He couldn't give my stare back.

He couldn't give it back! Beetle couldn't look at me! Not without flinching. Wonders of the world!

'Just say it.' My voice was hard, not caring. Told you I was losing it.

He forced his eyes to mine, and then said, 'I've got something for you.' He pulled his baccy box from his pocket and place it in my hands.

'Can't take it,' I whispered. 'Can't ...'

'It's for you.'

Beetle had carried his drugs in this old Black Cherry Rough Shag tin box, from the days of our time at Droylsden State, high school for unachievers. Within its closed-up darkness he had carried Jammers and Vaz, Fluff and Shadows, Feathers and Haze, all the things he could lay his hands upon. Contained within, all of his dreams. His treasure box.

'I can't take this, Bee.'

'Open it up,' he said.

Box opened with a satisfying click, and a nice feel in the hands, and I expected to find a real mess in there, a jungle of dark drugs. Instead a single feather lay on a bed of cotton wool.

'Bee!'

Feather was a deep blue-black, with a sheen of pink. I picked it up with shaking fingers, loving the way it fluttered in my hands, like the dream-bird was still using it, flying the Vurt waves.

'Bee!'

I turned it over to read the white label.

Tapewormer.

'Bee!'

I realised I was just saying his name; saying nothing, too shocked to think.

'You know I can't go back, Bee.'

'I've been up to my eyes in it, lately,' he said. 'Couldn't stop using it.'

'What's it like?'

I was crumbling under those hints of yesterday.

'It's a jewel Vurt, Scribble. But I was getting hooked. Just couldn't stop reworming that tape. Makes everything beautiful. But you know me, I can't stand getting hooked, well, not to single pleasures.'

'I don't know if I . . .'

'Des is in there,' he said, pointing to the feather. 'Well, you know, kind of.'

'And here's me trying to give up.'

'It's just for . . . just for . . .'

Guy couldn't say it.

'I know,' I said. 'Old times. Stash Riders.'

'Right.'

And he turned away, back to his old self. He made his way back to the food bench, telling Barnie the Chef he was a cool genius, in the kitchen of the gods.

Forgiveness.

It was forgiveness the Beetle was asking for, and my heart melted.

'You don't need that,' said the brogue voice.

'I do,' I answered, to the shadow that was forming. 'You just don't know why.'

'I know the secrets,' said the Gentleman, back again.

'I need this!'

'You need the gift. But not the Vurt.'

'And why not?'

'You've got the Vurt inside you,' he said.

'What do you mean?'

'You don't need feathers. You could tune in. Direct. This has happened already, yes?'

'Yes.'

Don't know why I said that!

'You've been there. Slipping in and out,' he said.

'It's getting worse,' I told him, again not knowing why, except that things had been going strange for me lately; lots of little slips, in and out of states. So that I didn't know what people were saying to me. And this feeling inside, like the world wasn't solid, it was an edge. It felt just the same when I was getting the Haunting. This isn't all there is. The edge was scary and I was living on it. No, not living *on* the edge, I was living *inside* the edge!

'Young man, the edge is real, and you don't know how close you are.'

'To what?'

'To the step. It's not getting worse; it's getting better.'

'You think so?'

'To where you lie. Your place, your proper place. The dream world, featherless.'

'I like it here on Earth.'

'Desdemona is waiting for you.'

'What?' *Oh Jesus!*

'She's waiting. Take a look.'

And the Gentleman led me gently to the balcony, where I gazed down upon the crowd, and there was Desdemona, waiting there, in the middle of the crush, perfectly still, her yellow blouse flecked with blood, and her face scarred and cracked. Sister was beckoning to me, from the dance floor, her two arms outstretched, urging.

'Desdemona,' I said.

'That's her,' said the Gentleman. 'She's waiting.'

I turned back to him, but already he was shivering, dissolving. 'Tell me who you are?' I demanded.

'Don't let the Viper get you,' he replied. 'Be careful. Be very, very careful. Keep it clean. Right under the rim. You know I never lie.'

'Just wait . . .'

But his eyes were over my shoulder once again, and I turned around to see Beetle and Suze hugging each other, but Tristan just looking, straight on, right into the eyes of the Gentleman. It was the look of love, that kind of doomed love that never leaves you alone.

'Tristan will tell you who I am,' the stranger said.

'Cat? Game Cat?' I said, turning back to the voice, but the voice was gone. Cat was gone.

That feeling again, that emptiness.

I peered over the balcony, searching for Desdemona. There she was, covered in smoke and blood, drifting away, into the smoke and the blood. And I couldn't help her. I couldn't fucking help her! Her scarred face misting over, dissolving, like the dreams of love, into the crowd, into the Vurt.

Losing her.

Losing.

Things we want the most, things that slip away.

And then I was taking the stairs, three at a time, dodging the rung-dancers, heading down to the floor and the fading sister. I was pushing into the crush, but they were welded tight by now. I think I threw some poor wraith aside as I squeezed through. The world was closing up and I ran straight into the arms of Bridget.

Bridget!

That smoky shape I had seen on the outskirts, from above; now she was in my hands and the smoke was rising from her skin, way beyond what I was used to, and her eyes were shadow-flecked and knowledgeable. She pushed away from me, back into the arms of her dancing partner, a handsome boy with curly brown hair.

'Bridget!' I called out.

'No,' the shadowgirl answered, and maybe it wasn't her. Maybe I was dreaming.

'You're just dreaming,' the voice in my head was saying. But it was Bridget's voice in there. She was thinking to me, through the Shadow waves, looking like the ghost of yesterday. I caught just a glimpse of recognition in her eyes, and then she was gone, fading away in a wave of smoke.

And a new face of scars taking her place, amongst the crush. Face of Murdoch. Shecop. Dog-torn. Penetrating. Real.

Moving through the crowd, like a demon.

HEAVY LOSSES

Where do you run, when the bad girl comes? Maybe you run home to Mummy. Maybe you run towards your lover. Or maybe, like me, you've got a Beetle in your life; somebody powerful, even if he was just this moment thick-bodied from the overuse of cheap Tapewormer feathers.

I took the stairs, three at a time, not caring about the cries of the crush, running into the arms of the main Rider. The Vurtglaze slipped from the Beetle's eyes, as I screamed the bad news at him. It was a sunblind being opened to a bright day, wonderful to watch, and he popped a couple of Jammers, already on the move. He pushed me through the crush, kicking some dancers over, just to make a way.

'Beetle! What about Mandy?' I said in the rush.

But his mind was on another trip, the jam was kicking in, and his eyes were scanning the pack for a way out.

'We can't leave her, Beetle!'

'Kid can hack it.' A quick breath, and then, 'There's gotta be a back way.'

We were cutting through the pack, as they made way under the threat of the Beetle's curse and the jammed-up energy in his fists. I heard a shout from below—'Out of the way! Police!' Some such. You ever seen a cop trying to cut through a dancing crush of semi-legals? I guess that Murdoch was having some problems down there. So suck on it, shecop! I was right up against the food tables now, and Barnie the Chef was giving me a bright stare. 'You liked my food, didn't you, Crew?' I told him that he was the King of the Feast, and that the angels were dining out on his takeaways. He pointed us to a back door. 'This way, Crew-cut,' he answered. 'Relish it.'

And we were clattering down a shining steel ladder of hard rungs, a fire-escape to heaven. Me and the Beetle, on a ride to-gether, old-days style. Felt like flying, and I guess I still had some Thunderwings in me. Then we were down on the back streets and running for sweet life.

I'm not telling this very well. I'm asking for your trust on this one. Here I am, surrounded by wine bottles and mannequins, salt cellars and golf clubs, car engines and pub signs. There are a thousand things in this room, and I am just one of them. the light is shining through my windows, stuttered by bars of iron, and I'm trying to get this down with a cracked-up genuine antique word processor, the kind they just don't make any more, trying to find the words.

Sometimes we get the words wrong.

Sometimes we get the words wrong!

Believe me on this one. And trust me, if you can. I'm doing my best to tell it true. It just gets real hard sometimes . . .

* * *

The very strangest thing about that night of running was this: that I could picture the Beetle better than myself. I didn't know where I was. But the Beetle was always, all of the time, very clear to me. I was following his movements through a clear-sighted glass, watching him burn a way down the darkness.

Me, myself, I was the Beetle's shadow, just hanging on to his flame, running through a black alley, back of the Slithy Tove restaurant. Something weighty and hard was banging around inside my jacket pocket but I didn't connect to that just then. I could feel a crowd running with me, but I didn't know who they were. Maybe I was still on Thunderwings, but that thin tickle should have long dissolved, into the blood stream. So what was I on?

What was I on?

Felt like the night was surrendering to me, filling me up with its pictures.

I was getting glimpses of everything.

I was Vurt-high, running through a dark space, with some crowd behind me, with nothing in my mouth, no feather in my mouth.

Cop sirens were sounding off, making bad music.

Whistles blowing.

The howling of a generator, as it pumped hard power to a set of arc lights.

Shadowcops shining down.

Feet clattering. Real human feet clattering over concrete.

Didn't know where I was.

Coming up hard against a brick wall, and turning away, and there was the Murdoch, scarred-up face glaring at me.

Dancers, former dancers, panicking behind me, in a crush, in a little crush, and then scattering. And me left there alone, facing the Murdoch's scars.

'I've got you.' The shecop's voice was hard from the chase, and the gun in her hand was crackling with shiny new life, like it had living bullets in the chambers.

I reached into my pocket without thinking, my fingers closing on Murdoch's old gun, the one I had stolen from the pad floor. But I had little knowledge of such things, and when Murdoch told me to drop it, I dropped it. It made a dead sound as it fell to the concrete, like I'd cut myself off from release but Murdoch's gun was well aimed and true. 'What's it gonna be, kid?' she offered. 'Dirty or clean?'

Murdoch's gun was the only thing in my life, the only thing worth living for. It gets like that sometimes, with instruments of death.

'What's it gonna be?'

Murdoch's gun was a raging hard-on, pointing straight at me, straight to the heart. There was just a glint of sun coming up, over a roof top, and a dark mist forming to her right. Other cops were moving into position. I could hear screams and cheers as people were brought down, or people were escaping. I could feel the Beetle's presence, way up close, but I couldn't see him anywhere.

'Best to come clean,' Murdoch said. The mist behind her right shoulder solidified into a twisting shape.

I knew that face, that shape.

Shaka! The blown apart shadowcop.

His smoking body was a mess of fumes, and his face was a grimace of smoke. He was waving in and out of existence, as his new-fangled box of tricks struggled to shine his broken body into the real world, so that it could lick there, feeding on secrets. They'd patched him up somewhat, but his beams were still strong and hot, and he fired them at me, somewhere towards me; I could feel them burning the brickwork just to one side of my head.

'He's mine, Shaka!' shouted Murdoch.

And wasn't it just my fate, to be the prize in a shooting contest,
between the real and its shadow.

Murdoch asked her gun barrel to focus, and I could hear the
whirring, as it found my centre, fixing hot bullets upon the heart,
that soft target.

'Turn around slowly,' Murdoch said. 'Towards the wall. No
surprises. I don't like surprises.'

Sure.

So I'm turning to the wall, just in the very act of turning, when
I sense Beetle nearby. That's how it was. I could just sense him!

The Beetle steps out of the shadows, holding his gun aloft, like
an offering.

Murdoch had seen that gun before and now here she was, once
again, on the dirty end. You could tell she wasn't too keen on it.
Same with the Shaka. He'd taken punishment from it; now here
he was, once again, on the dirty end.

Made me feel good; just to be free, for once, of the dirty end.

Shaka was flickering on and off, his shot memory banks struggling against his mechanisms. His box of tricks was being held by
some new dumbfuck partner, who was obviously way out of cool;
he was shaking, and the aerial box was shaking with him. Shaka
was doing his best to keep his beams in line. You could tell from
his half-lit face that humans left him kind of cold at this precise
moment.

Murdoch was sweating; fluid was running down the claw marks
in her face.

At the junction of Wilbraham Road and some poor bugger's
driveway, rested the mobile kennel van of Dingo Tush and his
pack of canine players. Hey, hey, we're the Warewolves, painted
on the side. Next to it I could see Tristan and Suze, their hair a
strong river flowing with moonlight. Suze had the two robohounds on a double leash. The dogs were almost as tall as she
was and baying for cop-blood.

I was dancing. That twitching dance that only the truly scared-to-fuck can manage. *But my mind was like a stranger, a cold hearted stranger with a gun in his hands.* That was the Beetle. Mandy came up behind him, her eyes darting from point to point, as she made out how the twin guns were poised; one on my heart, the other on a shecop's head.

Moon was still, full, and voiceless.

I'm taking this one moment at a time, step by step, because it's difficult, and because it's so important.

Murdoch spoke up. 'You're going down for the murder of a police officer, Beetle.'

'So take me,' the Beetle answered. Just like that. Beautiful.

Murdoch let the sweat droplets roll down her face, down her arms, down her fingers, to the trigger on the gun. It was slippery. The whole thing was slippery.

'Give me inpho, Shaka,' she asked.

Shaka obeyed, firing a thin shaking beam, straight to the gun in Beetle's hands. 'IT'S A GUN, MURDOCH,' he replied.

'For fuck's sake, Shaka!'

SORRY MA'AM.

I guess we caught that Shadow real good.

Thin beam travelling once again; Beetle just letting it happen, like he knew somehow, what was about to happen.

FOUR BULLETS LEFT, beamed the Shadowcop.

'You taking a chance, Murdoch?' asked the Beetle.

'Well, I guess so,' she answered.

Somebody was gonna get killed, hurt, or arrested.

Maybe it was me. Most probably it was me.

Some things just seem bound.

This is how we lost Desdemona, and found the Thing. Yes, time to tell it.

* * *

Sister and brother flying down through a feather's embraces. Into the Voodoo world. To land softly in a garden of bliss, walled in by ancient stones, surrounded by colours and perfume, a jungle of flowers. Bright yellow birds were singing bright yellow songs, from the trees that were growing, visibly, even whilst we walked. Deep in the countryside, an English garden . . .

'It's lovely, Scribble!' announced Desdemona. And indeed it was; everything you could wish for. Desdemona took my hand, and then my mouth, filling me up with kisses. The garden was playing with our senses, making them into a tapestry. The flowers were pollen-heavy, and so was I. I took Desdemona into my arms, letting her fall, gently, to the floor of petals, me following her down, into the petals.

Her cunt was pressed against my cock, and the world was beautiful.

I've done this already, I thought, maybe this is the Haunting? Maybe I'm inside the Vurt just now? But I dismissed that thought real easy, so I couldn't have been, could I?

Could I?

Then I slipped inside of her, the sister, feeling the walled garden close in to caress my penis, until the sap rose to the top, and the garden was flooded. The air was heavy with pollen; the whole world was copying itself, over and over, through the act of sex. And we were enfolded in the system, sucking where the bee sucks.

We were being watched.

I rolled off Desdemona's slick body, onto the ground, feeling the earth clutching at me, like it wanted to feel my seed. I was sinking, and a hooded figure was standing some five feet away, watching, just watching.

I lifted myself up, just to get a better look, only to find myself sinking into the figure's gaze. Like being eaten.

The figure was draped in purple robes, head to foot, hooded, so that only the eyes showed. Yellow eyes. Twin suns, glistening with knowledge. 'Your names, please?' the figure said. It was a woman's voice. I nudged at Des, and she sat up, straight away, no fear. There was no fear involved.

'My name is Desdemona,' she said.

'My name is Scribble,' I said. It was the most natural thing, no problems.

'Thank you,' said the figure. 'Welcome to English Voodoo. Do you know why you're here?'

'We do not,' I answered. I could not lie.

'You have come for knowledge,' the figure said. 'There will be pleasure. Because knowledge is sexy. There will also be pain. Because knowledge is torture. Do you understand what I'm saying?'

'Yes,' answered Des. 'We understand.'

Did we?

'Good. Join us.' The figure said this, moving her arms, to indicate the garden. Other figures were appearing, moving in from the distance, like images growing on a photographic plate, taking on life. They were all hooded and covered the same, head to foot, so that you could not distinguish between them. Only the yellow eyes peering out from beneath the dark cowls. Desdemona and I stood up then, to be on the same level with the figures. 'We are the keepers of the garden,' they said, all at the same time, but I was just getting the messages, no words, just thoughts. *What are these creatures?*

Birds were twittering in the trees, and one of the gardeners called out in a small bird-like whistle. A yellow bird, a canary, flew down into his hands. He stroked it carefully, until the bird was happy. Then he gently plucked a feather out of its plumage. It was a yellow feather, and he held it up for all to see. It was a small and gentle golden feather, kissed by the English sun. It really got to me. Looked like a dream. The figure opened his hand to let the bird fly free. Then he raised the yellow feather to his lips, darkened by the hood. He sucked it in, and then was gone, sinking into the earth, into a hole that opened up, and then closed again, as the figure disappeared beneath the soil. Flowers bloomed again over the space, growing in super motion. The golden feather was left there, floating in the air, free of all restraints. The next figure plucked it from the air, stroked it in, then was gone, sinking. The feather floating. The next figure took it up, stroked it. Gone. The next figure took the feather. Stroked it. Gone. The feather still floating. And so on, until only the initial figure remained.

'Where are they going?' Desdemona asked.

'To the past, the bad past, in search of knowledge,' the figure answered. She had the feather in her hands, and she was offering it to Des. 'Why don't you try it?' the figure said.

Desdemona hesitated for a second, and then took the yellow feather into her hands. She held it against her lips. 'What will it do?' she asked.

'The past is waiting,' the figure answered. 'You can go there, and change it. That way knowledge lies.'

Desdemona placed the feather between her lips.

'Des ...' My voice calling to her, in the garden. 'It might be dangerous ...'

'Yes, it is,' said the figure. 'It's a Yellow feather.'

'It's a Yellow feather, Scribb!' Des replied. 'Haven't you always wanted to take one of those?'

'Yes, but ...'

'How many chances do you get?' my sister asked.

'Not many.'

'You get one chance,' she said. 'And this is ours. Let's do it.'

'Des ...'

'It is not for the weak,' the figure said, but the sister already had the feather between her lips. Desdemona turned to face me.

'I want to go there, Scribble,' she said. 'I want you to come with me. Will you come?'

'Please don't go, Des.'

Did no good.

Desdemona pushed the golden feather in deep, to the limits. Her eyes flashed yellow, just the once, and then the ground was opening up beneath her feet, and weeds were pulling at her, yellow weeds, spiked with thorns. Desdemona was screaming; 'Scribble!!!!' But what could I do? The tendrils were wrapping themselves around my sister's limbs, drawing blood from a hundred places, as the spikes pierced her skin. This wasn't the easy passage the other figures had achieved; they hadn't gone down screaming. It was going wrong, the day was going wrong!

What could I do?

The sister was being pulled down by the yellow weeds; creepers and thorns clutching tight on her body, dragging her down to the world beneath the soil.

'Knowledge is torture,' the figure said. 'Didn't I tell you that?'

I was running towards Desdemona, trying my best to reach her.

The flowers won.

They dragged her down into the soil, until only her hair was left, her beautiful hair, and then even that was gone, strangled by the weeds, until only the weeds were left, the blonde flowers. They grew over where she had buried herself, smothering the space in a second.

The figure had the feather in her hands, and she was offering it to me.

'Go fuck yourself!'

My words.

'Very well,' the figure said. 'You are too weak. Maybe one day . . .' And with that she pushed the feather into her own mouth. Her eyes flashing more golden than the sun on a hot day, and I was alone, in the garden, the English garden.

The feather floated for a moment, and then started to fall. I reached out for it.

I reached out for it.

A yellow bird flew down, a blur of speed, caught the feather in her beak, and then was gone, flying back to feather some nest.

And who will feather my nest, now?

The garden was empty.

I stayed there for two, three hours, I don't know. A long time. And then I jerked out.

How can I forgive myself? Why did Desdemona leave me? All the hours I have spent wondering this. What had I done wrong? Wasn't I enough for her? What else did she want?

Some things are just bound.

This was how we lost Desdemona. And how I came to wake up, smothered by a Thing from Vurt, some heavy shit.

Exchange rates.

Some heavy losses.

Murdoch slowly swung her gun away from me, towards the real threat. Twin guns now, both of them pointed towards each other, mirrored in the same need. Beetle and Murdoch.

I heard the moon howl.

Dingo Tush was in the area. His jaws were split wide so that the inside was visible, slavering. He was calling up dogs from all over the Fallowfield, howling at the moon. Felt like the moon was howling.

I could hear the dogs responding.

The Dingo van came open and a pack of hybrids shot loose,

charging the concrete with their claws. I guess Murdoch got some visions of the Karli Dog just then, and she didn't fancy a repeat play of the last pad debacle. The gun reared up in her hands as it spat smoke. Then the noise of it. Then the bullet reaching out for a new home.

The Beetle answered her.

More or less the same time. Not quite the same time.

One gun fired.

And then the other.

One gun was later than the other.

Listen carefully. This is the secret of how to live: fire your gun before somebody else does.

The Beetle reeled back from the bullet.

His shoulder exploded. It was a warm flower opening on his flesh. I got flecked with some Beetle blood, across the cheeks.

There was a siren ringing in my head, behind my closed-up eyes, and the howling of wolves, as the dog pack ran riot.

There were bullets, suddenly, flying everywhere. I had a high pitch inside of me, a high-pitched screaming, like some woman had caught a stray shot.

Wonder who that was, caught that bad gift?

Hope it wasn't Mandy. Hope it wasn't . . .

And I felt myself being lifted up, lifted up above everything. Above the world of rain. Above the world with its screamings and its sirens. And all of its pain, dripping away, like the last few raindrops, into a small quiet pool of sunlight.

Where was I going? And who was taking me?

I'm walking through the leafy lane of a small town. Children are playing on the green. The postman whistles a jaunty melody. Mothers hang washing on lines, birds sing from leafy sundrenched trees. I walk towards the post office. Its sign calls it

Pleasureville Post Office. And I know where I am now. I'm in Pleasureville, a low-level blue Vurt, nothing special, totally legal, been there before, years before, when such things excited me. But never like this.

Never like this. Not without a feather. I was just there! Totally there. With no pain, no anxiety, no hassles. Smelt like sweetness.

I was walking the quiet lanes of Pleasureville, only the tiny laughter of kids to trouble me. No trouble. I can handle that. And the whistle of the postman, and the singing of the birds. No trouble. I can handle that.

And the knowledge that I was there, that I knew I was there, in the Vurt, and that another world was waiting for me, if I so wished; a world of pain. I could pull out any time. Or stay here forever.

That's forever.

Which is a vicious temptation.

G A M E   C A T

There is a dream out there, of a nation's second rise; when the dragon is slain and the good queen awakens from her coma-sleep, to a land capable of giving breath to her. The followers of ENGLISH VOODOO worship the new queen. The queen is the keeper of our dreams. Through her portals you can see a paradise of change, where trees are green, birds do sing, and the trains run on time. Also, lots of sex; that special kind, with a delicious English thump. The Voodoo is a Knowledge Feather. It leads to other worlds. It cannot be bought, only given. You wanna go down there? Into the English Voodoo? Fine. And beyond? Fine, very fine. Just take precautions. That wet trip is a demon-path of bliss and pain, equal amounts. Be careful. Be very, very careful. Those sugar walls will squeeze you to the bone. Cat knows. Cat has been there. And lived. Just. You want to see the scars?

Well yes, I guess you do.

Status: black, with sexy pink, and with glints of yellow. It's got some doors in it, through to the Yellow worlds. Step softly, traveller, don't get yourself swapped.

Not unless you want to be.

ON THE CUTTING
OF DROIDLOCKS

The first time that I came down, I came down into a dog world. Smelt bad, real bad after the sweet, feathery aromas of Pleasure-ville.

There was a dog face looming over me; mixed in there, amongst the fur and the jaws, were some bare traces of the human lineaments. This only made it worse, the shock of seeing that face, one of the many heads of Cerberus, leaning right over me, and that breath, that stench on my face.

They tell me that I screamed then.

Maybe I did.

I was too busy getting out of there, out of my head.

The Pleasure postman greeted me with a cheery hello.

'Anything for me today, Postie?'

'Just the one, Mr Scribble,' he replied, handing me a letter. I opened the sun-golden envelope, and pulled out a birthday card. The card was the brightest yellow I had ever seen. The words Happy Birthday were written in a dark and clotted red hand across the yellow.

I opened the card to find out whose birthday it was.

The second time I came down, I was in a travelling kennel of mad dogs. The stench was still there, ten times worse, but at least the dog face had left me alone.

I was pressed against the rear doors, like I'd been the last to get in the van. There were no windows, but I could feel us moving, at some speed, some law-breaking speed along a bumpy path. Felt like a well jammed-up Beetle was at the wheel, the old style, and I was glad for that.

I raised myself up on a pair of skinless elbows. *How did that happen?* I really thought the police had got me, and I expected to see Murdoch there, grinning, surrounded by her dumbfuck cronies.

All I got was the fleshy hindquarters of dogs. *There are times in life when this is all you get.* They were tight-pressed in that small space, maybe seven or eight of them, difficult to tell, what with the van lights broken and the mishmash of their bodies. All of them had bits of dog mixed in there, and bits of human, only in varying degrees, and they were crowded and pressed over some other forms.

What the fuck was under there?

Then I saw Beetle's face through a gap in the fur.

But surely, the Beetle was driving the van?

I was getting bits and pieces of the story then, coming back to me through the pain and confusion. Beetle's face, that sudden glimpse of him, was full of suffering, and my heart jumped.

Jumped.

Jumped.

Beetle had been hit . . .

I couldn't . . .

Couldn't . . .

Looked like they were licking him!

Then his face was covered by the closing fur once again and I saw Mandy for the first time. She was crouched against the van wall, holding on to nothing, just like the old days.

Old days! Three weeks ago!

'Mandy . . .' I whispered, my voice drifting.

She turned to me slowly. She turned her wet and beautiful eyes towards me, and I saw the hurt in there, way beyond the dream.

That's when Tristan screamed. From the dogs. From the middle of all those canines, those half humans. What were they doing back there? And why was Tristan screaming, like he'd been hurt, hurt real bad. It was the worst scream of all time.

Then I remembered the stray bullet, and that maybe someone had been caught by it. And maybe that someone was Tristan.

It was. But not in that way.

Then Mandy reached out to me. In her hands she held a scrap of clothing. It was a black cloth, made dirty by some other substance, some kind of dark fluid.

Blood.

Beetle's blood. And that was a piece of his favourite jacket, the black cord jacket, with the six buttons up the sleeves, and the double vents, and the tailored waist.

Mandy's hands were smeared with Vaz and blood. Like she'd been stroking his black clotted hair.

But it was the cloth that held me. There amidst the blood and the dirt hung a lump of glitter. It was hard and slightly rounded, flickering green and violet, with a long tongue of gold protruding. The thing was fastened to the cloth with a tarnished brass pin and I knew it then for what it was.

Snakehead.

Dreamsnake trophy.

He cut that fucker off!

That was too much. Had to get out of there.

I opened up a birthday card in Pleasureville. The sun was overhead, birds were singing, kids playing. The Postman was already whistling along the road to the next letterbox. Felt like a holiday, like a birthday. But whose birthday? I opened the card and read the message scrawled there in blood-thick ink.

I could hear her voice calling, through the ink:

'Happy birthday, Scribb! Bet you never realised, uh? You were always forgetting. Me, I'll never forget. Sorry I couldn't get my present to you, but will this do? Until we get back together? Don't stop looking, Scribb. I'm still waiting. We'll be together one day. Promise? Your loving sister, Des.'

There were tears in my eyes. Must have been the first ever tears in Pleasureville. Nobody cries there. I wanted to keep the card so I reached into my pocket for something to exchange, to leave behind.

I pulled out Beetle's baccy box. I clicked it open and pulled out the Tapewormer feather. This I shoved back into my pocket. Then I closed the box and laid it down on a nearby streetbench.

I looked up at a cherry tree. Its berries were ripe and bulbous under the eternal sunshine, and just then Pleasure started to stick in my throat, like a jagged chicken bone so I went back down again, pulling the jerkout cord.

The third time I came down, I came down to the breakfast table. I was back in my new flat, shovelling a bowl of JFK flakes down my throat. I came down with the spoon halfway in my mouth and the crispness of the flakes against the coldness of the milk made me feel like a king, like life was actually worth something, worth getting up for. That good, those flakes.

Twinkle's eyes were looking at me, from the other side of the table. 'Happy birthday, Scribb,' she said.

'How did you know that?' I asked.

'Beetle told me.'

'Beetle!'

'Calm down, partner,' she said. But I was on my feet anyway, the cereal bowl tipping over and spilling its milk all over the table-cloth.

'Where is he?' I demanded, everything coming back. I was back in the alley for a second, hearing the gunshots, listening to the dogs howling, seeing Beetle's shoulder explode, feeling the wall scraping my elbows away, as I fell . . . as I fell . . .

'Where the fuck is he?!'

I was screaming, and it wasn't very dignified.

Well listen; fuck dignity. Fuck dignity to death.

'He's in your room,' Twinkle said.

'What's he doing in there?'

'He wants you.'

This is a love story. You got that already?

Took me a long while to realise; all those presents that I was getting.

How many people have you had that are willing to lose something, just so that you can carry on for a little while?

Count them.

That low, uh?

Listen, I'm an expert on this.

I went into my bedroom, and found the Beetle there. Mandy was with him. She was sitting beside the bed, on an old wicker chair, painted green. It wasn't my paint; I'd moved into these Whalley Range rooms only three weeks ago, on the run from the cops, and the Riders. Here we find ourselves.

I loved that chair.

Beetle lay in the bed. That old damp and tattered bed with its mattress full of bugs, and its springs all loose and rusted.

How I loved that bed. Its short respite.

The Beetle was lying in my bed with his eyes closed, a feather stuck halfway down his throat.

'What's he on, Mandy?' I asked.

'Tapewormer. What else?' She sounded well pissed off. 'All he does these days is ride that feather back. It gets kind of boring, Scribble . . . for a way-ahead girl.'

Yeah, I guess it does.

I pulled back gently, on the sheets, revealing the wound. His shoulder was a sprawling mess, but the strips of flesh were held together and bandaged with some kind of web. Looked like a nest of dog fur. The blood was congealing behind there. Some kind of healing, maybe. My eyes were wet. I could barely look.

'What is that stuff on him?'

'Dog people put it there,' said Mandy. 'Said it would help.'

I looked close. His wound was tight-bound with strands of fur, crisscrossing, making a hold against the blood flow. The fur was glued in place with dog spit. Made me feel nauseous, except that it was saving him. Well, I could only hope so.

'Why are they doing this, Mandy?' I asked. 'Why are the dogs helping him? He hates the dogs!'

Mandy just shrugged.

I looked deeper into the Beetle's wound and saw tiny snakes moving there, a rainbow of worms, baby snakes. They took me back some way, like the maggots we bought by the handful, Bee and I, when we were just two kids planning a fishing trip. It made me pull back.

'Christ, Bee . . .'

He made no sound.

I turned to the new girl. 'Mandy? What is that?'

'Where?'

'In his wound . . .'

She was leaning in.

'There's nothing there, Scribble. What's wrong?'

And when I looked back the wound was clean, under its bed of fur.

'Beetle . . . Beetle . . .'

My voice was searching, and I guess the Beetle must have picked up on it, down in the darkness, because he was mumbling words around the feather. They came out clogged by the Vurt, so I pulled that feather out, jerking him away from the dream. Just like he used to do with me, when I went in alone. The play was shifting, and I knew how bad it felt, to have your dream dragged from your mouth.

He came back to us with a slow rising, as though he was used by now to being dragged back, maybe by Mandy, as though he was riding the feathers real easy these days.

'What is it, my man?' he drawled.

I managed an answer, but it came out awkward.

'Is there no end to the trouble, Bee?' I asked, with a breaking voice.

'No end . . . Scribble . . .' replied the Beetle, slovenly, from the depths of his pain. His eyes weren't even open. 'Not since the schoolyard. Remember that?'

His eyes were slitted, crusted, just a glimpse of eyeball showing through, between the twin layers of bloated skin.

'I remember, Bee. You used to bully me something rotten.'

'Aye. Good days. Good days . . .' He was drifting off again.

'Beetle!'

His eyes flicked open, halfway, pushing apart the lids. 'How's Murdoch, Scribb,' he asked. 'Is she dead yet?'

'I don't know,' I answered.

'Maybe she is. Maybe we finished her.'

'No, not yet,' said Mandy. 'I didn't see that.'

'What did you see?' I asked.

'That was some bad theatre, back there.'

'What are you after, Mandy?' I asked.

'What's it to you?' she answered.

'It's everything.'

'Don't give up the fight, Scribble,' said the voice. It was the Beetle's voice.

'How could I?' I replied.

'Keep on finding them. The Brid and the Sister. And the Thing. Don't give up on me.'

'Bridget was in the Slithy Tove,' I told him.

'What do you mean?'

'Bridget was in the Slithy Tove. I saw her there.'

I was expecting him to say I was going off the edge someway, that I was feeling the pull too much, the pull of Tapewormer. Which is like willing the past into life.

Guy should know. He was the one hooked.

Except I got an entirely different answer.

'Talk to the Dingo about this.'

'What's that, Bee?' I said, puzzled. 'The Dingo? Does he—'

'Yes.'

'What?'

'He might know something.'

'Brid's still alive?'

'Maybe she is. I caught something in the van. They thought I was out of it.' He smiled. It was a painful smile. 'You know me, Scribb. Down, but never out.'

'I just want to give in, Bee. It's too much for me.'

'Is life like that?' the Beetle asked.

'I don't think I'm up to it,' I replied, hating every word but knowing each one to be true.

'Tristan needs your help, Scribb.'

'Tristan does?'

Somebody caught a stray bullet.

'Help the man.'

Then his eyes closed. His lips closed. The Beetle was sleeping, and it was my time to leave.

I stroked the Tapewormer back into his mouth, gentle-like. Well, why not? Guy can only take so much. I was watching his face smile at the fake memories.

'This is a neat piece,' announced Mandy. And when I turned to her, she had Beetle's gun in both hands, lining it up to the shadow clock on the far wall. 'Neat. See the way it self-focuses?' So I watched the chambers of the gun slide and whirr, locking on.

'You know about guns, Mandy?'

'Some. The Bee told me loads. We going into action soon, Scribb?' Now she was rubbing some Vaz from the Beetle's bed-side jar into the firing mechanism.

'Soon. We move in the early morning.'

'I'm glad for that.'

'I didn't think you were that bothered about Des.'

'I'm bothered about you, Scribb.'

'That right?'

She put the gun back down on the bedside cabinet, and then looked over at the Beetle. He was smiling, so let him smile some more.

'I've been thinking some crazy things, Scribble,' she said.

'Yeah?'

'Like how you got me in here, in the Riders. You really sold it to me.'

'You want to get out?'

'What?'

'I can see that. Things have turned bad. You wanna go, just go.'

She was quiet for a moment.

'Scribble ...'

'Just say so.'

'This is the most fun I've ever had.'

Fun?

'I'm not getting the picture, Mandy. What are you saying?'

'I know I was just here to stand in for your sister. But that's okay. I've been worse things. All the times I've been looking for something ... something better than me ... you know what I'm saying?'

'Kind of.'

'Just this kind of constant search for a man ... a man who's tougher than me. I never met him of course. So when you introduced me to the Bee ... well ... you know the feeling?'

I knew it.

'It's the same with you and Des, I guess?' she asked.

This girl was getting to me, and I didn't like it too much.

'You don't have to answer,' Mandy told me. And then she turned back to look at the Beetle. He was still smiling, and the colours of his wound were vibrant and shocking. 'I hate to see him like this. All that energy going to waste. Look at him! He's almost laughing. It just makes me sad. A man like that ... living in the past. Tapewormer sucks. I'm not the past ... I'm the future. Do you understand me, Scribble?'

I nodded.

'I think I want to kill Murdoch.' She had the gun in her hands again, and the threat looked so sexy . . . it was an immense pity that I just wasn't up there, in the toughness stakes, far enough for this soldier.

'Is that bad?' she asked.

'No. No it's not. It's real.'

'I don't want to lose him. Not ever.'

Her eyes were getting wet, so I took her into my arms. 'No way will that happen. Believe me.'

Dingo Tush was waiting for me in the corridor.

He'd just come out of Twinkle's room, and he had Karli the robodog in his arms. The bitch was flopping upside down in his half-human paws. Karli's tongue was loose and sloppy, and a constant low pitched whine was falling out from her jaws. Dingo's face was caught in the blue light cast from a small table lamp; those famous cheeks and muzzle sculptured and lit to perfection. He looked so very beautiful, and often I had thought, in those early days; if only I could have just that bit of dog in me. Then I would be truly beautiful, and the women would love me.

Not to be. Only human. Still clinging to the hope of being only human.

'Karli's pretty upset,' whispered Dingo.

'She's just a dog.'

Oh shit! Silly thing to say!

'I will forgive that slight indiscretion.'

'Beetle told me you might know about Brid and the Thing. Where they are.'

'Why should I know that?'

'I'm just following the Beetle. What do you know?'

'I know a good record when I hear one. What do you think I know? I'm a pop star, for fuck's sake. And if you don't mind, I have an all-nighter to get to.'

'I don't know who to believe.'

'I think you should learn some manners when talking to a Dog-star. One who has just saved the life of your friend. A somewhat small life, if I may add.'

'You best not be lying, Dingo.'

'Ooh! Big. Tough.' He gives me his famous smile, the one with all the teeth on show.

Holy shit!

'I would have you for breakfast, dear boy.'

I opened the door to Twinkle's bedroom. Tristan was sitting on the bed. In his arms lay Suze, his one love.

Their hair lay all around like a wake.

It was matted.

Blood-matted.

Tristan looked up at my entrance. His eyes were a pair of wet diamonds.

'Can you help me?' he said.

'What's happening?' I asked.

'Suze,' he said, was all that he said.

Somebody caught a stray bullet.

'Suze got hit?' I asked.

'Yes,' he said. It was that simple, that deadly.

'Bad?'

Tristan didn't answer. Instead he reached out his hand towards me, offering a pair of scissors. 'I want you to do this,' he said.

I looked down at the body of Suze, held there, upon his lap, unbreathing. I wanted my voice to come easy, but my mouth was scorched and the words came out like smoke. 'Tristan...do you...is that right?' I didn't know what to say.

'Just cut this for me, will you?!' His eyes were glaring. 'Don't keep me waiting!'

'I don't think I can do it, Trist.'

'Nobody else will.'

Tristan's eyes . . .

So I took the scissors in my trembling hands.

There are only two parts of the body that don't feel pain. One is the hair, the other is the nails. Both are made out of Keratin, a fibrous sulphur-containing protein. It occurs in the outer layer of the skin and in the hair, nails, feathers, hooves, etc. From the Greek *keras,* meaning horn, meaning that which can be cut without tears.

Let me tell you about that.

I have seen the tears at the cutting.

Karli slipped through the gap in the left-open door.

I had a rope of thick hair in my fingers. It went on forever, between Tristan and Suze, and then back again. That hair was living. Nano germs were calling out for mercy. I swear that they were. I could hear this screaming in my brain. Well then, friends, I guess you never felt anything like this before?

I worked the scissors through a severe angle, slicing the droidlocks. It took some kind of strength to do it, and I was kind of proud. And it took some time. Because the hair was thick and clogged up with debris; spent matches, jewels, hairgrips, dog fur. And that just in three weeks since the last washing. I pocketed one of the hairgrips. Why? A voice told me to do it. Which voice? The one that never stops.

That droid hair was so thick it was like cutting through the night.

Until, eventually, I separated them, Tristan from Suze. Karli the robobitch was licking at the face of the corpse, tying to wake her.

Nothing would wake her.

MY FIRST WORDS

I'd come down from Pleasureville two, or maybe three o'clock in the afternoon. I'd attended the sickbed of my best and worst friend. I'd cut some hair. Cut two people in half. You know, just one of those days. Now I was tired, so tired and I just wanted to sleep, even though I knew we should be moving on, out of there, *because the cops have got your number, Scribble, and you're maybe on a death list. Murdoch's list.*

So guess what, Murdoch? You're on mine.

All this added up and I shouldn't even have been thinking about lying down on that couch, fully clothed. My eyes closing, heavy with the world, thinking about how this story started; Mandy coming out of that all-night Vurt-U-Want, dodging dogs and cops.

Christ! I was playing it back already.

I got up suddenly, startling Karli, who was playing with Twinkle.

'Fetch me some paper, kidder,' I said, whilst searching my pockets for a pen. I had some debris from the trip in there, and I placed them all out on the table top. My birthday card. The Tapewormer feather that Beetle had given me. The fool card. Put that down as well. Took a long stare down at the collection.

My mind was like a stranger.

Twinkle put an old school exercise book down on the table, and then reached for the birthday card. 'Aw! Scribb! You got a birthday card! Who's it off. Let's see—'

I caught her with a hard slap to the face.

Shit . . .

She backed off, holding her cheek, her eyes dribbling.

Oh Christ . . . shouldn't have done that . . . what was happening to me . . .

'Mister Scribble . . .' Twinkle's voice.

Did my best to ignore what I'd just done, picked up the pen, opened the book, and then scribbled down some words, the first I had written in weeks. And I remember thinking, that if I ever get out of this with body and soul still connected, well then I was going to tell the whole story, and this is how it would start:

Mandy came out of the all-night Vurt-U-Want, clutching a bag of goodies.

Okay, so this is twenty years later, and I'm only just getting round to it.

I closed the book, put down the pen, picked up the birthday cad, read Desdemona's message, put down the card, picked up the feather, and the tarot card. I was moving like some cheap made-in-Taiwan robo.

I went back to the couch, lay down, the feather in one hand, fool's card in the other. Twinkle's voice, 'Mister Scribble . . .'

I didn't look.

'What're you doing?'

'Going in.'

I took one last look at the fool's card; the young man stepping it lightly towards the abyss, all his world wrapped up in a shoulder sack, his dog snapping at his heels, trying to stop his fall. I'm getting the picture, dead Suze. Cheers for the card. So you thought that I was a fool? Very well. I'll act like one. I'll be what you wanted, Suze.

'Can I come? Can I?' pleaded Twinkle.

'This is private,' I said to her, and then sucked the feather in real deep, down to the shaft. I know my times and my places. And this was a time to get out. Out of that time, out of that place.

The Tapewormer feather was halfway down my throat and I could feel the waves approaching over the music's swelling main theme, intercut with the credits. But then the waves were moving backwards, taking the music with them, so I was getting the fade, and then the hit of each note, and I was in there somewhere, losing the sense of trouble, the sense of now.

I was being inverted.

Mandy came out of the all-night Vurt-U-Want, clutching a bag of goodies.

That's fine. It's just that sometimes we want to change things a little. We want things to be better. How they should've been.

That's no crime?

That's just a moment of stupidity. That's all.

I mean who hasn't, at some time, wanted this? To feel the fade before the hit?

I gave the feather one last push and then I was gone, wave deep, swimming the surf back home, as the main theme and the credits dropped away . . .

T A P E W O R M E R

Desdemona came out of the all-night Vurt-U-Want, clutching a bag of goodies.

There was no trouble, a nice clean pick-up. Des is an expert and we love her for that.

We rode the stash back to the flat, the fearless four of us; Beetle and Bridget, Desdemona and I. The Beetle was up front, the van pilot, Vaz-smeared for extra performance. I was on the left side wheel housing, Brid was on the right. She was fast asleep, so what's new? Desdemona was sitting between us, slightly forward, with the treasure sack in her lap. It was a smooth road.

'What's in the bag, sister?' I asked her.

'Beauties,' she replied. 'A Yellow.' Her voice sent a shiver through me.

Just like . . .

'Let's have a look,' I said.

Desdemona pulled out a feather, a pure and golden flight path. 'Oh wow!'

'What is it, Scribble?' shouted the Beetle, from the pilot's seat. 'Did she do good?'

'Oh Christ! Did she!'

'What's she got, Scribb? Ask her for me.'

'What you got there, sweet sister?'

She was moving the sun feather in her hands, gazing at it like the relic of a god.

Which it was.

A sun god.

Light shards thrown off the passing streetlamps, changed to black by the van's mirrored windows, found themselves caught, for a second, upon the feather's one million flights. Then they were reflected, in fractals of gold, bouncing off the sides of the van like ricochets from the sun.

When Desdemona spoke—with her face so pretty in the feather light—her voice was inlaid with gold, and burnished to a fuck-me-please shine.

Just like . . . just like she's . . .

'Takshaka Yellow,' she said, all quiet like.

There was a suck of breath as we all breathed it in, all those perfumes, those pleasures to come.

'Takshaka?' I said, unbelieving.

'Takskaka fucking Yellow!' screamed the Beetle, letting the wheel slip for a second. I felt the van careen over to the pavement, and then the jolt as it took the curb at speed. For a second or two we were travelling in chaos. Then the Beetle popped a Cortex Jammer, and grabbed the wheel like a murderer his gun. So we were back on the track, the road, the King's highway, with a vengeance.

'Beetle! You shouldn't be doing that!'

'Tell me why, little man?!' he screamed. And then; 'Awooooooh!!!!! Let's rock!' And he drove that van into a let's all go out in a blaze of yellow glory.

'Because this is supposed to be perfect, Bee,' I answered. 'That's why.'

'Fuck perfect! Let's ride this sucker!'

Bridget was still fast in sleep. Desdemona was foreplaying the feather, getting it on strong.

'This is my trip, Beetle!' I said. 'Let me ride it.'

Why was I saying this? It wasn't just me. I wanted the group with me.

'Nobody goes alone, Scribb,' he replied. 'Nobody goes in alone.'

'This is private!'

This is private?

I was getting voices. Outside voices. Where the fuck were they from? And in my hands I found a pasteboard card, the image of a young man, a sack of things on his shoulder, a barking dog at his heels, the edge of a cliff beckoning.

Where did I get that from?

'This is beautiful,' whispered Desdemona. 'Takshaka Yellow. The marinade of God.' Her voice was saffron-rich. 'You read the Cat on this one, Scribb?'

'Kind of,' I answered

'Utanka was a young student . . .' Desdemona started.

'What's she saying, Scribb?' shouted the Beetle. 'I can't hear her properly!'

'She's telling us a story, Bee.'

'Woh! What story?!'

'Story of Takshaka.'

'Woh! Keep telling it!' the Beetle screamed, jamming that van through the Curry Paths. All the scents of India assailed us, as we rode that jasmine chute. Desdemona was talking with a saffron tongue, and I wanted to kiss my sister's voice, because it was so very beautiful. She told us the story of young Utanka, the Asian student. He travelled into the realm of snakes in order to steal back the earrings of the queen. The king of England had forged these jewels out of the most precious ore, as a birthday gift to his beautiful wife. Utanka had been given the task of carrying the earrings to the queen. Unfortunately, upon the way to the royal bedchamber, the earrings were stolen by Takshaka, the king of the snakes, who was as long as a river, a violet and green river. His bite was deadly to human flesh, carrying poisonous dreams along the veins until the mind was polluted with violence.

Takshaka carried the jewels down into his kingdom, the world of the Nagas, the dreamsnakes.

'What happens next, Des?' I asked her.

'Your mission, Scribble Utanka, should you wish to accept it, is to journey through into the jasmine valley of the dreamsnakes, armed only with a ball hammer, some snakeweed juice, and a forked branch, and to retrieve those earrings. Do you accept this task, oh great warrior, Scribble Utanka?'

'I'm not sure . . .'

The rest of the Riders were laughing by now, but I was taking it straight.

'Just do it, brother,' said Desdemona.

'I don't think I can,' I replied. 'The Cat says that you can die in a Yellow . . . for real.'

Then she leaned over to kiss me.

Sister kissed me and I felt some petals falling on me, inside the van, falling, falling, inside my head, from some unimagined Vurt.

Flowers were falling.

It surely is the sweetest colour. It was giving us flavours, flavours of the feast to come. Things we'd never tasted.

The living room was amber lit, with flowers of gold falling off the wallpaper, so many thousands of them that they made a carpet of petals on the floor. There was a hole in the carpet. And although we all knew that falling through a yellow door was bad, still we fell through it anyway.

!!!!!WARNING!!!!!

Shit! What was that?

I was walking through a palace of gold, my three companions at my side. In my hands, a ball hammer drenched in snakeweed, only known antidote to the dreamsnake bite. The other three were loaded up the same, and we were warriors in, bad world, and I felt full up of hunger and blood.

Everything was shining yellow, shining with the smell of saffron, in the world of the Nagas.

Game Cat tells us that the Nagas are a fabulous race of snakes. They are powerful and dangerous and usually appear in the form of ordinary snakes, but sometimes as mythic giants, long twisting forms of violet and green. Sometimes they turn into human shapes, just to fool us. The king of the Nagas is called Takshaka. Sometimes the Nagas get caught in the human world, and this makes them very angry, because they cannot stand the light of our world. We call these exiles the dreamsnakes.

!!!!!WARNING!!!!!

What was that? I was getting voices. Maybe I was getting the Haunting?

Please, my Lord, don't let this be a Vurt. Let this pleasure be real.

Having entered the limitless world of the dreaming snakes, we found it to be full of admirable establishments for games, both large and small, and crowded with hundreds of porticoes, turrets, palaces, and temples.

Jasmine flowers were falling, as I sipped at God's
this chariot towards Takshaka, with the best set of
locked tight to mine, her tongue going in, like a fe
That good.

Don't let me lose her.

What?

What did I just think?

'Let's ride this beauty,' chanted the Beetle, so
chance to question my doubts. We rolled the bea
a Rusholme Garden port, behind the flats, each of
the rust deposits settling, for a few moments, as we
the pleasures to come, the saffron-drenched pleasu

Rust was falling.

Drenched pleasures. These would be mine tonight,
various guises.

Beetle broke the mood, 'Let's do it! Inside!' he sh
ing the feather out of Desdemona's hand. 'Let's
the Yellow! Come on!'

We made an easy, snakeless flight up the stairway
which welcomed us with a show of lights. Now Bri
on the settee, slow-gazing at a three week old cop
Cat. Beetle was standing by the window, stroki
feather. He charged up the flights real good with
he fed it to our mouths, each of our mouths in
with his own last of all.

I felt the opening credits roll and then the pad
and my last thought was; this is beautiful and I wa
want it forever. Then the Yellow kicked in . . .

The fearless famous four of us are swimming in th
getting ourselves marinaded, getting ourselves pa

All this beauty; not a snake to be seen. Only their soft slith-erings in the yellow shadows, invisible. My left ankle was tingling, like it had a message for me, a message I had long since forgotten.

WARNING. YOU ARE NOW INSIDE A
METAVURT.

'Did you hear that? Anyone?' I asked.

'Hear what?' said Desdemona.

'That voice.'

'Heard nothing.'

'Come on, you two,' said the Beetle. 'Less of the billy-cooing. Let's hammer some snakes!'

We stalked that gilded world, with our weapons of steel and weed, and our fear and our sweat. Bridget started to sing her song, a tingling hymn of praise to the unseen Naga snakes. They were smothered in pride by the song from Brid's lips. But they would not return the earrings, and the snakes remained in the shadows, entwining.

A jasmine powder was dropping on us, from the palace's ceil-ing, but I was getting voices . . .

WARNING! YOU ARE NOW IN A METAVURT,
RUNG TWO. THIS IS EXTREMELY UNWISE,
AND SHOULD BE VACATED FORTHWITH.
THANK YOU. THIS HAS BEEN A PUBLIC
HEALTH WARNING.

'You heard that,' I said. 'Didn't you?'

'What's up, love?' asked Des.

'That voice! Listen to it! Can't you hear it! We're in a Meta-vurt!'

'Don't be silly now.'

And as she said it, she held my hand in her own. Her fingers were soft and long, with sharpened nails, that dug in, just slightly, just enough.

'Okay, lovebirds. Enough words,' announced the Beetle. 'Here come the fuckers!'

And the snakes came, unravelling from the shadows, from the golden shadows, all violets and greens, giving a shine to the world, a poisonous shine. They were coming in hundreds, but so tightly knotted, it would take more than a human span to count them.

I tried to run. I think I tried to run.

But something held me back; this could only be perfect.

Takshaka the King rose up, his great head all mutilated and bleeding. He seemed to be made out of smoke, not flesh, a snake of smoke.

YOU ARE REALLY GETTING ON MY WICK!
PLEASE VACATE THIS META-LEVEL
IMMEDIATELY.

Beetle let loose the first blow, swinging his ball hammer down in a hard graph, the muscles in his arms standing out like plague swellings. The head of a young snake caught the blow, and then cracked open, so that the weed could get through, dripping sap into the system, until the snake split apart, and there was snake juice everywhere, all over the warriors. But it looked so good, that splatter, we all just had to join in, bringing hammers down on the heads of snakes, dodging the fangs, revelling in the juice that was pouring over us, like a marinade of rain.

We hit that first line of snakes like a flesh hammer, and it all seemed so easy, so very easy for a Yellow, so maybe Yellows aren't all they're cracked up to be. Or maybe I was dreaming all this. Maybe I getting the Haunting again, seeing the dirt through the glass.

No matter.

Some dreamsnakes died that night, let me tell you.

Of course we did well, we did good, we did it like warriors, like heroes. We didn't get Takshaka, King Snake, but we hammered some bad fucker cronies. And we got those earrings back, and delivered.

The Beetle was draped all over with snakeskin, layers of it, stuff he had flayed with his own hands. He had a snakehead pinned to his jacket, a personal souvenir of the victory.

'That was some theatre, Des!' he said. 'Thanks for finding it.'

'No trouble, Bee,' my sister answered.

We were all slumped out; Brid fast asleep on the couch, me in my favourite armchair, Desdemona on the rug by the fire. Only the Beetle was lively; he was pacing the room like a jammed-up panther, looking for something to eat.

'I feel like squeezing the juice some more,' he said. 'Come on, Bridget. Time for bed.' She rose up to follow him, and the door closed behind them with a soft sound.

Desdemona and I, all alone then, against the world.

'You wanna go to bed?' I asked her, copying Beetle.

'Yes please,' she answered. And my pulse sang.

This is just like she's never been away.

We fell into each other's arms, under the sheets, with a warm breath blowing from the open windows, like an English balm.

Just like she's never . . .

And afterwards—as we lay stomach to back, my right hand on her breasts, my left scrunched up against her neck, my right leg draped over her legs, my left tucked up neat against her thighs, her breathing moving to mine like a twin clock—a man came into our room.

Desdemona was fast asleep, and so was I, but I could feel him there, in the darkened air, like a taste on the mouth long after the feast has gone.

'Young man,' the ghost said. 'I am most disappointed in your conduct.'

My eyes wouldn't open; I was locked in fear.

'No doubt you have an excuse,' the darkness said.

'Desdemona...' I asked. Or tried to ask. Or thought that I might have asked. Or didn't ask. No matter, Desdemona just slept right on through anyway.

'Open your eyes, young man, when you're looking at me.'

Something made me do it, some outside force.

My father was looking down at me, from the foot of the bed.

Oh shit! Oh fuck! Oh Christ!

I couldn't seem to move. Why can't I move?

Stay calm. Can't be. Can't be.

Not my father. Just some older man.

Father wouldn't have just stood there watching his children in bed. No. He would have pounded me. Not out of any common decency, no, but out of jealousy; having bedded his daughter a few times anyway, along with all the cuttings to her—

'Be careful,' the man said.

I knew that voice.

I was sitting upright now, the sheets caught up around me. Desdemona stirred beside me, but did not awake.

'Who are you?'

'Be careful. Be very, very careful.'

'Game Cat?'

'Indeed. You remember me.'

'I've never seen you before.'

'Why, we met only this morning. At a rather sleazy affair I'm afraid.'

'Leave me alone.'

I was coming down from the fear by now, and getting pictures; me standing on the balcony, looking down; the man standing beside me No! I wasn't having that! This morning I was sleeping next to Desdemona, this very bed.

'You know that Tapewormer is a young boy's feather?'

'Tapewormer?'

'Presumably you have heard of it?'

'Of course, it's a—'

'You're in it now.'

'No. This is—'

'Young man, you are in the Vurt. Listen to me. This is the Game Cat speaking. When am I ever wrong?'

I looked over at Desdemona. She was peaceful. She was there. 'Cat! Tell me I'm not in Vurt,' I pleaded.

The Cat just smiled.

'Please! I'm not on Vurt. Please! This is for real.'

'Don't fight it, kittling. You just did a Yellow. You just did Takshaka. Think about it.'

'So?'

'That was a Tapewormer Yellow. Has to be. You'd be dead otherwise. Yellows do not come that easy.'

'Please!' I was hugging Desdemona in her deep sleep. 'I don't know what you're talking about! You're not talking about me! Desdemona is here! She's here!'

'Did you not get the voices?'

'I . . .'

'You know that you did. Inside Takshaka. The voices warning you about going Meta. That was the Sniffing General speaking.'

'Who?'

'The General's in charge of the layers. You made him very, very angry. You heard him, didn't you?'

'Yes. But—'

'And the others—the Stash Riders, is it? How very quaint—they didn't hear the voice. I wonder why?

'Because they . . .' But I was feeling it bad.

'Because you are indulging in Tapewormer. Alone. The others
are just figments. Nothing is real.'

I couldn't take it any more. I was trying to get up, struggling
with the wet sheets. 'Get out of my house!' I screamed, but the
Cat just laughed. He pushed me back easily, with one finger. I
collapsed back onto the bed, beside Des. She still hadn't woken,
and I suppose I should have seen it by now.

The Game Cat was looking down at me. His face had turned
cold.

'You ever heard of Curious Yellow?' he asked.

'What? No ... I ... vaguely ...'

'It means nothing to you?'

'Isn't it some high-level Vurt. A yellow feather? Why? Should
it mean something?'

The Cat sighed, wearily. 'Let me tell you about Curious Yellow.
It's a sucker fuck, my kittling. A testing ground, if you like. A rites
of passage game. It's painful. We are at this moment inside Tapewormer. It's makes the past beautiful. It takes out all the bad stuff.
Exaggerates the good. Curious Yellow is the exact opposite. It
makes the past into a nightmare, and then strands you there, with
no hope of release. Only knowledge will get you out. Listen, I've
been there. It takes all you've got.'

'So?'

'That's where your sister is. Curious Yellow. Trapped there.
Suffering. Dying. And you, young man, are spending your time in
wanker feathers like this one, making believe that she is safe. That
disgusts me.'

This speech had finished me. It felt like I was being told some
ultimate truth; I knew it to be true. And yet it went against the
world I was living in.

Maybe I just wanted to deny it.

'Am I getting through?' the Cat said.

'You're confusing me.'

'I had to do this, Scribble. Tapewormer is not the way. I need you out there.'

'Where?'

'The real world. You'll be pulling out soon. And when you do . . . all this will make sense. I have something to ask of you. Will you look after my brother for me? No, don't protest. His name is Tristan. In this version of the world you never meet, but in reality you do. We are . . . well . . . we're not very close. Not these days. He has just suffered a great, great loss. I would like to offer some condolences . . . alas, it is not to be. He needs help, Scribble. Would you do this for me? No, no, don't say anything. Just remember these words. Consider this a dream—it may be easier that way—and that soon you will awake. Do you understand?'

'Almost.'

'Good. Let Sirius guide you.'

Game Cat reached inside his jacket and pulled out a feather. It was a silver feather. 'Do you have anything to give me?' he asked.

I shook my head. The feather was holding me, the way the lights were dancing in it.

'That card will do.' He was looking over at our bedside table. The strange card was lying there, the one with the fool and the dog. 'Give me that.'

I gave it to him and he placed the feather in my hands. It rested in my palm like a sliver of the moon.

'Do you know what it is?'

'It's a Silver. An Operator feather. I . . .'

'I know. It gets to you, doesn't it?'

'Never seen one before. It's very beautiful.'

'It's name is Sniffing General. The General is a Doorgod.

Perhaps one of the most powerful. Be very careful, when dealing with him. You may find need of him one day.'

'Where did you get it?'

'Hobart gave it to me.'

I was so shocked, I almost dropped the Silver.

'You've met Hobart?!'

'Sniffing General is Hobart's servant.'

Everybody knew about Hobart, but nobody knew anything. Just the hundreds of rumours that surrounded the name: Hobart invented Vurt. Hobart is alive, Hobart is dead. Hobart is a man, a woman, a child, an alien. Some have called her Queen Hobart, and they have worshipped her. To others Hobart is a dream or a myth, or just a good story that somebody made up, so good that it stuck around, became truth.

Nobody knew anything.

'What is Hobart, Cat? I asked. But his eyes were far away, his mouth set into a tight line.

'Some Viper is coming in the system, Scribble. I'm getting it. Bad messages. I really don't need this, young man. This is your fuck up! This is what you get when you go Meta. We're getting some leakage from Takshaka Yellow. May I advise a jerkout?'

'Wait! Game Cat! What's happening?'

'It's all yours, Scribble. It's your show.'

There was a noise coming from beyond the door.

'Game Cat!!!'

He'd vanished.

Oh Christ! What was that?

There was a light shining under the bedroom door, and I knew that I'd turned all the lights out before following Desdemona to bed. It was a green and violet light, and I could smell saffron in the air as drifts of smoke found their way in through cracks.

I turned to wake Desdemona.

She had slipped away from me, unseen.

I was alone. Everything was slipping away; the room, the world, the love.

I was in a Vurt, haunted.

That terrible sadness.

Takshaka exploded through the door, a great rush of colours and mists, writing around the room, even as the room started to fade and I was pulling out . . .

Come on! Do it!

Couldn't find the way out.

King Snake wove his long body around the room, almost like he was showing off. His head was three feet across, with a cruel mouth split by two spear-like fangs. There was a knowing look in his unblinking eyes, like he was laughing at me. And something else there; something that stirred a bad memory for me; I knew that look! From the real world—

Come on, you bastard! Let me out of here!

I was working the jerkout switch but getting nowhere, stuck between worlds, knowing in my mind exactly what I was, even whilst my body clung to the Vurt.

And somebody calling my name . . .

Takshaka opened his mouth wide to show off the bloated poison sac at the back of his throat.

'Scribble!' That voice.

Help me. Voice, help me. Takshaka closed his mouth slightly until I could see his eyes again and catch the look that was there—

Shadowcop!

'Scribble! Come out! Please!' The voice calling to me. Twinkle's voice!

King of the Snakes soaring down at me—

Do it now, do the jerkout! Do it!

'Scriiiii—

Intense wrenching somewhere in the body and I was—

—iiiiiible!'

—*falling onto the settee as though from miles away.*

Shaking, shaking. Twinkle was shaking me. 'Scribble? Stop it!'

'What? Huh! Christ! Hurts—'

'I've got you now. Calm down!' Twinkle holding me tight as I held on to the real world, like it was my mother, holding me back from the dream.

Tapewormer.

It was all just Tapewormer. All the kisses and caresses of Desdemona, they were all just false dreams, a poor boy's dreams.

Desdemona was still captured and this was reality.

I was stretched out full length on an old settee, in a rented room in Whalley Range, and Karli the robobitch was licking my face, and Twinkle was bending over me. 'Are you alright, Mister Scribble?' she asked.

Couldn't answer. Didn't know if I was or not.

She forced something into my hands. 'It's from the Beetle. He can't use it any more. Not with his bad arm.'

I bought my hand up to my face. The Beetle's gun in my hand.

'He says to tell you . . . happy birthday.'

Beetle had given me this?

'And from me,' Twinkle said, slowly, like it was hard work. And then I remembered hitting her.

'I'm sorry for hitting you, Twink. Stuff was getting to me.'

'I can see that.' And she could. Girl was growing.

I weighted the gun in my palm, feeling its power. Opened it up, saw three bullets left there. Mine to use. *This time, I won't drop you in panic or fear.*

In my other hand, a silver feather lay waiting. Sniffing General. Doorgod. Key to the Cat.

'Scribble! You brought back a Silver!' cried Twinkle. 'Well done!'

Well done?

Well then . . . yes . . . well done, well fucking done! I was coming through!

It's all yours, Scribble. It's your show. Let Sirius guide you. And I knew exactly what he meant. The dog star.

I'm coming after you, all my lost ones.

DAY 23

'A glass of fetish. Clean drugs.
Good friends. A hot partner.'

FEATHERED UP

Midnight. Closedown. Stepping out of the house, locking the door behind me. Alone. The streets of Whalley Range shimmering to a dark haze. Some few streetlamps still functioning, most of them long dead. The warm clammy air hung like a Sunday's curse over the town, full up with the smell of rain. It sure was building up to a comedown. This was going to be the longest Sunday of my life.

Let's do it!

I reached into my pocket, pulled out a tube of Vaz, looking up and down the street, searching out a potential victim. I saw one some twelve cars away, a nice bright Ford Transit, parked half on, half off the pavement. I started to walk towards it, thinking; come on you bastard, you Game Cat, give me some knowledge! Let me know how it feels! I was seeking out a Vurt along the way, something to jump into, featherless.

If I could just manage it . . .

By the second car along I was trying for Crash Master. Did no good. Couldn't reach it. Too high to reach, too black. By the fourth car I was trying for Jumpstarter. No use. Too far to go.

Shit to fuck! What was I doing?

I didn't have a license, or anything. Beetle had given me some lessons, during which he'd cursed like a demon, grabbing at the wheel, and here I was, hoping to pull a Taking Without Owner's Consent.

I drew up close to the Transit.

I put my hand on the door handle and called up Baby Racer.

Baby Racer was a real low-down theatre, a learner's Vurt. Should've gotten right on in there.

Easy.

Left ankle was twitching. Felt like the wound down there, seemed like miles away, maybe it was opening, and I could feel the Vurt in my veins, the blood in waves, chopping, just inches away from my fingertips.

Couldn't reach it. Tried hard. Just couldn't.

The waves were going out, back to the sea. I was left up dry, human dry, with a beautiful blue and white Transit sitting right there on the curb and nothing to show for it. Felt like the rain should start, and right now, and on me, just on me.

That bad.

We had to carry the Beetle down the stairs, just like the old alien days, me on one end, Mandy on the other. Mandy was on the feet. I kept dropping him of course, or so Mandy kept telling me.

'What are you on, Scribble?' she asked.

'I'm on the head,' I answered. 'What are you on?'

'Very funny.'

'Yeah. Fucking hilarious!' shouted the Beetle. 'Just get me down easy.'

Behind us were Twinkle and Karli. Behind them Tristan, carrying the body of Suze, her long strands of hair falling free at last, from the lover's knot. He had some bad things in his brain, you could see them moving, just behind the eyes. I had to turn away from it, back to where the Beetle was making a sad call, 'Keep a fucking grip, you two! I am the wounded warrior and I deserve your respect.'

'Beetle, actually I think you can walk now.'

'The fuck I can walk! I'm a registered invalid.'

'It's your shoulder, Bee . . .' I said, dropping him.

'Youch!'

'. . . not your knees.'

Beetle's head was resting awkwardly between two steps. 'Actually, Scribb darling,' he said, looking up at me, with the light of his face falling into shadow. 'I'm feeling pretty bad. Something's happening. My shoulder . . . shit . . .'

When I looked down into those black eyes, it felt just like the old feeling, like I was being dragged into the darkness by him.

'You got a car for us, didn't you, Scribble?' he drawled out, on a whisper of breath.

'Yeah. Sure,' I lied. 'Got a beauty.'

Just that I couldn't get inside it, couldn't start it up, couldn't drive it. Apart from that . . . the world is rosy.

I looked over to Tristan. Maybe I could ask him to drive? Then I saw the weight he was carrying, the weight of lost love, and I gave him the miss on that.

'Carry me, carry me,' sang the Beetle.

So we carried him. Those last few steps, and then out the door, into the hot streets. The van was there, ten cars away, just waiting.

'I can't see no van, Scribb,' said the Beetle.

We had laid him out on the pavement, and the rest of the

group were standing around, all of them looking at me. As though
I was the warrior. *Shit, man, maybe I just can't handle this.*

'You got somewhere for the Suze to lie?' asked Tristan. His
face was dripping sweat in the night, from the weight, from the
tenderness.

'I got somewhere.'

'He ain't got fuck all!' hissed the Beetle. 'Babe is a failure! I'll
tell you something, Tristan. Kid sure ain't no Stash Rider.'

'Well fuck you, Bee!' I answered back.

'Who's in charge around here?' he asked.

'I am.'

With that I took off up the street, towards the van.

'Oh good,' I could hear him calling after me. 'I'm glad somebody
is.'

His words were stinging me as I moved through the waves of
heat. My shadow was gathered by one streetlamp, and passed on
into the burnt out darkness of another.

I was full up with hate. Hate for the Bee. Hate for the job. Hate
for the loss and the failure. Hate for failing Desdemona, and
Bridget, and the Thing, and all the others that were waiting, those
that I had yet to fail, but would surely do so, when the crack came
around.

That was when I felt it. The flash. Sudden image. Me riding in
a stolen Merc, doing a wheel twist around a corner, not giving a
shit, putting deliberate dents in the posh parked cars.

I was in Baby Racer.

I was right on in there! Driving!

Totally feathered up, living on the dub side.

The hatred had fired me, jump-started me.

I Vazzed open the van hood, disconnected the alarm system.
How the fuck did I do that? Cut one wire, spliced it to another,
poured some Vaz from the tube into the door lock, slipped into

the van. I reached into my pocket for the hairgrip of Suze's, dipped it in the Vaz, fed it to the starter. It worked smoothly and suddenly I was in control, full up on knowledge, shifting those pedals like a young kid on a bad estate. Felt like bliss as I turned the wheel, steering the van out of the gap, no scratches, driving back to the team on a smear of Vaz, my head singing with it.

I opened up the back door, the same smooth way, and Twinkle and the dog were the first on board, first cargo. I lodged Beetle's head on the floor rim, then stepped into the back myself helping to pull his limp shape inside, Mandy steering the rudder of his legs. She climbed in after him. Beetle made some noises during all this, but I had the shades down. I was climbing back out when Mandy called me over. 'Scribble? The Beetle . . .'

'What is it?' I asked.

'His wound. Look . . .' The worms were glowing there, and turning into colours. All the colours you could name. 'What's happening to him?' Mandy asked.

'Never mind the Beetle just now. You know we've got some work to do.'

In other words . . . I just didn't know.

'What's wrong with you people?' cried the Beetle. 'I'm feeling top notch! I'm on the case! Just a little pain, is all!'

I climbed back out of the van, to where Tristan was waiting, Suze in his arms.

'How you doing, Tristan?' I asked.

He just turned those steel-driven eyes onto me, and I saw the answer there. A bad answer.

'We're doing it, okay?' I told him.

He kept staring.

'You know what she wants,' I said.

He nodded.

We worked her gentle body into the van; it was like some kind of ceremony. Tristan followed her, stepping high, but sluggish. They were all in.

Good.

First phase over.

I closed one door, reached for the other. 'Keep the faith.' That's what I said, don't know why, just said it.

Keep the faith.

I closed the darkness on them and walked around to the driver's door. I climbed in the cab. Reached up, for the Vurt. Come on down. Felt it coming down, the flood of knowledge, Baby Racer knowledge. My hands were turning the hairgrip key, working the clutch, feet on the pedals, wishing for a start.

Vurt came flooding down.

'Yahhhhhhh!!!!!!!!!!!!!!!' My voice screaming.

Baby Racer.

The engine caught. Gunned it.

'Be careful, Scribb,' called Twinkle from the back, trying out her best Game Cat impression. Sounded nothing like him, but never mind that.

Be careful. Be very, very careful.

'Fuck careful!' I shouted, driving.

Driving!

My hands were instruments of Vurt.

I parked the van some few feet away from the original space, where the old van, the Stashmobile, had found her last resting place. Heavy tires crunching glass as we came to rest.

I heard the back door opening.

Seconds later Tristan appeared at my window. I wound it down, letting his sad-eyed face come close. 'I'm gonna sort some things out,' he said.

'Yeah. Sure,' I replied. 'You alright?'

'I'm fine. Fine.'

'You don't look it, man.'

'Just keep looking after Suze.'

'It's done.'

Then he was away, striding out, into the darkness. I watched him disappear into the stairwell. A kind of loneliness closed in, all around me.

I switched off the engine. The Vurt dropped away to a whisper, but still there, on the edge, just waiting.

I could hear the whimpering of Karli Dog. Maybe she was licking the wounds of Suze. The dead wounds.

I didn't look back. Couldn't afford to.

All around, the shimmering dark towers of Bottletown were calling to me.

'Can I get out the van, Mister Scribble?' asked Twinkle, from the darkness.

'No. No, stay in the van,'

I heard Mandy bringing some comfort to the youngster.

Through the windscreen I watched Bottletown going to bed. Light by light. All along the crescents lights were going out, one by one. Seemed like some kind of mystic code was being played out there, on the high-rises, until only the fat moon was left glistening.

'Are we doing anything, Scribble?' asked the Beetle, from the back.

'Sure, Bee,' I answered. 'We're doing the daily crossword. Now everybody shut the fuck up.'

Everybody shut the fuck up. Even the Beetle.

We were waiting on something, each of us, in the moments before the rain.

Tristan had been gone half an hour.

What the fuck was he doing up there?

The first wet spots hit the screen. Big hot coins of it, splattering the glass.

'Where is he?' asked Mandy.

'He's coming,' I answered. 'Stay cool, gang.'

Not believing a word.

I could see shadows moving, along the lines of glass.

'What the fuck's going on, man?!' screamed the Beetle. 'What the fuck is going on out there?'

'I'm in control, Beetle.'

'Well fucking show it, man! I'm getting impatient. And my fucking shoulder is killing me!'

'The dogs looked after you.'

'It's worse than that.'

Didn't know what to say.

The rain was falling hard now. I stepped out of the van, away from the voices, and the rain felt so good against my skin, I just wanted to shout out loud.

Tristan had been gone three quarters of an hour.

I walked over to where the first van had been fired.

The ground was well crushed with glass.

I was looking for clues, but could find none. Just a spill of oil on the tarmac, capturing rainbows.

But that was ages ago, the fire, and surely this fresh oil slick was from some other vehicle, some more recent crash, and anyway, maybe the Brid and the Thing were dead already, and I was just playing a pair of deuces. Maybe that's all I ever get to play in this hand?

Tufts of dog fur were caught on the shards of glass, and something had painted the words Das Uberdog on the pavement.

My feet were getting cut.

My ankle was aching again, so I rolled up my jean leg to see the wound dripping, like those tiny holes were reopening.

Tristan still wasn't back yet.

I could hear Beetle crying out in pain from the back of the van, but I just paid him no mind. Shades down. Other problems.

The black rain was dripping from my eyelids, into my line of sight, forming a beaded curtain. I hear a noise over to my right and I turn to see a man walking towards me. At first I think he's a bad guy, he looks that mean. Then I see the dogs coming, two of them, leashed to one of his hands. Over one shoulder he carries a shotgun, over the other a canvas bag. In his other hand a spade. And as the stranger approaches other details fall into place: the smears of paint on his face, in stripes: the look in his eyes, a look of pure momentum, like an animal.

He takes those last few steps, the ones that bring us near to each other, the difficult steps. I see then his bald head shining in the moonlight, jabs of colour here and there, bits of blood it looks like. 'Tristan?' I ask. 'That you?'

The stranger doesn't answer me.

'What you done, man? Where's the hair?'

'Shaved it.'

The two dogs were straining to be set free, howling towards the moon, feeling their blood pulled in waves by its gravity.

'That's drastic action,' I say. 'I guess you needed to do that?'

Tristan's not looking at the moon. He's not looking at the stars, or at the flats, or at the van. Tristan's looking at me. I'm his sole intention.

'You know what I want, Scribble,' he says.

Yeah. What we all want. A glass of Fetish. Clean drugs. Good friends. A hot partner. All that.

Something more.

A squaring of the tides.

GAME CAT

Sneak preview. I'm getting word of a new theatre. Hasn't got a name yet. Working title is Bootleg Dreams. I've met the hero figure. His name is Scratch, and he tells a well wicked story. The names have been changed, to protect the guilty. This is how it starts: Wendy comes out of the all-night Vurt-U-Want, clutching a bag of goodies. You're a member of this gang of young hip malcontents. They call themselves the CRASH DRIVERS, so that's what I'm calling this new feather trip. The hero's name is Scratch, and this is one yellow shining journey. Golden yellow. Boy, have you got problems! First off your sister, Shona, has been caught in Metaland, swapped for a lump of lard alien. Your job is to get this Shona back to base Earth. Of course that's virtually impossible; nobody's managed it before. Still you can't stop trying anyway, because of the deep love. Then there's the fact that the evil shecop Moloch is after you. For putting scratches in her face, no less. Your best friend, The Weevil, isn't helping, with his constant desire for the gutter. He wants to drag you right down next to him, keep you there, in the dirtiness. It's a hard life, and most probably you're going to die in this crazy Yellow. Be very, very careful. This ride is not for the weak. It's a psycho. A bit like real life.

Well maybe not quite that bad.

ASHES TO ASHES, HAIR TO HAIR

Some bad things buried out on the moors. Some good things as well, some innocent things. Some things that didn't want to get buried. Some that did. Some that got buried by accident, by snow-fall or rockfall or soil slippage. Some that buried themselves, wanting the darkness to fall over their all-seeing eyes.

Plenty get buried there, out on the moors. It's where you go, when you come from Manchester, and you want to bury, get buried, or be buried.

On the way through the night, we talked about the wound. The way it was turning, spiralling out from its point of entry, coming in colours like a rainbow, crumbling at the edges in paisley shapes.

'I'm on a spree!' said the Beetle. 'Stop complaining.'

'It's not getting better, Bee,' I heard Mandy say back, but some change was coming over the man, and it was making him ramble. 'I don't want it to get better!' he shouted. 'I like it like this. Hey, Scribb! You seen my new colours?'

'Sure, Bee. Looking good.'

I had to chance random glances now and then, along some straight path of road. And then back to the wheel.

The air outside was dark pitch, flittering with passing shapes, like grey ghosts; trees, houses, signals. And it was a good job I was feathered up to the Racer, because that meant that some-body else was holding the van, some expert, some young kid expert.

At least the rain had stopped. Stopped some time in the night, leaving the roads wet, slippery.

I took another glance back, and the colours were glowing, spreading out from Beetle's shoulder, taking charge of him, reach-ing almost to his elbow on one side, to the back of his neck on the other. Mandy was cradling his head in her palms. The dark air of the van suffused into a soft aura around his body.

I turned back to the road and the driving.

Didn't really know where we were going, just knew we were getting there.

Baby Racer.

'I do think it's bad, Bee,' Tristan was saying. 'Extremely.'

'Shit! Don't scare me, man,' Beetle replied. 'It feels good. The pain's drifting away. You get that, Trist? No fucking pain! Listen to me!'

We were listening.

'You know what that means?' said Tristan, quietly, almost like he didn't want the Beetle to hear.

I was waiting for the Beetle's reply.

Took an age to come, and it was quiet, like the shadow of a voice, 'Not me . . . I'm pure . . . tell me I'm pure . . .' You could feel the hurt in there, as the Beetle's mind played against the wound, but I didn't look back. No way. Just kept my eyes blacked out to everything but the road ahead, losing myself in the darkness and the Vurt and the driving.

Please, somebody, take me away from this. Give me a straight road, a well-lit road, a sign-posted road, anything but this wounded road.

Tristan pushed through the gap, and settled into the passenger seat. He had the shotgun in his lap and the bag over his shoulder, and he was holding on to both of them real tight, like he was scared of losing them. From the back I could hear the dogs whimpering over the dead Suze.

We let some darkness pass, out beyond the lamps now, deep country.

'It's a Mandel Bullet,' he whispered, keeping it secret.

'I was trying not to think that,' I replied.

'Murdoch's got him.'

Jesus! Does it have to be like this?

'No one escapes it,' Tristan said. 'Once bitten, that worm just keeps on growing, spreading, multiplying. You can't stop it. No way. He's going fractal.' Sounded final, like an official result in Vurtball, beamed in from the judge's bench. 'It's a slow death,' Tristan added.

'Don't say that,' I whispered back. 'Please. Don't say that.'

No use. Just no use.

I was driving through the night, listening to Beetle's laughter, as the worm took over.

'There's no antidote, Scribb,' said Tristan.

No answer. No antidote.

Beetle was doomed.

I guess he knew that anyway, being the Beetle, being au fait with everything. That's the twister; you might know all the details of Mandel bullets, still didn't stop you enjoying the trip as they killed you. Mandel Bullets were designed to take advantage of the near miss, the wounding shot. If at first you don't succeed, put a parasite in there. Let that parasite suck the last remnants of life away, crumbling the skin into fragments. Each bullet contained a fractal virus. It takes maybe five seconds for the program to unload, direct to the cell walls. With twenty-four hours, forty-eight at the most, the entire metabolism has been taken over. You're dead. And how. The deepest cut was that those last twenty-four hours of your life were going to be the best you'd ever lived, as the fractals lit up like a rainbow, giving you visions of glory, and that was why the Beetle was singing now, his mind taken over, singing the praises of life.

Even in the midst of death, singing praises...

'You've been talking to my brother,' Tristan said, calling me down from my thoughts. I took my eyes off the road for a second. Baby Racer kept his eyes there for me.

'What's that?' I asked.

'I saw you there, at the Slithy Tove.'

'The Game Cat? You saw him?'

'Oh yes. I can see him. When Geoffrey wants me to see, that is.'

'Geoffrey?'

'Yeah. His real name. The Cat's best kept secret. Call him Geoffrey next time. He'll most probably kill you.' I could hear Tristan laughing as I clenched my hands around the wheel rim, driving on air, dark air. 'Did he mention that I was his brother?'

'Yes. I didn't believe it at first. But I've seen him since, in the Tapewormer.'

'What did you talk about?'

'He said that he felt for you. That he—'

Tristan exploded. 'That man should stay out of my life!' His voice was driven by fire. 'That fucker only brings grief!'

'Sure, sure . . . whatever, Trist . . .' I said, cooling it down some. We drove forward in silence for a few minutes.

'You want to talk?' I asked. Tristan turned his face to the side window, watching the black fields go by. 'About how come you lost each other?'

When he spoke, it was coming from the depths, and he couldn't stand to look at me. 'He went too far.'

'What's that mean?'

'He went too far for me. So far, I couldn't follow. You got that?'

'I got it.'

Got nothing at all. Except that Tristan wanted to talk about Game Cat, about Beetle, anything to stop the thoughts of Suze.

The lost love.

'You've got some dog in you, haven't you?' I said.

'Just a trace. Enough to know.'

'You ever made love to one?'

He was quiet for a moment.

'You ever made love to a dog, Trist?' I asked.

'Years ago,' he answered. 'But then I found the Suze, and nothing else came near.'

I knew that feeling.

Then he went all quiet on me, as he lit up a Haze joint, wreathing himself in honey smoke. Then he said this to me, 'Suze was expecting.'

At first I thought he was saying that Suze expected to die, but then I got the real story. 'Christ! Trist!' I said. 'A baby? You had a baby on the way?'

'Listen to me,' he stated. 'I'm alive for one thing.'

'You're going after Murdoch?'

'I don't have to, Scribble. She's coming after you.'

'What's in the bag, Trist?'

'My hair.'

Figures.

'You got bit by a snake, yeah?' he asked.

'I got bit.'

'So you got some Vurt in you?'

'So they say.'

'Geoffrey told you?'

'The Cat says lots of things,' I answered. 'I don't know how much to believe.'

'Believe everything. He's been all the way.'

'Meaning?'

'Geoffrey took a bite too. From a snake.'

'He's got some heavy Vurt in him, no argument.'

'Wasn't just any ordinary snake bit him.'

'No?'

'Not at all.'

'Tell me about it.'

Tristan turned back to the window, so I let the van drift on easy, secure in Baby Racer's arms. A night bird flew across the headlights; a sudden vision of life, moving on black wings. 'It happened years ago,' Tristan said, his voice coming on like a slow recording. 'When we were both young, me younger than him, but both of us hooked on the feathers. Couldn't stop taking them. You know that now I'm totally opposed to it, but there's a reason for that.'

'Geoffrey's the reason?'

'He was into it more than I was. But I was looking up to him so much, I couldn't stop following. He would go out on bad journeys, down to the low life, buying up the blackest Vurts he could find. One day he found a Yellow. Our first Yellow.' Tristan paused for a moment. 'He paid heavily for it.'

'I thought you couldn't buy them?'

'Depends what you pay with.'

I let that settle in my mind. *Depends what you pay with.*

'I was scared of the feather,' Tristan continued. 'We carried it back home, and Geoffrey was so excited. Our parents were asleep by then, so we had the room to ourselves. I was young and in awe of my brother, so I took the feather with him. But I was scared, so scared.'

'Which feather was it?'

'Takshaka. You know, where the dreamsnakes come from?'

I didn't reply, my eyes on the road.

'You ever done Takshaka, Scribble?' he asked.

'Yeah. I've done it.'

'Really?'

'No. Not really. Only in the Tapewormer. I went Meta.'

'That's nothing. That's just a joke Yellow. Takshaka kills. It's famous for it. I was scared but we went in anyway. Geoffrey got bitten. Not by any normal snake. Oh no, not my brother. Takshaka himself, the king of the snakes, sank two fangs into his arm.'

'That should've killed him.'

'Geoffrey took it on board . . . worshipped the wound. Fed it on bones and flesh. I think he fell in love with the poison inside him, and it fell in love with him. Maybe one in a thousand is capable of this. The Game Cat talks about it one time, in the magazine.' I caught on to the change of name. 'He says that some flesh is sacred to the Vurt; it can live with it. It's like a kind of marriage. So he says. Whatever . . . my brother got addicted then. Craving more. Having once tasted . . . well, you know how it is.'

'I know.'

'He was seeking out more and more dangerous feathers. I think he went too far. I had to fight back.'

'What did he find?' I asked.

'It was too much for me, Scribble. What my brother was doing . . . I had to take measures.'

'What happened?'

'He found Curious Yellow.'

Oh Christ!

The van skidded on a wet bend and I could feel paintwork being peeled off, as the struts of a fence clawed into us. Seconds of my life went by in a rush as I clamped down on the wheel, spinning it. Did no use. I was totally alone and human. Human! The passengers from the back were calling out and cursing me, and then the dogs joined in, all three of them. Sounded like a zoo on wheels. I could see the trees sliding near as we hit a rock, or something, and then this big oak trunk in the headlights, dancing, straight in front of us. Seemed like the whole world was screaming, me with it, and the Beetle singing along from behind, his colours exploding. But then the Vurt came down, hard! and the wheel seemed to know where to go under my fingers until I was rolling once again, cool and easy does it, over the black roads.

'Nice driving, Scribble,' Tristan said.

I was taking in massive breaths of air, feeling the sweat all over my skin. Mandy was calling me all the bad names she could think of. Twinkle was adding some of her own. The Bee was still singing, and the dogs were whimpering along with all three of them.

'Christ, Tristan . . . don't do that!' I could hardly get the words out, but Tristan had sat through it all, like he was stone cold, set on a fixed path.

'So we did the Curious,' he was saying, but it took some yards of easy driving before I could really get my grip on what he was saying.

'Was this inside English Voodoo?' I asked.

'Yes. He forced me into doing it.'

'What happened?' Knowing full well . . .

Tristan's slow, sad voice; 'I came down alone.'

'Curious got him?'

'I think he let it. You know what I'm saying, Scribb? I think he wanted to stay there. It was the worst thing I'd ever experienced, but for Geoffrey, with all that Vurt in him anyway, from Taksha-ka . . . I think he preferred it there. He felt . . . I don't know how to put this . . . he felt at home. Something like that.'

'What's Curious like?' I needed to know.

'It's the past, your past . . . but magnified, all the bad things magnified. The good things vanish.'

'How did you get out?'

'The Cat threw me out. He was glowing with power, messing with the feathers, even in the pain.'

'Why do people want to do this?' I asked. 'Go through all that pain?'

'Because they're crazy. They think it's going to bring them knowledge. It's like rites of passage, all that crap. All that Queen Hobart rubbish.'

'What is Hobart?'

'Don't get involved, Scribb. Some crazy religion, that's all. They think Vurt's more than it is, you know? Like it's some higher way, or something. It's not. Vurt is just collective dreamings. That's all. Christ! Isn't that enough for them?'

Tristan went quiet again.

I let him be for a while, but something was nagging at me, something he'd said. 'The Cat was taken into Vurt?' I asked. Tristan nodded. 'But you said that you'd come down alone? If the Cat was swapped . . . he must have been swapped . . . that's how it works . . . exchange rates . . . there's no escaping . . .'

I think he knew what I was going for, but he took his time in answering.

'I came round in our living room. No, I wasn't alone.'

I waited.

'There was a woman beside me, well, a girl actually. Because this was years ago. She was embracing me so tightly, and I was doing the same to her, and we were shaking you know, from the trip. I was still feeling the pain, and I think she was feeling the same. The pain of being forced through, from the dream, to the world. It's painful. But her embrace was powerful, and I gave back the same. She was lovely. That was years ago. I . . .'

His voice faded, to silence. And then I got a memory, of a woman who had got right inside me. Who had known everything about me. Who had eyes of gold . . .

'This was Suze?' I said.

Tristan nodded.

Suze was a Vurt being! An alien. Just like the Thing, but one thousand times more beautiful. 'Didn't you try for a swapback?' I asked.

'I didn't want to.'

'Why not?'

'This woman meant too much to me. More than my brother did. Can you see that, Scribble? Can you? Suze was the best piece of luck a man could ever wish for. And out of all that pain, we made a love. I vowed never to lose her. Not for one day'

I saw the strands of hair locking them together.

'I could not let her go. Just in case the Vurt claimed her back. Do you see that? Not for one second would she leave my sight. I thought it would work. I really thought it would . . .' There was a catch in his voice, and I kept my eyes on the road. I don't think he wanted me looking at him. But I could feel him pulling himself together, sitting up straight in the seat, hugging his little bag of hair, before speaking again; 'It was the real world that got her.'

I did look over then. Tristan was crying. Oh God, Scribble! What am I going to do?' he broke down. 'Suze . . .'

There are no words to add. You can't help that kind of pain. You can only make it worse. Or bury it.

We had left the trees behind, and the night opened up, into a black expanse of moorland. Even the skies were crying now, a dark fall of tears against the windscreen.

'This is the place,' Tristan said.

It was a shallow grave. Because that was all that Tristan could manage, scraping away with his thin shovel, against the layers of dirt.

All around our circle, shadows were dancing.

The rain was turning the earth into mud, and Tristan was struggling. I'd tried to help, we all had, but Tristan had pushed us away.

We watched as he lowered Suze into the shallow grave. Then he opened the bag, and took out the thick tresses of his hair. He let them fall into the earth, so that they landed softly on her body. He took a small wooden box from the bag, and placed this also with the body.

Tristan mumbling his words of farewell, over the grave, the falling soil that he was shovelling back into the ground.

Ashes to ashes. Hair to hair.

The trio of dogs howled into the night, howling for the lost mistress.

All of us gathered around the grave, silent, our minds full up of want.

Tristan had the two grown up dogs on a double lead. I could see his fingers starting to slip.

'What are you doing?' I asked.

His fingers were loosening, one by one.

'I'm letting them go,' Tristan answered.

'We may need them.'

'No. No, not at all. We're doing this alone. Suze wants it like this.'

'I'm keeping Karli,' says Twinkle.

Tristan nodded.

So I'm watching the two dogs disappearing into the darkness. Twinkle comes up close to me, fingers tight on Karli's collar, pulling her back from the urge.

The young bitch was yelping, wanting release.

'Stay, good girl. Stay!' whispered Twinkle, but the dog wasn't taking it too well.

Tristan's shaved head was splattered with raindrops, but his eyes were dry, focused, tight. I could feel the need coming off him.

The bad need.

GUN STROKE
(SUFFERING
FROM)

The dancing crowd-crush could just fuck off.

That look on Dingo's face, when he realised.

Just fuck off you dancing fools, because I was there, with both hands around the grip, two sweaty hands; one finger, dry, on the trigger.

Dingo didn't even know yet. Didn't even know yet that a gun was pointing at him.

The Tushdog fans were dancing. I had squeezed my way amongst them, into the pit, close to the stage, covered in sweat and dogbreath. It was bad, but close enough to see his eyes as he sang, and that was all I wanted.

I just wanted to see his eyes as he saw me there.

Then he caught a glimpse of metal from the crowd.

You ever looked down the barrel of a gun? Into the dark fluttering that waits there, the bullet in the chamber waiting there, waiting for the flash of powder which will set it free, waiting there?

You ever been on the wrong end of a gun?

Feels like a tunnel is about to open up, and you're going to get sucked in, and there's nothing you can do about it. There's just nothing that you can do.

Dogmusic spluttering to a close. The Dingo hooked on the thing in my hands.

'You know what I'm after, Dingo?' I called.

The crowd were sensing me now, and they were moving back, forming a circle, scared, feeling the funk.

Felt good!

Dingo Tush the superdog, the high barking king of dogpop. Well just take a look, loyal fans; see how he shakes now.

It felt good and bad to be doing this. Good because of the power trip, bad because of the betrayal, betrayal of a saviour.

Some bad things you've got to do, just to speed up the life, in the face of death.

'You know what I want,' I said, louder this time.

Above Dingo's head a sad mirrorball spun, flinging out lines of light like a broken halo.

It was just gone five in the morning. Dingo Tush was playing an all-nighter at the Fleshpot, a lowlife dogtruckers' stopover, down by the canal side, storming through a rush of music; big hits, planet samples, cover versions; all done up in hardware beats. But now the music stops.

Now the music fucking stops, dogstar!

Dingo tried to move.

I held the gun steady but inside I was sweating heaven out from my pores, thinking, *Shit! I've never fired a gun before. Please, Lord, don't let me hurt anybody!*

'Don't move, dogman!' I screamed. 'You know what I'm looking for.'

Dingo's eyes were darting to and fro, looking for escape routes. And then he latched onto some movement out in the crowd, and his fangs broke through as he smiled.

I didn't dare risk even a sideways glance, but I guess someone had called the bouncers and now they were moving in. So it was comforting to find Tristan at my side, his shotgun primed and heavy, and then Twinkle moving up close, her little hands straining on Karli's lead. Karli was a brutal handsome devil by now, and she did us proud; a fine show of daggered teeth and foaming jaw slush. And then Mandy pushed through the crowd, leading the Beetle by the hand. His colours shone out, loud and proud from his spreading wound. It was the best light show the Fleshpotters had ever seen and they couldn't help but dance under its radiance.

I guess the bouncers saw the way it was going. Nobody was bothering us.

The crowd were showing a suitable hush. Somebody screamed, then went quiet, sudden like, as though somebody else had jabbed her in the ribs. It was a suitable hush and I was pleased with that. I was pleased with the effect I was having. It felt like release. 'What do you want?' asked Dingo Tush. His voice was stretched, halfway between dog and human. Whichever; he was well scared in both modes.

'You know what, dogfucker,' I shouted.

Maybe he didn't like the use of that bad word. Maybe he didn't like the way my gun was rock steady upon his face. Maybe he didn't like me betraying him like this. Maybe he didn't like the look in my eyes.

Well, neither did I. But it was there, so let's fuck it to hell.

'You can't fire that thing, baby,' he said. Somebody from the crowd shouted, 'Right on!' and then they all joined in, mocking my incompetence, like this was just some mad part of the show, the latest Dingo Tush gimmick; mock assassination attempts. They were calling out to me:

'Go to it, dude!'

'Fire that fucker!'

'Let's see it!'

'Kid's a loser!'

'Baby can't fire.'

Other such stuff, and the Dingo was urging them on, goading them into mocking me. *And something came down then, into my blood stream, filling my head with knowledge; how to load, clean, aim, fire, and kill with a pistol.*

With a black jolt I was in Gun Stroker; a well-black feather, but featherless.

'Guy can't cut it!' said a crowd voice.

There was a burst of light coming out of my hands, and then the crash of air, as the bullet escaped my grip. I thought the sun had blown itself apart. It was just the mirrorball exploding above Dingo's head, a rain of glass falling down upon his bristling fur. 'What are you after?' he shouted.

'Brid and the Thing.'

'How would I know?'

'Dogfucker,' I said, 'Tell me where.'

I could see a few seconds of resistance in his eyes, as he contemplated his denial. But I had the gun, and he didn't. I guess it makes some kind of difference.

'Cosmic Debris.'

'No games, Dingo. The address.'

'That's the lot, pure boy.'

I pulled on the trigger.

Just a little, mind. Just a tiny Gun Stroker squeeze; enough to activate the red firing light. Enough to get the crowd gasping and the Dingo to start screaming; and to end the screaming with a blurted out message, the address.

I eased the trigger back into safety mode; the red light fading to cool mode.

'I would have told you anyway,' shouted the Dogstar.

'Just to make sure, Dingo.'

Just to make sure.

Because I already knew where Cosmic Debris was. I'd been there. I'd shopped there. We'd bought that old worm-hive settee from there.

Now we were going back. In search of some smoke-damaged shadowgirl and a second-hand Thing-from-Outer-Space.

'Stash Riders! Out of here!'

I was kind of loving this.

Outside, into the swirl . . .

Sunday mornings, starting at five a.m., they have this car boot sale at the Fleshpot canal site, down by the Old Trafford docks. That early all the illegal dealers turn up, selling off cheap feathers and Haze. Along with various domestic items. The sale was in full swing as we rushed out of the truckers' club. People were crowding the shore, looking for bargains. It was a crash of faces and noise. Cars were pulled up, tightly packed. Whole families were out in force, buying and selling. Felt like I was staring into a kaleidoscope, searching for a single crystal. Colours were swirling. Shouts and banter from all angles were calling to me, as I led the Stash Riders through the crush, back towards the van.

I pushed some people aside but it didn't take too much effort. What with The Beetle's colours, and Tristan's shotgun, and Karli's teeth and Karli's growl, I guess we made a pretty picture. The crowd made a clear path for us, over towards where the van was parked.

I was heading for the back door, ready to let the crew in, but I was getting this bad feeling, like there was something wrong with the number-plate, or something wrong with my eyes. I couldn't fathom it. Something wrong. I was staring at the number plate, and the numbers were flickering. Like they were living numbers. Couldn't work it out.

Then I got it.

Shadowcop!

There was a beam of inpho firing onto the number-plate. I looked around and there was the Shaka, working his mechanisms.

What now, big leader man?

'Stash Riders!' I was calling. 'Let's move!'

I was running through the crowd, away from the van, forcing a path. People yelling out at me, but I wasn't listening, just running on. Twinkle and Karli close behind, could feel them. And the Beetle's colours leading the way.

Where was Tristan now?

Never mind that.

Didn't know where to run to.

Except that the sun was glinting on the water somewhere, beyond where all those boats were moored.

That's where I led the Riders, not even knowing why.

There were sirens playing in the morning air.

Cop sirens.

Dozens of boats were tied up along the bank; the floating families selling off stuff, just to make a small life. Some were selling food from barbecue boats. Some were selling love, the downmarket version; cheap sluts and rabid studs on deck. And a boat of flowers; a floating garden.

I was looking all ways, searching for a way out. Cop sirens were playing my all-time least favourite tune.

I caught a broken shadow dancing along the edge of my vision.

I turned to get that image fixed. There was the Shaka, floating over the market, with the shecop Murdoch close behind, gun in hand.

Man, I was getting some serious Vipers in my system.

They were parting the crowd swirl by force and daring, and the look on Murdoch's face was pure, and raging; like she was aiming for a big thrill.

'Crewcut!' said this voice, from over by the boats. 'This way! Relish it!'

I turned back to the water.

'Crew baby! This way!'

I was searching for the voice, the needling voice in the boat-stack. Then my eyes were following the sound to its likely source, finding the sign on the mast-head: 'Food O'Juniper. Chef Barnie.'

I ran towards the boat, dragging the posse on.

Chef Barnie was on deck, waving us aboard. A young girl child was standing next to him, her fingers working the lines loose. 'This way, Crewcut. This way!'

We clambered onto the swaying vessel, and I was almost certain I had brought everybody with me. Twinkle? Yes. Karli with her? Yes. Mandy? Yes. Tristan?

Tristan? You there, my friend?

Seems not.

It seems that it is not to be.

The young girl cut the line.

'Wait!' I called.

But called it late, way too late.

And as we were drifting away, I watched the Tristan stepping out from the crowd, his gun lodged in his arms, firm and solid.

'Tristan!' I screamed. Guy took no notice. He had the shecop in his sights, and he wanted payment, payment for the loss.

Tristan let loose that shotgun.

It made a pretty flame in the morning's light.

Car booters were screaming and running.

A pile of house trash exploded on a makeshift trestle table as the bullet hit. Murdoch dived behind the body of a family saloon, away from the fire. Other cops were coming in. Tristan was jigging the gun mechanism, readying for another shot. Too late. Too slow.

I was catching all of this from the widening water.

Too late. Too late and too slow. The both of us.

The cops were grabbing hold of Tristan, wrestling him to the floor, holding him down. Barnie was putting some water between us and the trouble. Now the cops where beating down on Tristan with hot spikes.

All I could do was watch.

I turned my eyes away. Barnie was there, at the helm, wheel in hand, turning it upstream. I studied his perfect facebones for a full minute. 'Where are you taking us, Chef?' I asked.

'Home,' he answered.

Home? Where's that then?

And the river was a vein of blood under the sun.

AN IDEAL
FOR LIVING

Eyes opening to a flicker.

Colours, shapes of faces, people laughing.

The television was on.

I'm sitting in a deep velvet armchair, in the corner of a small living room, watching through half-open eyes. The television was a matt black model, with chrome trim. A real collector's item.

The kids down on the rug were screaming with joy. The dog's tail wagging.

Noel Edmonds was on the television. With his whirlpool of hair, and that cheeky grin, he was asking questions of a happy family. Every time they got a question wrong, a rude noise sounded, and this bright red pointer moved closer to the symbol of a pile of sick. Above the family rested a giant bucket. It was steaming. Below the bucket, in large blue and red letters, were

the words Noel's Spew Tank. Even when the television family got
a question wrong, still they laughed and giggled. Down on the rug
the three kids and the dog were laughing along. The dog laughed
by wagging her tail. I was laughing as well. My god! I hadn't seen
this since my childhood. What was happening?

I opened my eyes fully then, trying to take it all in. This room,
this house, this wallpaper of flowers, and the people who were
gathered there. It was all so familiar, like a memory. Like I'd been
here before.

The oldest kid was a teenager. Her name was Mandy. The dog
was called Karli, and the second girl was called Twinkle. I didn't
know the name of the youngest kid. And I suddenly got this picture; they've never seen this before! Never seen the hair of Noel,
the cigar of Saville, the magic of Daniels.

The living room door opened and Barnie came into the room.
He was followed by a woman. She was carrying a tray of food,
and Barnie had a bottle of wine and some glasses. The woman's
hair was green, emerald green, and it reached down to her fifth
vertebrae; it stirred up some feelings in me. Like I'd known her
before, and very closely. Couldn't place it. She put the tray down
for me, on a small glass coffee table. The food went with the
room. Plates of meat and fish, spiced vegetables, crispy salads,
ginger and garlic pastes, fruit and nuts, crumbling cheeses, apple
pie with a cinnamon custard.

'You awake now, Crewcut?' Barnie asked.

'Yes. I . . .'

'You were out cold. All of you were. When's the last time you
slept?'

'Slept . . .' I couldn't remember. 'What time is it?'

The woman answered. 'Half two.'

I jerked upright then, out of the chair's soft embraces. 'Half
two! Is that afternoon or morning?'

The woman laughed.

'It's the afternoon, Scribb. You dumbo!' This from the older kid on the floor, whose name was Mandy.

'You want to dig into that food, Crew?' asked Barnie.

I did. It was ages since I'd eaten.

'Where's Beetle?' I asked.

'Beetle's in the bedroom,' Barnie told me. 'This is our home, and this is my wife . . . Lucinda.' The woman smiled. Her mouth was wide and opulent. 'And this is our child, Crystal.' At these words from Barnie, the young girl pulled her face from the screen for a second, to give me a smile.

I started on the good food, feeling it ease my need. I could feel food dribbling down my chin, and I suppose I must have looked a little bit of a mess. 'I can't stay here,' I mumbled through a big mouthful. 'I'm in a hurry.' Some oil was dripping off my chin. I had to get back to Brid and the Thing. That was all that counted. But I didn't even know where I was.

'You fell asleep in the chair, Crew,' Barnie said. 'We didn't like to distrub you.'

'This is our home,' Lucinda added. 'You are most welcome.'

'Have I seen you before?' I asked her.

'Oh, most probably.' She smiled again. She had a perfect face. So did Barnie. The child also. They were all smiles. The room where they lived was a hive of comfort. The paintings on the wall told the same story; half naked women coyly glancing, horses leaping the waves, swans gliding down rivers of gold, big-eyed puppy dogs chewing on stolen slippers. The room was drenched in age-old colours.

Just then the television family got one too many questions wrong, and Noel's Spew Tank started to fall. It covered them in gunge, and they loved it. The audience roared their approval. The kids on the rug following suit.

And it suddenly came to me that not even I had done this before; never seen Noel, Saville, or Daniels. All this is way before my time. I'd just seen the re-runs. So what was going down? And why was I going down with it?

Déjà Vurt.

That's the name of the feeling you get sometimes, in Vurt, when you've done this one already, but you're in the Vurt anyway, remember? And you're thinking it's real. So a loop is made in the head, and it becomes a kind of Haunting. Memories of your previous trips start to play on the feather dreams, shifting them out of phase, like a feedback wave. Maybe this was the answer. I'm in a Vurt, getting a real cool Haunting.

'It's not a real television,' Barnie said. 'It's just pre-recorded tapes.'

'This isn't real,' I shouted. 'It's just not real!'

'That's right,' he answered, as though proud of it, before lifting up his arm to me, and with the other hand he peeled off a section of the flesh, showing me the workings underneath.

'This is what I am,' he said.

I was looking into this hole in his skin, gazing into a pool of wet plastic; the nanogerms popping along the veins of his blood, the synthetic bones flexing as he lowered and raised his arm for me. 'This is what I am,' he said again, slow this time, with a hint of sadness, like he'd left something behind, something human.

Robo! Barnie was a robo. A robochef!

'Inside of here,' he said, tapping his tight skull, 'are all the best recipes of all the best chefs on this world. I am their depository.'

As though in response to this, the young child, Crystal, ripped some flesh off the back of her neck. It was almost like she was playing, it meant that much to her.

'This is Roboville, Crew,' Barnie said. 'I think the pure call it Toytown, isn't that right?'

'Don't let Barnie scare you,' Lucinda was saying, but it was too late for all that. I was almost retching.

The roboman took a step towards me. 'Isn't it funny?' he said. 'The way that the pure react to robo? You'd think we were dirty or something, given their reaction.' I didn't know about that, only that I had to get some distance between us, back to where Shadow and Thing were waiting.

'Tell me the way out of here,' I asked. 'Got something to do.'

'Don't think that's possible,' said Barnie. 'Beetle's in a bad way.'

'He isn't that pure,' Lucinda said. Was she referring to me, or to the Beetle?

And I saw myself in a boat on the water, watching the shore, useless gun in hand, watching Tristan getting dragged down by the cops, heading for the station. Where they turn the screws on your feelings, until you can't feel any more. It wasn't a Vurt. It wasn't a dream. The world was real, and my eyes were wet from it.

Oh for a little less Vaz in my life, and a touch of glue. Maybe then I could stick hold tight of somebody.

The kids were laughing out loud at the television family's misfortune and I didn't know what was real any more.

There were chains and handcuffs arranged along the walls of the bedroom. A collection of whips lay spread out on a bedside cabinet.

Beetle was strapped to the bed, with six strong tethers. He was flat on his back, and the colours were pouring out of his skin in blades of light. Seemed like half his body was taken over by now, alive with fractals.

'Scribble! My babe!' he said. 'Good to see you up and about. You gonna loosen these ties a little? I feel like walking some.'

'I guess not.' The virus was getting to his mind now, making him feel like a super hero. 'It's for your own good, Bee. Don't want you jumping off tall buildings.'

'Yeah! That's me. The Shining Man. That Barnie did a real good job. Hey, maybe he's a bondage freak! You seen his wife, Scribb?'

'I saw her.'

'That is one sexy player! Remember that one?'

'Remember what?'

'Shit, babe, you don't recall that one? How could you forget that dream? Maybe you're all shrivelled up. I read that happened, sometimes, you didn't use it enough.'

'Do you know what's happening, Beetle?' I asked.

'Happening? The world's happening. And I am a major player. And if you don't undo these ropes, Scribble . . . I'm just going to flow right under them anyway. I'm floating, babe! You cotton me?'

Yeah. I got it.

'I know the final score, kid,' he continued, his voice changing, becoming quiet, serious. 'That shecop bitch really laid one on me. I guess this is cheerio time. Shit, babe, but I feel good! That's the twister.'

'It does that to you,' I said, just as quiet. And his colours were burning on my face. My tears were warm as they trickled down my skin, evaporating in the glare.

'I know it, Scribb. But you know what else? I feel like going out and stealing back shadowgirl and the alien. I feel like going out strong. In a blaze. You got that?'

'Coming soon, the Beetle,' I whispered. 'Coming real soon.'

He kind of nodded then, like he wasn't really there. 'Don't lose Mandy,' he said, at last.

'I won't.' His fingers were hot as I clenched my hand around them, feeling the colours shifting freely, back and forth between us.

But I kept my hand there anyway, taking the heat.

Which was like taking hold of spectrums.

I wash away the dirt of days, dry my skin, and take a long stare at what I look like these days. My face coming back at me, reflected in a bathroom mirror.

I peel back the lids and skin of my left eye. I move closer to the mirror, directly under the sink light. I stare into my own eyes, looking for clues.

'Found anything?' The soft honey voice from behind my shoulder. I spin around, almost banging into her. Her body was close to mine, and again I felt that memory coming back. I was trying to pin it down, explain it, but the best I could manage made it into a memory of something that had never happened. 'Don't you like us?' the voice said.

'I like you,' I replied, chancing a look into her eyes, expecting a steely metal glint. Instead an intense human gaze met mine.

'I'm not robo, you know?' she said. 'Did you get that?'

'I can see that.'

'That Twinkle's a nice kid. Maybe you should find a good women, and settle down some. With the kid in tow. That wouldn't be a bad life.'

'What's the story with Barnie?' I asked.

'He's a good man.'

'I know that.'

'He cut one finger off when he was young, just peeling the veg. The cafe paid for a replacement, put some nano-plastic in there. The kid got hooked. It happens. You get some plastic in you, you just want some more. This is what Barnie tells me. Some more of that strength. Because that's what it is. Strength. The strength to persist. Don't you ever feel like giving up, Scribble?'

'I feel it. Sometimes.'

'Get some robo in you. All that drops away then. So they say.'

'I'm in a Vurt now? Is that right?' I asked.

'No. This is real.'

'How can I trust you? It's feels like a Vurt.'

'That's because of what I've got inside.'

'Which is?'

'Can't you feel anything?'

'I feel . . .'

'Yes?'

'I feel like I've known you already.'

'In what way?'

'It's . . . it's embarrassing.'

'You know Barnie sleeps around?'

'Does he?'

'That's okay. So do I.'

'Do you?'

I was holding myself back from her.

'He has this thing about shadowgirls. Maybe it's because he's a robo. He likes that softness against his hardness. Soft smoke, hard plastic. It works well. And of course the shadowgirls love him back. It's got to be robo or dog, to keep a shadowgirl happy.'

I thought about Bridget and Beetle. And then seeing Bridget dancing with that new man at the Slithy Tove. What was he?

'Did you find anything?' she asked.

'What?'

'In your eyes.'

'No. Nothing.'

'Let me look,' she said, and stepping close, too close, she reached up to stroke my face. Lucinda looked into my eyes. Which meant I had to look into hers. They were green like apples from a sun-drenched orchard, somewhere far off. It was too much for me.

'Stop shaking. Let me see,' she insisted.

Lucinda gazing into me. I was hard already, and what I saw in her eyes, up close, just made it ten times worse.

'No. Nothing,' she said. 'Your eyes are blue, perfect blue. Like a summer's day, but without a hint of sun. That's strange. I could have sworn . . .'

'That I was Vurt?'

'Yes. It feels right, but not a trace of yellow.'

'There's yellow in your eyes.' I had seen the tiny flecks there, as she gazed deep into me. They had sparkled like fragments of gold.

'You've been here before, haven't you?' she said.

'I can't explain it.'

'Let me show you something.'

'Lucinda . . .'

'What's wrong, baby?'

'I . . .'

'What is it?'

'I shouldn't be doing this.'

I should be seeking out Bridget and the Thing. And Desdemona . . .

Lucinda took a hold of my hands, gently leading.

The back bedroom was draped in purple, with a stone slab bed and a statue of the Virgin Mary. Her white alabaster body was dripping blood from the eyes.

I felt myself reeling, and then getting hard at the sights.

'I'm in the Vurt!' I mumbled. 'I know I am!'

'No,' Lucinda replied. 'You just think you are.'

'But this is Catholic Fuck, isn't it? An Interactive Madonna Vurt?'

'That's right. Don't you get it yet? The living room?'

'That was the early nineties, wasn't it?'

'Correct.'

'We're talking Nostalgia Trap?'

'You got it. And the room where Beetle sleeps? With the straps and the whips?'

'That's got to be Mistress Pervurt. I've done all of these!'

'Look closely.'

And then I started to get it, the feeling of being cheated. I looked closely at the Catholic Fuck room. The blood didn't look that real any more. I smeared some on to my fingers, sniffed at it, 'This is paint?'

Lucinda laughed. 'Barnie had these rooms designed for me. They're copies of best-selling feathers. It's fun, isn't it? And Barnie gets off on it, I think.'

'He can't do Vurt?'

'You got it. Barnie is flightless.'

'I knew it. That look . . .'

'It's not so bad, you know? It makes him very real. Very powerful. In that old-fashioned kind of way. No wonder the shadow-girls love him in bed. I know I do. And these rooms . . . well they certainly make him come good.'

But all I was seeing was the sadness in Barnie's eyes, that sense of missing out on the dream. But not in the sense that I knew. He liked missing out on the dream. The dream was weak and the chef was solid. Now it all came together; Barnie was featherless. I had to pull myself back from the feelings. 'You've got the Vurt in your eyes, Lucinda. What are you?'

'I'm the star. I've got just enough Vurt inside me. I can connect the living with the dream. They call me Cinders.'

Cinders O'Juniper.

And I saw myself in her arms, making love to her in feathers, countless soft and pink Pornovurts.

'I'm a Vurt actress,' she said. 'That's my job.'

Having her there in front of me, for real, it was making me ache.

'I know you've got some Vurt inside you,' she said. 'Despite the blue eyes. Maybe you're not ready for it yet. I felt it though, from the first glimpse. I'm feeling it now.'

'How do you know?'

'Because I'm tingling all over.'

Didn't know where to look.

K A R M A C H A N I C S

Cinders led me down the canal paths, beyond the gates of Toy-town, down to where the car mechanics and the rubberwear manufacturers work and play. That was during the day, but now it was early evening; the world was half-lit, and the pathway was ours alone.

We were walking a thin cobbled line between the canal and a railway bridge. The bridge was pitted with a row of arches, and each of them taken over, and boarded up against the nighttime thiefs. And the water at my left hand side was the colour of a bad Vurt dream, you know that kind, when the feelings turn to mud, and you can't fight your way out.

Cinders was quiet and distant as she led the way, walking some two feet ahead of me, her body full up of wonders and sex dreams. This was the partner of my fantasy bed, countless times, and I was following like a dog. I guess I felt pretty low down. Totally unresisting.

You got that feeling?

'Nearly there, Scribble,' Cinders said. 'Can you feel it yet?'

And I could.

'I'm feeling apprehensive, Cinders,' I replied.

'Don't worry, Scribble, there are no snakes around these waters.' She was tapping a message on an archway door.

'You're sure of that?'

'Sure I'm sure.'

I was looking at the sign above the door.

Karmachanics.

Two old cars and an ancient ice-cream van were parked outside.

'Why so sure?' I asked, shivering.

'We caught all those fuckers long ago.'

The door swung open a fraction and Cinders slipped inside. I followed her, into a dark red room. The roof was arched above us, the stones slick with damp. Smoke was drifting through the tight space, bringing visions to my eyes.

Icarus Wing was at the smoke desk, mixing it.

'You brought that dog, this time?' he asked.

'Not this time,' I answered, shaking.

'Or that bad arse guy?'

He meant the Beetle. 'No one,' I said.

'Then come right on in. You are welcome.'

'You two met already?' asked Cinders.

'Hey, this kid really threatened me, you know,' replied Icarus. 'But that's okay. No grudges.'

In the shadows I caught dry glints of violet and green. Also, the sound they made, skin against skin, skin against soil and glass; slithers in the night. Bad dreams.

I was sweating, holding it all back in, against the fear. Along one entire wall of the arch they lay, a triple bank of old fish tanks, each one containing either a single snake, or a knotted mass of them.

'Don't be scared, Scribble,' said Cinders. 'These are your friends.'

'I'm not sure about that,' I stammered.

'Vurtboy is scared shitless,' laughed Icarus.

'You sold me a bad Vurt, Icarus.'

'Sold you?'

'That Voodoo feather was a pirate copy. Nothing but a cheap dream.'

'Hey, how was I to know? I just buy the things in, you know? You're standing there, threatening one of my best snakes with a pumped up robodog. What do you want? I hadn't even had time to test that new stuff. Leave me out of this.'

'Icarus is editing this morning's rushes,' said Cinders. 'You want to see some?'

No. Is it alright if I just run a million miles away?

The archway was studded with silver feathers in racks, and used-up cream feathers littered the floor. Dream smoke was drifting in layers of colours; blue, then black, then silver. And in the dark roof gulf a few wisps of gold fluttered against the wet stones.

Yellow smoke! That rare and precious mist.

'We shot some beauties this morning,' said Icarus, mixing the smoke, 'We're calling this one Bitch On Heat. It's right close to the edge. As hard as you can get, and yet still put on the top shelves at Vurturama's. Go ahead, take a look.'

Anything other than those ugly twisters, so I lowered my face into the Vurt mist. I felt its fingers caressing me until I wasn't there any more, I was walking on my splayed paws over to where

Cinders was waiting on all fours. Her green hair was dark with sweat and her lips were wet. I was salivating and my cock felt good and strong, as it unsheathed itself. I could feel the fleas jumping in my fur but I paid them no mind. All I wanted was to rut. Her haunches were jutted at just the right angle for entry and I followed my cock back to the source, peeling the lips back as I pushed forward, my front paws on her shoulders, my hind legs slipping and sliding on the lino, trying to get a purchase. Felt like sinking into tenderness, into the night, into some hot meat dinner. Awhoooh!!!!! I was howling, and the woman was jerking back against me and moaning with it. Awhooohhh! Good rutting tonight! Awhooooohhh!

Then I was jerking out, sick of myself, back to reality, sick of the wanting, and Cinders was laughing at me in the archway. I saw Icarus with a ball hammer in his hands. The stench of snake-weed in the air. He was opening up one of the cages. 'There's some stuff we need to take out there. Or else we say goodbye to general release.' But I wasn't listening that well. The room was misting over and the dream smoke was clogging my mouth, bring-ing the Vurt back down. I needed air, clean air, and as the snake came out, caught under Icarus' snakeweed spell, I was fighting for the door, struggling with the latch, heading out somewhere, into the open. Just anywhere would do! I caught a whiplash glimpse of the snake as it whacked its body against human flesh. I had a hard-on to make Zeus jealous as I forced the door and felt the hot wet night falling on me.

It took five minutes for the feelings to soften in the rain. I was standing by the canalside, drawing breath, watching the water slap listlessly against the stone. It was a turgid outgoing tide, sweet and rank. Debris bobbed along, not really getting anywhere. One piece looked just like a human forearm.

Over the water I could see the opposite bank, where, earlier, some way downstream, we had lost the Tristan to the enemy. Lights were playing faintly there, as some other kinds of people led themselves a normal life. I needed some intake so I reached into my pocket for my ten pack of Napalms, my fingers falling instead on the soft flights of a feather.

I pulled the feather loose and held it up against the moon. It was silver to the very edge. I think the moon was a little jealous, because it hid its face behind a ragged cloud. I thought about the Game Cat.

What had he called it?

The silver flights made a merry flickering.

Sniffing General.

Just do it.

Just do it. Just take it in. Into the mouth. Get the latest message. Go visit. Move along the path some way. Just do it. Find out what the Cat has to say.

The feather was resting between my parched lips, under the moon, by the waterside, edge of Toytown, when I heard Lucinda's voice calling to me. 'Didn't I please you enough?' she said.

I took the feather out of my mouth.

'What's it called?' she asked.

'Sniffing General.'

'That's way up the scale, young boy. Sure you can handle it?'

I didn't answer.

'You ever done a Sucker, Scribble?'

'What's that?'

'Sucking feathers. It's how we make the Vurts. They work like normal feathers, but in reverse. Instead of giving us dreams, they steal our dreams. Then they bring me in, or some other unfortunate. Somebody with a bit of Vurt in them, just to make it real. They mix me into the dreams, Scribble. I'm very good. It's a sad life, but a good living. Maybe you could try it.'

'I don't think so.'

'I think you could do good.'

'It's not me.' I was denying everything.

'I must have really pissed you off, in that Dogvurt?' Cinders asked.

'No.'

'You just don't like talking to me any more? Is that the thing?'

'Not that.'

'Oh wow, Scribble . . . you really know how to make a Vurtgirl feel wanted.'

Sudden thought: maybe I could swap this woman? She's got so much Vurt in her, and so much worth; maybe I could steal her away, and do a swapback for Desdemona.

'I'm real, Cinders,' I answered. 'You've seen my eyes.'

'Oh you're so real, kid. So why all the fuss? How come you're so scared of the flesh?'

'I've had women,' I cried.

'Sure.' Her voice was mocking me.

'I've got myself a woman,' I said. 'She's a good woman.'

'Where is she? She's so good, so where is she?'

I couldn't answer.

'Pussy got the tongue?' she asked.

'I can't see why you're coming on like this. I've got other things to do.'

'I don't like people running away from my art.'

'I got scared.'

'That's what I said, wasn't it?'

Her eyes were sending me fiery signals. All I wanted was to pull away and be out of there. But her voice was pulling me back; 'The saddest thing is, I could really take you somewhere. Somewhere good. Don't you want that, Scribble?'

Her eyes were a deep lunar green in the watery light, flashing with stars of yellow. Lucinda came close, in the soft rain, and kissed me. Her lips had a honey taste to them, and I felt myself slipping. Slipping into the rain and the water, and the Vurtflesh. Her fingers were playing along the small of my back like the ripple effect of the moon's tide, as it pulled and pushed at the waters of the Ship Canal.

Just do it.

I pulled my lips away from hers with a soft sound.

Her eyes were looking at me, and I just couldn't believe it.

'I'm going back to the house,' she said. 'Barnie's working to-night. And then he's going to visit Shadowtown. You want to come back with me?'

'I'm not very good with women,' I whispered.

'Try it sometime,' Lucinda said. She was a pale shape in the darkness, but her words cut me to the heart.

Try it sometime.

Just do it.

And I was sorely tempted. So much so that I looked deep into those eyes of green and yellow, and I saw something new there, not of herself. Lucinda was taken over and blue eyes I knew so well were staring at me from behind the green fronds of hair.

'Desdemona?' I cried. 'Is that you, sister?'

It was that old Desdemona look of love and lust. I was drawn forward into her arms, falling into memories. I could do nothing but follow her back to the house, where we made love against the statue of Virgin Mary. We were doing a Catholic Fuck, and this from a total unbeliever. Never mind. I was making love to Cinders O'Juniper, the queen of pink feathers. I'd done it before of course—what young kid hasn't tried this one?—but this was for real now, too real. So much so that I could barely take it, especially with Desdemona flickering inside of Cinders' eyes, call-ing out to me. And when we reached the peak, and the woman's voice was screaming 'Save me, oh save me!' I couldn't tell if it was

Cinders or my sister that was doing the calling. And that made
the ending bitter and sweet at the same time, with the Virgin's
blood falling on to my skin, until a moment of release burst within
me and I sprayed it all out, into the dream and the real, until both
were saturated.

I woke up in my sister's arms, or so it felt, until Cinders turned
her face to mine, sleepily. 'What happened then, baby?' she asked.
    'I don't know.'
    'I felt like I was somebody else.'
    You were. Well, kind of. Partly. Halfway. I didn't have the
words to tell her what I was feeling.
    'Felt good,' she said, but I didn't feel any pride, or anything.
Because I knew that Desdemona was in there, somewhere, using
the Vurt in Cinders to get to me.
    'This is just a one-off?' Cinders asked.
    'I think so.'
    'You've got other things to do?'
    'Some.' And I told her about my sister and how I was trying to
get her back. And all about the obstacles in my way. And then
Lucinda said this, and it killed me, 'Maybe you could swap me
back?'
    What could I do to answer that?
    'I've got the Vurt in me,' she said. 'I think I've got the worth.
Enough to satisfy Hobart. Let's do it. This life tires me.'
    I was dumbstruck.
    'No. No, it cannot happen.' I actually said that. Cinders meant
too much to me. Even if I never saw her again. Too much.
    Her eyes were closing on the world, and when she spoke, it
was from far down inside the dream, 'Find what you want.'
    'I'm trying to.'
    'Keep the faith . . .' Her last words before sleep.

I climbed naked out of the Catholic bed, trying to find my scattered clothes in the grey light. Through the bedroom window I could see the moon shining through a ribbon of clouds. Maybe it was too late. I picked up my jacket and pulled the silver feather from the inside pocket. I took a last look down at Cinders.

What was I doing, leaving this woman?

I checked the time from the flower clock and then pushed the feather deep, between my lips.

Going silver.

Falling . . .

Hit by darkness . . .

A ROOM IN ENGLAND

What . . .

Nothing here . . .

I'm . . .

Darkness . . .

Nothing here . . .

There's nothing here! For fuck's sake!!!

Darkness . . .

Falling . . .

I'm not here. There's not even me here. Just the thought that I might be here. I think. Or don't think. No, don't stop thinking, Scribble! Because then even you won't be here any more. Don't stop thinking . . .

No. Not falling, floating . . .

In the darkness . . .

Where the fuck am I?

You're here, thinking about here . . .

Keep thinking . . .

But who's doing the thinking for me . . .

You are, Scribble . . .

Right . . .

Who's Scribble . . .

You are . . .

Right . . .

Get me out of here!!!

Darkness . . .

A single star of light . . . up ahead . . . where's up . . . where's ahead . . . where is my head . . . this is my head . . . and the star's inside my head . . .

Twinkle, twinkle . . . little star . . . how I wonder what you are . . .

The little silver star was writing letters in the night . . . in my head . . . just like . . .

What was it like?

   LOADING SNIFFING GENERAL . . . PLEASE BE
   PATIENT.

Right . . .

Silver star . . .

Just like a cursor . . . that's it . . . I'm in a feather . . .

I *am* a feather . . .

The silver star is scrolling . . .

   1. EDIT

   2. CLONE

   3. HELP

   4. DOOR

   5. MAP

   6. ESCAPE

   PLEASE SELECT . . .

I'm thinking about the number four ...

Four for a door ... remember that ...

Why ... just remember it ...

> THIS OPTION WILL ALLOW YOU ACCESS
> THROUGH DOORS BETWEEN THEATRES ...
> PLEASE SELECT ...
> 1. BLUE
> 2. BLACK
> 3. PINK
> 4. SILVER
> 5. LIFE
> 6. CAT
> 7. YELLOW
> 8. HOBART

Five is alive ... five is alive ... remember that ...

I'm thinking about the number seven ... because I can't resist it ...

Why not ...

Because of Desdemona ...

Who ...

> I AM SORRY ... INSUFFICIENT CODING
> ACCESS ... PLEASE RESELECT ...

I'm thinking about the number eight ... just for the hell of it ...

> I AM SORRY ... INSUFFICIENT CODING
> ACCESS ... AND ANYWAY HOBART IS IN A
> MEETING JUST NOW ... PLEASE RESELECT
> ...AND STOP WASTING MY TIME ...

I'm thinking about the number six ...

> THAT'S OKAY ... LOADING ... PLEASE HOLD
> ON ...

What ...

Christ!

Falling . . . falling . . . really falling now . . . down through the layers of darkness . . . more and more stars in the sky as I rush through . . . silver stars . . . more and more of them . . . until the darkness has drained away . . . and I'm falling like a stone through the silverness . . . getting my thoughts back . . . one by one . . . until I know where I am . . . and who I am . . . and where I'm going . . .

A door opening in the silver . . .

Through . . .

Sniffing General was sitting at his desk, pushing something around with his paper-knife. He was a small man, not much hair, thick glasses covering his eyes, and he didn't bother to look up as I came into his office. 'You've got a nerve,' he said. It was a thin voice, edging towards a whine.

'I want to see the Game Cat.'

'I mean, asking to see Hobart. That's ridiculous.'

He'd finished with the knife now, and he was gazing down at his desk, almost lovingly. I stepped closer. A line of blue powder on a small shaving mirror, that lay face-up on his desk, and I couldn't tell if he was smiling at the Choke powder, or his own reflection. There was a door in the wood panelling behind him, fitted out with frosted glass. The words Game Cat were etched onto a small brass plate, fixed just below the glass.

'Is he in?' I asked.

'I don't like people wasting my time,' he said, rolling up a ten pound note. 'Do you think I haven't got work to do?'

'I am a personal friend of the Cat's.'

That made him look up. He'd already stuck the note up his left nostril, and what with that, and the thick glasses, it was all I could do not to laugh.

'Oh they all are, they all are,' he replied. 'They all claim to know the Game Cat. None of them do, of course. Only I know the

Game Cat.' With that, he lowered his head, and sniffed up the line of Choke.

'Tell him that Scribble is here to see him.'

The General looked up again, his eyes behind the glasses coming alive now, turned up by the powder. 'I've had trouble from you in the past,' he said.

'Is that right?'

'Oh yes. Tapewormer, I think it was. I've got the details somewhere.' He was shuffling through the piles of paper on his desk. 'It was you, wasn't it? Yes. Scribble. That was the name. It's all down here somewhere. You went Meta on that one, into Takshaka. Didn't you hear me calling to you?'

I had done. But I wasn't about to give him the satisfaction.

'Messing about in Takshaka is not recommended. The cops don't like it.'

'The cops?'

'Takshaka is a Copvurt. They store all their information there.'

'The cops own the King Snake?'

'Well they think they do. Really it's the other way around. Takshaka owns them. But let's keep the cops happy, yes?'

'I just want to see the Game Cat, Sniffing General,' I said. 'I have an appointment.'

'Oh they all do,' the General replied. 'You wouldn't believe the number of appointments I have to deal with. Of course the Game Cat has never heard of them before. It's all so tiresome. And then there was that other incident, wasn't there?'

'Which one?'

'That Curious incident. Yes. That was most difficult.'

'What are you saying?' I asked.

'Really, Mister Scribble . . . vehemence will get you nowhere. Yes. English Voodoo it was. You lost somebody very worthy that day. She went through a door into Curious Yellow, if I recall. Got swapped. You know that Hobart has to work out all the details of these transactions? Hobart has better things to do. And do you know who gets blamed for it? That's right. I do. I got a right dressing down that day, let me tell you.'

'Pity about the Game Cat then,' I said.

'What do you mean?'

'I thought the Cat did the same? Got lost in Curious Yellow. Isn't that how he ended up here?'

The General was silent for a moment. Just the sound of his nostrils sniffing up the Choke powder, deeper and deeper. 'You seem to know a lot, Mr Scribble?'

'I've been around,' I told the General. And then, 'Tell Geoffrey that I'm here.'

That clinched it.

'Geoffrey?' he asked.

'Yes. Tell him I've come to visit.'

The Sniffing General considered it for a moment, and then pressed a button on his desk. He spoke into an intercom; 'Game Cat ... ahum! ... yes, yes ... sorry to disturb you ... there's a somebody out here, wants to see you, sir. Calls himself Scribble ...'

I heard the Cat answering from the speaker, but it was all lost in static.

Sniffing General seemed to get the gist of it, 'Game Cat will see you now.'

There is a room in England somewhere, but it's nowhere to be seen. It exists only in the mind, and only in the mind of those that have been there. This is where the Game Cat lives, surrounded by his objects. Swapped objects. Kitchen sinks and golf clubs, stuffed animals and antique globes, fishing rods and bus tickets. All the paraphernalia of England that the Cat had gathered around

him, swapped in countless desperate deals, from all the people
that had come to visit, seeking solace.

I was just the latest.

'Scribble,' the Cat said. 'So nice of you to make it.'

Game Cat was sitting in a wicker armchair, with a balloon glass
of deep red wine in his hand. He was wearing a purple smoking
jacket, and—get this—he had tartan slippers on his feet.

'Would you like a drink, young man?' he asked.

'You know what I want, Cat,' I answered.

'You should drink more wine, Scribble. Oh I know that Fetish
is all the rage these days, amongst the children, but really . . . only
wine does the job. It certainly eases the pain, my kittling. Ah!
How the children love that talk.' He held his glass up to the light
from a table lamp. The lamp was the shape of a golden dancing
fish, and its glow was soothing. Another gift, I guess, from another
grateful visitor.

'Yes, certainly,' he said, reading my mind. 'When people visit
me they usually bring something along . . . some gift . . . some small
thing.' He gestured towards the array of objects in his room. 'Did
you bring anything along, Scribble?'

'Nothing.'

'That's a shame. You sure you don't want a drink?'

'You know what I'm thinking, Cat.'

My, my, those are violent thoughts.'

'Give me that fucking Yellow!'

'Really, I will not stand for this. Shall I call the General?'

'Do what the fuck you like! Just give me the Curious!'

'He will have you removed. It is quite painful, if I remember—'

'Cat! I want Curious! Now!'

'Scribble . . .'

'The feather!'

He looked at me. 'I don't have Curious Yellow.' And there was something in his eyes, some injury . . . maybe he was telling the truth. No, he was lying!

'Liar! Tristan told me. You're hooked on it!'

He took a sip from his wine glass, like he didn't care.

'You know where Tristan is?' I asked.

'I know.'

'He got captured.'

'I know, yes.'

'It means nothing to you?'

I was playing him along, trying for a reaction.

'Young man,' he said, 'you can never play me.'

How was I going to handle this?

'I don't think you can handle it, Scribble. I know the rules of the game better than you. I know all the rules. The secret ones . . . the ones that don't officially exist.'

'Okay. You win.'

Keep it simple.

'Yes. Let's.' He took another sip. 'I went down to visit him, you know?'

'Your brother?'

'Yes. In his cell. I am not totally without feelings, Scribble. They had . . . they had hurt him somewhat . . . he had . . . he had wounds. Bruises, really. A bit of blood, not too much. He's alive.'

'That's good to hear.'

'But he seemed very sad and weary to me. He had a collection of very bad thoughts, like it was all coming to an end.' He paused. 'We have no secrets, of course, my brother and I.' Another pause. 'I told you to help him, Scribble.'

'I tried.'

'Did you?' The Cat knew how to hit me.

'Losing Suze was too much for him,' I said.

'Yes, I can imagine.'

'Can you?'

'Yes. I can imagine.'

I was getting the picture of a man without connections. Someone to whom real life was some kind of hideous prank, played by a cruel god. And so, from a very early age, the Vurt must have seemed like heaven, like the touch of a strong hand, leading him to feelings. He must have clung to the feathers, revelling in the strength they gave him, the intensity, until feathers were everything. And real life was a bad dream. Takshaka's bite must have seemed like a gift, and the chance of getting lost, getting swapped, was all too much. Cat had taken it, fallen into it; going through the door into Curious Yellow with no regrets; losing himself to the Vurt.

'Well that's quite an interesting theory, Scribble,' he said. 'Doesn't it remind you of somebody?'

'You never told me about Curious Yellow. That you got lost in it.'

'Why should I tell you?'

'Because that means you know how to get Desdemona back.'

'Yes. I do know.'

'Tell me.'

'It's quite simple. Find the Thing. Find a working copy of Curious Yellow. Combine the two. Swapback. Quite simple.'

'Well fuck you, Game Cat!'

'Oh dear.'

'You managed to get Tristan out of Curious. He said that you were working the feathers.'

'Scribble, my dear ... even at that age I was a master of the feathers. You haven't even started yet.'

'I want Desdemona back!'

'How very poetic.'

'You bastard!' My hands were twisted up into tight fists.

EVERYTHING OKAY IN THERE, GAME CAT,
SIR?

Sniffing General's voice coming over the intercom. The Cat nodded at me as he pressed the speak button and I felt something pulling me back, the Cat's room dissolving around me, intense pain in the body. 'Cat! Please!' I cried out.

Game Cat smiled, and the pain eased slightly.

'Everything's fine in here, General,' the Cat was answering. 'Thank you. We're just discussing possible gifts that the visitor might be willing to donate. Get back to your ledgers, General.'

WILL DO, SIR. JUST CALL IF YOU NEED ME.

'I will.'

The Cat closed off the connection and then looked up at me. With a heavy sigh he raised himself out of the wicker chair, and walked over to an antique wooden cabinet. There were five drawers in it, one above the other. He pulled open the top drawer. 'This is my collection,' he said.

I walked over to the cabinet. I was standing by his side, gazing down into the drawer. It was divided into sections, each section separated by a panel of wood, each section lined with purple velvet. It was a series of nests, and in each nest lay a feather. In this first drawer all the feathers were blue, various shades of. It was like looking into the sky, seeing the glints of the day there. Along the edge of each section, embossed on a brass plate, were the names of the feathers. And, these feathers being blue only, I knew most of the names by heart, having travelled them.

'People come to me for feathers,' the Cat said. 'Special ones. Dreams. Dreams that they think will save them. They give me gifts in return.'

He closed the top drawer, and opened the second. Black feathers lay glistening there. Like looking into the night. Closed that one, opened the third. Pink feathers. Like looking into the flesh. The names brought back some sweet memories.

'Of course this is only a small part of my collection. The major part I have in storage. You are seeing only the current favourites.'

He opened the fourth drawer. Silver feathers. Like looking into the moon. One of the sections was empty. The name read Sniffing General.

'I'll have to ask for the Sniffer back, I'm afraid, when you've finished with it.' He closed the fourth layer, opened the last.

Gold.

My eyes dancing, catching the waves.

Golden feathers.

Like looking into the sun.

Their very names alone bringing a dream to my head.

'Yes, that's how powerful they are,' the Cat told me. 'I've heard that some people take them anally. Of course one doesn't like to think about such things.'

Only two of the names meant anything to me: Curious and Takshaka.

The section marked Curious was empty.

'You had Curious Yellow?' I asked.

'I am a keeper of the feathers. Of course I had a copy.'

'Where is it?'

Game Cat closed the drawer. 'Tristan stole it from me,' he said. 'Didn't you know that?'

'No. I . . .'

'It's quite obvious,' the Cat was saying. 'Tristan didn't like what Curious had done to me. My brother is a very conservative man, Scribble. You must understand this. Despite the hair and the Haze, and the guns . . . he is the white sheep of the family. He had the impression that he was losing me, to the Vurt. In fact it was the other way around; I was losing him to the pure world.'

'He wasn't that pure,' I said. 'He told me that he had some dog in him.'

'Oh yes. Just a trace. I'm the same. Our great grandfather was an Alsatian. Of course it's very far down in the blood stream by now. Sometimes I like to chew on a bone, more than is governed by dinner party etiquette. That's about the extent of it, thank God. And of course he's very jealous of me, being at a lower level, you see? Stuck to the real.'

'Tristan stole Curious Yellow?'

'He did.'

'Where is it now?'

'I have the impression that he wanted to save the whole world from it. He is an innocent.'

'I just want to know where it is.'

'He threw it away.'

'Where?'

'You saw him do it.'

'What?'

'You were there.'

'Stop this—'

'You think that I'm not helping you. In fact I'm doing all that I can.'

I looked deep into the Game Cat's eyes, and saw the answer there. It was way deep, but I managed it. Because really it was inside of me, and that was where I had to look. 'My God!'

'Indeed. You were very close.'

He smiled and nodded. 'You will come back to me, won't you, young man? This is your proper place. Really, you are a natural.'

'I would prefer the real world, and Desdemona.'

'Ah yes. The draw of the physical. Of course I could come down and give you a hand now and again. My brother . . . you understand?'

'No. This is mine. No feathers. Nothing. Don't even consider it, Cat.' I was heading for the door.

'One last thing, young man,' the Cat said.

'Yeah, I know. Be careful. Be very, very careful.'

'You got me, my kittling.'

G A M E   C A T

There are only FIVE PURE MODES OF BEING. And all are equal in value. To be pure is good, it leads to a good life. But who wants a good life? Only the lonely. And so therefore we have the FIVE LEVELS OF BEING. And each layer is better than the one before. The deeper, the sweeter, the more completer.

FIRST LEVEL is the purest level. Where all things are separate and so very unsexy. There are only five pure states and their names are Dog, Human, Robo, Shadow, and Vurt.

SECOND LEVEL is the next step. It happens because the modes want to have sex, with other modes, different modes, otherness modes. Except they don't always use Vaz, so these babies get born: Second level creatures. Or sometimes the modes get grafted together. There are many ways to change. Whatever, Second level beings go one better in the knowledge stakes. There are ten Second level beings and their names are Dogman, Robodog, Dogshadow, Vurt-dog, Roboman, Shadowman, Vurtman, Roboshad, Robo-vurt, and Shadowvurt. Chances are you, the reader, are a Second level being of some kind.

But you just want to have sex, right? Which delivers the next level, the THIRD LEVEL, of which there are ten modes also; Robodogman, Shadowmandog, Dogmanvurt, Robo-dogshadow, Robovurtdog, Shadowvurtdog, Robomanshad, Robomanvurt, Shadowmanvurt, and Roboshadowvurt. These are the middle beings, where most creatures get stuck; they just haven't got the spirit to go beyond.

Except of course, some few just can't stop having sex. Which gives birth to the FOURTH LEVEL, of which there are only five modes, each missing only one element, and their names are; Flake, Dunce, Squid, Spanner, and Float. Hey, what did you want? More big mouthfuls. Fourth level beings are deep beauties, and I should know, because the Cat is one. Which kind? Hey, what is this, gift week? You'll be asking who Hobart is next. I know, I'm a tease. That's how I make my living.

Beyond all this lies the FIFTH LEVEL. Fifth level beings have a thousand names, but Robomandogshadowvurt isn't one of them. They have a thousand names because every-body calls them something different. Call them what you like—you're never going to meet one. Fifth level beings are way up the scale of knowledge and they don't like to mingle. Maybe they don't even exist.

The Cat? He calls the Fifth level Alice. Because that was my mother's name, and it's the thing we all spring from, and try to get back to.

You got a problem with that name, reader?

So make up your own!

ASHES TO ASHES, FEATHERS TO HAIR

Cinders was still asleep when I came down.

I stroked her soft and green hair for a few seconds as I checked the flower clock on the wall. Only five petals had fallen. Seemed like I'd been in the Silver for an hour or more, but that's the Vurt for you; it does strange things to time.

I leaned over to kiss Cinder's face, and then went into The Beetle's room. He was struggling against his chains, desperate to get out of there. But still too fleshy, too human. He couldn't quite make it.

Not without my help.

I guess I'd always wanted him in this position, dependent upon me, but now it brought no pleasure.

'Time come, Scribb?' he asked.

'Definitely,' I answered.

'If you let me loose, Scribble, I'll be your friend for life.'
'I don't think you've got much life left, Beetle.'
'I feel beautiful,' he said.
'That's good. Could you do some last things for me?'
'What's that, baby?'
'Steal and drive a van for me.'
'I thought you were the expert these days.'
'I want to go bareback. No Vurt.'
'Crazy mother.'
'Damn right. You wanna go for it?'
The shining colours in his eyes lit up even brighter as he smiled,
'Let's go ride some stash!'
His voice was singing.

I led the Beetle down along the canalside, towards the last arch-way. That old clapped out ice-cream van was still there, like a tin corpse. Icarus's face had appeared at the door, boasting a bad look of fear. So I just waved the gun around a little, just to keep him inside, whilst the Beetle breached the van. He didn't use Vaz, beyond that now, and the hood seemed to open up for him, like a slow seduction. He reached inside and I saw some colours shin-ing. They flowed from his fingers, touching the wires inside, and then the engine choked into a small life.

'You know what, brother?' he said. 'I really feel some juice tonight.'

So we used that juice to drive out to the moors again, me and Twinkle and Mandy, and the Beetle up front, just like it should be.

'Where are we going, Mister Scribble?' asked Twinkle.
'On a picnic. We're going to sell some ice cream.'
'It's a bit dark for ice cream,' she answered.

It was nine o'clock on the Sunday night, and the trees were fading into silver.

'I like this van,' the Twinkle said. 'It's the best van yet. I always wanted to ride in an ice-cream van.'

'I saw you with that Lucinda woman, Scribble,' Mandy said.

'Do you have to bring this up?'

'Why not? You're quite the lover, aren't you?'

'What's happening?' asked Twinkle.

'Scribble got himself a—'

'Mandy!'

'What is it? What is it?' Twinkle shouting.

'Nothing!'

'Scribble got himself a woman.'

'Scribble!'

'It's not . . .'

'Scribble, how could you?' Twinkle's eyes were staring. 'What will Desdemona say?'

That left me empty.

'Good question,' said Mandy, with a smile.

I looked from the young woman, to the young girl, and then out through the ice-cream van's hatch window, watching the fields go by.

Desdemona. Forgive me.

Beetle rode the van along the same tire tracks of the morning's ride, coming to a perfect stop some ten feet away from the grave.

I stepped out alone, telling the crew to keep the engine turning.

The mound of soil.

My hands digging into the soil, bringing up clumps of mud; scraping the mud onto the earth, moving on, sod by sod, until my fingernails were black and fragile and the world was opening up beneath me.

Found her body there. Suze's.

Strands of hair mixed in with the soil. Her sweet face rising out of the dirt as I brushed the traces of earth away from her, my hand hitting against hard wood. The little wooden box.

Waiting...

It was lodged against Suze's neck, hidden amongst Tristan's hair. And Suze's hair had fallen over his, so that the box was entangled within.

Waiting...

I pushed my hands into the thick mat of hair.

Suze's eyes were closed and her body warm from the earth. She's just sleeping. That's all. I'm just making a steal from a sleeping woman's body. That's all...

Christ! This was getting to me.

The complex folds of the hair, the sweat falling from my brow to my hands, the fact that I could hear the van door opening, Twinkle calling to me, the look on the dead woman's face; all these things conspiring against me, until I was tearing at the hair, cursing. Twinkle's voice from behind me, asking me what I was doing? But I had to get this box loose, you see, I just had to do it!

'What's going on, Mister Scribble?'

Then I had it.

Waiting... Desdesmona...

The last few strands of hair fell away and the box was in my hands. It was hand-carved from mahogany, the top etched into the shape of a howling dog. No lock, just a small brass clasp. I clicked aside the clasp, and then lifted the lid...

Yellow!

A glint of yellow amidst the darkness.

Yellow! The Yellow feather! It was small and neat, just like I remembered, its golden flights enwrapping me, burnishing the air with colours and dreams.

Twinkle came round to see, and I guess her eyes must have seen the look in mine as I gazed at the feather, because all I heard was her sharp breath.

Curious Yellow.

I have you!

Waiting for me ...

COMING IN COLOURS

We were. We were that. Coming in colours. Beetle up front, just like the old days, but this was something new, something else altogether. Felt like I was riding home, riding home in the back of a clapped-out Mr Whipping van, with a golden feather in one hand, Beetle's gun in the other, two bullets left.

Beetle was working the wheel with a hot touch. His spectrum was widening, his skin crumbling at the edges. I'd persuaded him to wear his black frock-coat, and to pull his hat down real tight. Mandy had wrapped a large scarf around his face. Cinders had given us the scarf and hat, along with a pair of neat sunglasses. The Beetle had these on as well. And his leather gloves. 'He looks like the Invisible Man!' Twinkle had cried. The Beetle just shrugged. Flashes of colour were seeping through the gaps in his clothing, but it would do.

We were speeding the Wilmslow Road at a Jammer pace, back towards Manchester and the address in my pocket. Except the Beetle wasn't on Jammers any more; he didn't need that shit, not with the bullet in him.

'We going after Brid and the Thing now, Scribble?' asked Twinkle.

'That's the score, kidder,' I answered.

'Oh good.'

That kid should be having a good life, not being thrown about in the back of a stolen ice-cream van. And it was me leading her there, into a dark place, just because I needed her help. What kind of behaviour is that?

Yeah, I know. Like shit.

We came onto the Fallowfield crossroads. The Slithy Tove restaurant went by on the left and got me to thinking about Barnie, and his wife. Cinders. Her green hair wet with sweat.

Lose that picture. Lose it!

We were driving up the Fallowfield hill now and I saw a phone booth coming up close on the right, outside the student residences.

'Beetle!' I shouted. 'Stop right here. I need to make a call.' He pressed down on the brakes like a Sumovurt, throwing us all over the Mr Whipping equipment.

Like I really need this battering, my man. Know what I'm saying?

The phone booth had been vandalised recently, but a drop of Vaz in the slot sorted that out. I had a blue Mercury Vurt, almost gone to cream, but the phone's mouth took the feather gratefully. Then I pulled the feather out, and placed it between my own lips. Ten units of value glowed in the phone's eyes.

Jesus. That was low.

POLICE. YOU NEED HELP? the floating head asked.

Yes. Yes I did.

POLICE. CAN WE HELP? repeated the voice, growing impatient. I was finding it hard to speak, and I knew just why. This was
the first time, in all my life, that I'd actually called the cops.

'I was just wondering . . . ,' I managed.

YOU HAVE AN ENQUIRY, SIR? LET ME PUT YOU
THROUGH.

Noises in the wave wires like the kissing of the sea. The eyes
telling me I had only seven units of call left.

DATA. CAN I HELP? A man's head replacing the woman's.

'Yes, please,' I said. 'I would like to know the situation regarding
a Mr Tristan Catterick. He was arrested yesterday. Could you
tell me please?'

HOLD THE LINE, SIR. I'LL GET THE RELEVANT FILE.

'I've only got four units left,' I said, but the line was playing the
national anthem, whilst the head smiled benignly.

So I waited.

The voice cut in again. WE ARE RETRIEVING THE FILES, SIR.
WE'LL GET RIGHT BACK TO YOU.

'I've got two units left!'

No response.

One unit.

HOLD THE LINE, SIR.

The music playing, and then the eyes glowing from cream to
blue again as the units came back on. Two units. Flicker. Four
units. Flicker. And then upwards until I had ten units left. Somebody was feeding units in, and it wasn't me. Must be coming from
the other side, from the cops, trying not to get me cut off.

They had a tracer on!

A glimpse of Takshaka's tongue flickering over the wires.

I pulled the feather out, doing a bad jerkout job. Shit! Time to
move.

We rode down Fallowfield hill like demons, down into Rusholme, past the Platt Fields, towards the curry chute. Every car that we passed had flags waving from the windows. Pakistani flags. Inside each car, families of Asians were laughing and shouting, and the cars were sounding their horns.

What the fuck was going on?

Now the traffic was slowing down, and we came up close to the old flat, the Rusholme Gardens. It gave me a bad feeling, seeing where we had come from, and how far, and I thought the Beetle was feeling the same because I could hear him cursing. Except it wasn't from nostalgia. It was from the cops. I'd clambered up to sit next to him, and I could see them there; working the road, diverting the cars down Platt Lane.

A real heavy cop presence.

'Stay tucked up, Bee.'

'I'm boiling, Scribb.'

'You're a shining example to us all, Beetle, but right now I reckon you should keep it tight.' I slipped the gun and the feather into my pockets. A shadowcop flickered onto our number-plate, but that's okay; that old ice-cream van was innocent. The Beetle kept himself well back in the shadows of the cab. A traffic cop waved us through, left onto Platt, taking it slower now, jammed between the Asian cars. Mandy came forward, poking her head between us.

'What's happening, Mandy?' I asked.

'Eid, baby,' she answered.

Oh right. What a night to pick.

'It's the end of Ramadan. The end of fasting. The people go a bit crazy, and sometimes it kicks off. That's why the cops are here. They seal the curry chute off, but it just spills over.'

Gangs of Asian kids were lining the pavements, cheering the cars and the flags, so Beetle found the button that worked the van's music. The kids really freaked out then. They waved us on like we were some kind of ice-cream chariot of the gods, dancing to the tune of Popeye the Sailor Man, played at fever pitch.

We got through okay, and then a slow right onto the Yew Tree Road. Cops were out of it by now, the roads were quiet. Right from Yew Tree, onto Claremont Road. I told the Beetle to slow it even more. He did so, with a sure hand, taking us to a gentle crawl, between the rows of terraces. Way ahead, at the top of Claremont, you could see where the cops had sealed off Wilmslow Road. Hundreds of Asians moving beyond the road-blocks.

'Kill that Popeye shit as well,' I added.

Silence coming in as the music faded.

'What number we after, Scribb?' asked Mandy.

'There's the one,' I said.

The van came to a smooth stop.

Karli started to whine.

Here we are. Sunday evening, the 1st of June. Ten thirty on the night of Eid.

The road was pretty much our own now. The house was three storeys tall, over the top of a junkshop called Cosmic Debris. A tight alley opened up between this house and the next, barred by a wooden gate, topped with wire. Dogfluff fluttered on the barbs.

Karli was really howling now, feeling something.

The house was dark but for the weak spluttering of a candle in a top floor window. 'Bad dogs, real bad dogs,' said Mandy, 'they don't like the light.'

This is it. This is where we come to.

'You want to try the back, Bee?' I said. Because who would invite this shining man into their household?

'Love to,' he answered.

'We go in first. Got that? No heroics.'

'What, me?' His colours were very beautiful. They always are, just before the death.

'You're doing fine, Bee.' I said.

'I do feel good.' Maybe he knew it. The ending. He wasn't letting on.

'I just wanted to say...' I started. But the words wouldn't come.

'Don't bother,' the Beetle replied. Cool as ever, right to the end.

'I'm proud of you, Beetle.' Managed it.

'Me too,' said Mandy.

Beetle took off the sunglasses. He looked at me, smiled, then over to Mandy.

He kissed her. It was sweet, and it lasted.

Then he turned back to the house. 'I haven't got all night. Let's do it.'

Oh Beetle.

'Are we really here, Scribble?' asked Twinkle from the back of the van.

I looked back to find her, but all I saw was Karli.

The robobitch was down on her stomach, rubbing the van floor like a snake. Her forelegs were stretched out flat, her hindlegs were raised up tall, tail aloft, her arse on view, pink and pouting. 'I think she's smelling something,' whispered Twinkle. 'I think she's on heat.'

Yes. We're here. And we're all on heat.

T U R D S V I L L E

Twinkle and Karli went to the door first. There was a kind of alcove, with the door to the shop on one side, and the door to the upstairs flat on the back. Above the door someone had pinned a printed notice saying PURE FREE ZONE. Below that was tacked a piece of paper with the words—you not got dog, fuck off!—scrawled in thick clumsy letters. Above the letterbox was an ornate iron scrollwork sign that said CHEZ CHIEN in a Gothic script. Below the box someone had felt-tipped the message—*Turdsville. Watch where you tread.* It was written in a human hand. Just to the left of the bell was a sticker, a photo of an Alsatian on it, and the words—*Go ahead, make my day!* Somebody had glued two blue human eyes over the dog's.

Twinkle pressed the bell.

You couldn't hear the bell, so you just had to believe it was working.

No response to that.

Mandy was standing behind Twinkle, and I was behind her. The Beetle was still sitting in the van, watching us through the window. The gun felt hot in my pocket, but that didn't stop the fear. I just couldn't stop shaking. Twinkle pressed the bell again, keeping her finger down this time.

Still no answer.

'Maybe they're not in,' said Mandy.

'Keep pressing, Twink,' I said.

Twinkle pressed.

No answer, so she lifted the letterbox and shouted through, 'Anyone at home?'

Nothing.

Until the door came open a little, held back by a heavy chain. Two dark, wet eyes stared out at us. 'What want?' the deep voice growled. 'What want?'

You could see the slaver dripping as he spoke.

Twinkle rose up like a true star to the occasion. 'We've got a young bitch,' she said. 'You want to buy some?'

There was a pause. The dog's eyes flicked up to stare at me. I smiled back.

'Let hear some,' barked the voice.

So Twinkle pressed the Karli up close to the door gap and let her sound off there. That bitch howled like a sex goddess, like a Pornovurt; like Cinders on an Oscar-winning bed scene. The doordog was whining back, full up of heat and want. He vanished for a second, and then the chain hung loose and the door yawned open, on a breath of rank air. You could hear the locks getting wet and slippery. That's when the smell hit us. The overpowering stench of dogs.

We went on through. The doordog had us trapped now, in a tight dark space. Behind him a set of stairs faded into the darkness. The stench was thick, almost physical, and the dogman's eyes were glinting in front of mine. Karli set off up the stairs, Twinkle down hard on the lead, pulling that bitch to a howling halt on the middle step.

The doordog had a heap of dog in him, a whole heap. He was standing upright, on two clenched hindlegs, and that was the just about the most human thing about him. His muzzle was long and matted with dirt. His teeth were crowding his jaw, his pink lips drooling a bath of foam. He patted each of us down in the small hallway. Finding nothing on Mandy and Twink, finding the gun on me. He took the gun away in his clumsy paws and hung it on a coat hook and then shooed us up the dark stairway, after the Karli. 'Top floor,' he growled.

I took one step forward, and felt the soft squelch as I brought my foot down.

Oh yuk!

The stairs were covered in dogshit.

So were my shoes.

So I followed Twinkle like a mad dancer, one foot here, one there, between the dungheaps, moving up to the dim landing.

The top step led straight into the kitchen. Along one wall were nailed the carcasses of dozens of dreamsnakes, shimmers of green and violet. Three dogmen were eating there, out of bowls at the table. The room was in darkness, but you could smell the meat they were eating, and lumps of it were falling to the floor as they slobbered at it. The smell was sweet to my nostrils, but I couldn't work out why. It was certainly having an effect on them; the more they ate, the more they howled. One of them fell on the floor, landing in some of his own shit. It didn't bother him, just kept on rolling around, like he was having some kind of trance.

I don't think they even knew we were there.

Karli took one sniff into the kitchen and then raced out of the room, following some more succulent dog scent, along a corridor, and then up the next flight of steps, Twinkle pulled along by the tight lead.

I hung back for a moment, Mandy just behind. There was a closed door to my left. The door ahead of me was slightly ajar, so I pushed it open. The room was bathed in darkness, with a smell like dog sex coming in waves. One whiff of it and I was back in the pink Vurt, Bitch on Heat, Cinders urging me on. And when she looked back at me, it wasn't Cinders, or Desdemona; it was the Game Cat there, smiling in the dog's eyes.

No.

Not now. Do this alone. No feathers.

I brought myself down.

A lone dog girl was lying on a black carpet, her long tongue licking down between her split legs.

The room smelt like porn. Dogporn. Porn for the nose.

The bitchgirl looked up at me.

She had eyes of the brightest human blue, set amidst a face of fur.

I couldn't look into those eyes.

I closed the door gently, and then turned to the door on the left. Mandy was no longer with me. *Where was that girl?* No matter. Do it alone. Check every room. Keep looking—

A tiny noise. There! Listen! A tiny noise just coming in, almost lost in the howling from the kitchen. I pressed my ear against the left side door. There it was. The sound of alien flesh rubbing up the wrong way against planet Earth.

I pushed the door open.

Slowly.

Do this slowly, holding the breath, keeping cool.

I went into the room.

There was a smell of bad meat, a rancid haze that clogged at the senses, bringing thoughts of death.

The Thing was in the room.

I could hear him calling me, in that strange tongue.

The room was dark, dark as all the rest, but I could just make him out there, his fat bulk. The curtains were closed, just a glimmer of a streetlamp filtering in. In the shadows I saw a thin shape moving. It was bent over near the Thing. A dull glint came from its fingers. The shape moved slightly as I stepped inside, lifting its head up towards me, and I saw the snout dribbling, a slow turn of its thin long face.

The shape howled, high pitched.

My eyes adjusted to the darkness. It was a young dogboy and he was crouched over a bed. The Thing was tied down to the bed with old dogleads. Dogboy had a breadknife in his paws, and he was cutting chunks from the Thing's stomach. Beside the bed lay a bowl. Some meat was in there already. My mind jumped back to the kitchen, what I saw there as we passed—the dogs eating and the sweet aroma of the meat.

Sudden flash of me arriving back down in the real, the Thing pressed up on top of me, that sweet aroma rising from his skin.

Those dogs were eating the Thing! Bit by bit. Letting him regenerate between meals. And then cutting some more muscle off, taking that featherless flight into Vurt, direct to the flesh.

Something snapped just then. Something happened.

Not sure what. But during it I felt the cut of the breadknife on my arm, up just past the elbow. Didn't hurt. Even though I saw the red spurting onto my jacket sleeve. The dogboy was howling as I picked him up.

Go take a flying fuck, dogshit!

Dogboy made a fat sound against the wallpaper, and then slid and crumpled. He lay there, broken, whimpering.

I went over to the Thing. My arm just starting to hurt now, but I managed the straps alright, cutting them with the breadknife. The Thing didn't move. Didn't even make a noise. He just lay there, weak-hearted. He'd lost a ton of weight over the lost weeks, eaten away; his alien metabolism battling hard against the cuttings, but not quite keeping up. I unwound the leads from the bed, and then wrapped them around his soft body a few times, making a harness. The Thing was muttering now, in that thick tongue of his. I tickled him on the stomach, where he liked it. Maybe it did some good. He was so thin I almost felt that I could carry him alone. So I slipped the leads around one shoulder, and then around the other, took a deep breath, and pulled him up.

I had him up there, aloft and free, his alien voice calling to me. Couldn't make out a word but it sounded like comfort anyway, like he was glad to be carried.

I walked back to the landing to fetch Twinkle and Karli.

Up the next flight to the top floor. Another two doors waiting. The floor had been cleaned recently, and it made a nice change, to be stepping lightly, free of the shit. I was covered enough already. A note pinned to the stairwell read 'No dirty paws beyond this point. That includes you, Slobba!' It was written in Bridget's hand. Both doors were closed, but the one straight ahead had a flicker of blue light around the jamb. And the slightest hint of dog smell coming through, mixed in with flowers.

The Thing was weighing down on my shoulders.

I heard Dingo's latest love ballad—Venus in Fur—playing softly.

And then the voice, 'Is that you, Scribble?'

Bridget's voice from behind the door.

I had the Thing. I had Curious Yellow. I could have just ridden out of there.

Instead I went on through.

DAS UBERDOG

'How could you do this, Bridget?'

She raised her sleepy head from the bed to look at me. Her eyes were loaded with dreams, and a red flush coloured her usually pale flesh. She was lying on a ruffled bed, wearing just a man's white shirt and a lace of shadow-smoke. The room was dark except for the play of light coming from the candle on the window ledge. It had an azure flame; the palest blue light gently shining over the room.

'The candle's there for you, Scribb,' she said. 'I knew you'd find me.'

'I guess it took me too long,' I answered.

There was a man lying in the bed, covered by sheets. He had a handsome face on him, long brown hair; maybe just a trace of dog. One hand lovingly stroked Bridget's neck, whilst the other held open a book. I could see the title in gold, embossed, the sonnets of John Donne.

The bedroom looked clean and human in the candle's glow, full of the smell of flowers and incense. I guess this was more of Bridget's work; an attempt to mask the smell of dog. The flowers did a good job, but only just; the aroma of dog lingered like one of Dingo's bass notes.

And I got the picture of Bridget gardening this small human space, in the middle of Turdsville. What was that girl on? What was the motivation?

And why am I the last person to ask this?

Karli was on the bed with the young couple. She was trying to nudge the sheets back, getting her nose under there, her pink arse on display, raised up. Twinkle was sitting in an armchair, watching Karli's game.

I was watching all this from out on the landing, through the now wide-open door, with the breadknife still clutched, tight, in my right hand.

Bridget lit a cigarette in the blue shadows.

'We've come to take you out of here,' I said.

Bridget turned back to me, her mouth full of smoke, giving me that old-time sleepy smile. 'Look at the Thing,' I cried. 'Look what they're doing to him!'

'Yeah?' she answered, her voice a slow drawl.

'They've been eating him!'

'Eating who?'

I took a breath. 'Bridget . . .'

'How's the Beetle these days, Scribble? He still pushing you around?'

'Beetle's doing fine.'

So what was I supposed to say? Beetle's on his last moments.

He desperately wants to see you again, before he dies of the colours, so why don't you just come easy?

Would that have worked?

And where the hell was that guy anyway?

'This is my friend, Uber,' she said to the man beside her. 'Scribble.'

'Good morning, sir,' his voice lightly dog-touched. 'May I say how pleased I am to be in your company.'

'Scribble, this is Uber,' Bridget told me.

'How could you do this, Brid?' I cried. 'Tell me!' Bridget turned her sleeping eyes full on to me, and in the blue light, they looked like jewels.

'Uber is so very good. He takes me places.'

'Yeah. To a dogshit hole like this.'

Uber threw the blankets back.

Karli was thrown with them, but he caught her in his human hands as he rolled out of the bed. He was a strong, young man, and he lifted the dog without struggle. Karli didn't mind. That robobitch was in love! She let herself be tumbled over onto his lap.

Uber was a beautiful creature.

A perfect split, straight across the middle. Sometimes it happens like that, once in a thousand matings. He was human from the waist up, dog from the waist down. He placed his fur-covered legs down on the floor, sitting on the bed, with the Karli in his strong arms. She was nuzzling up close to him, licking his face with a pink tongue. Uber moved his head away from her, giving me a slow look.

'I have been so looking forward to this,' he said, in that dark voice. 'Bridget tells me stories about you. I must say, I do find them rather amusing. She has a high regard for you, sir.'

I didn't answer.

The shadows changing on the candle's breath.

He held out a long fingered hand. Sharp claws pushed through the soft pads of each finger, and when he smiled, his teeth were pointed, tiny shards of dog lodged in the human. 'What's wrong?' he said. 'Won't you shake my hand, sir?' He could retract the claws at will, and he did so now, presenting a soft hand to me, but still I wasn't tempted. 'Don't you like me, Scribble? After all, I'm the one who saved Bridget.'

'Saved her from what?' I asked.

'Why, from the pure life, of course.'

'I'm taking Bridget back,' I said.

Uber turned his face to the candle. He closed his eyes slightly against the glare. 'Ah yes,' he said. 'I was expecting this. Dingo warned me thus.'

'It's going to happen.'

'Put down the food please, sir.'

'I can't.'

'Why's that?'

'I need the Thing.'

'You call him a thing. That's shows little respect. Food is most precious, and should be treated accordingly.'

'Fuck you.'

Uber closed his eyes fully, for a moment, whilst stroking Karli on his lap.

'This is a luscious robobitch,' he said. 'I thank you for bringing her to me.'

And as he spoke, he was moving his fingers between Karli's hindlegs.

'Scribble?' said Twinkle, from her chair.

'Don't worry, kid,' I told her. 'It's under control.'

'Is it, indeed?' said Uber. 'Under control? Is it under control? Oh good. Whose control?' And each word came darker than the last, and more dog-like, like he was losing it, the human, and getting one serious rag on.

'I'm walking out of here,' I said.

'Don't push him, Scribb,' said Bridget.

'I'm taking the Thing with me,' I said. 'You ready, Twink?'

'I'm ready,' she answered. And then turned to the pet. 'Karli!' she called.

Karli pricked up one ear towards Twinkle's voice, and then refolded it. 'Come on, Karli!' Twinkle tried again. But I guess that dog was too happy.

'You coming too, Bridget?' I asked.

She didn't even look at me.

Twinkle was on her feet, by my side.

Uber was stroking Karli on the neck, the underside, where she loved it the most. He blew out the candle, even from that distance, with a dog's breath. When he turned back to me, his human face was split by a pure canine grin.

'Don't let me do this,' Uber said, tightening still further. And at first Karli let it happen, thinking it a touch of love. But then feeling it for what it was; an act of torture. Uber's fingers were squeezing on the windpipe, and his claws were coming out, pricking tiny jewels of blood from Karli's neck. He had an expert's knack of finding the soft flesh between the plastic bones.

Karli was whimpering now, struggling to get loose.

Uber parted his thick lips, showing those chiselled teeth. 'I am Das Uberdog,' he growled. 'The world is my shitting place.' And his eyes were wild, wild and free, as his claws tightened on the wet throat.

I made a struggling move, under the digging weight of the Thing, but Twinkle beat me to it. She launched herself forwards, hurling herself at Das Uber with all her young strength.

Uber bent a powerful dog-muscled leg in two, like a levered machine, so that Twinkle was pressed up against it, struggling to get Karli loose. Then Das Uber unflexed his leg, quickly and with a finely tuned force, that sent Twinkle screaming, backwards, to land at my feet.

'What is your reading of the situation, sir?' asked Das Uber. Blood from Karli's neck was leaking between his long human fingers.

'I think you smell like shit,' I said.

'Thank you,' he replied.

So I turned around.

Twinkle was clutching at my legs, trying to stop me, crying out, 'Scribble! Scribble! Don't leave us!'

But I just turned around, and walked away.

Some things are more important than others, and if that makes me bad, then let it stand.

I was heading back down the stairs, the weight of the Thing on my shoulders and back, almost pulling me over.

Cold, like stone.

Twinkle was crying from above, but I was down on the first landing now, carrying the weight. Felt like I was carrying Desdemona herself. That's how I pictured it, the swap already made, just to get the blood pumping. Past the front room where the bitchgirl was licking herself to a frenzy. I could hear her whining from under the door. Around the corner, along the corridor, towards the kitchen, where all three dog people were now down on the floor, rolling around, travelling some mutant Vurt, fuelled by the Thing's flesh.

Where was Mandy? Where was Twinkle? Where was the Beetle? Where was the Bridget? Why was I doing this alone?

And then Uber's howl, from the top storey. Sounded like a

siren's cry, refused in love. The scrabbling of his dog claws on lino and floorboards. Me taking a lurching race for the last stairs, where the front door lay waiting, and the doordog was turning to see what all the howling was about.

Thing was, he was just a little bit busy.

Because Mandy was happily wrapped around him, one hand reaching down stroking him between his legs.

Thanks for the help, Mandy. Appreciate it.

But then I saw that her other hand was reaching for the coat hook, and I changed all that around. *Do it, girl! Do it!*

I could hear the dogs getting close behind as I raced down, stumbling under the burden of the Thing, slipping on dogshit, making a slide of it, heading straight for the doordog. His eyes were so wide, felt like I was going to slide right on in there. Something was grabbing at me from behind, pulling at the Thing on my back, dragging hard, so we were pulled up, and back, half-way down the stairs, lodged against the two walls. A strong, white, human hand reached around and grabbed my neck. My face was jerked back, and I was looking straight into the eyes of Das Uberdog. That's when the lights came on.

A scorching brilliance.

Every lamp shining down with a fierce radiance, dazzling in rainbows of colours.

Beetle! Was that your work, my man?

I heard dogs behind me howling in pain; sounded like a bad jerkout.

But not Uber.

He took it, unblinking, and I felt his claws digging in at my throat.

I brought my right hand up, and backwards, in a sweeping arc, the breadknife lodged solid in my fingers.

Das Uber saw it coming, moved his face with a dog's jammed-up instinct, whip-fast, away from the blade's path.

Too slow, sucker!

The knife went in, hard against the flesh, somewhere on his left cheek, hit bone, slipped, cut through, into the jawline.

Blood on my face, Das Uber howling, me twisting the knife, hard!

I was free of the grip now, so I heaved the Thing back up, letting go of the knife, and started for the door again. The doordog had struggled free of Mandy. He was shielding his eyes from the glare with one forepaw, struggling up the stairs, his other paw flailing around in front of him.

That's when Mandy delivered. Delivered good.

Do it, girl!

First the flash of bright hot light, then the exploding air, the noise of it enough to kill, then the howling scream of Doordog as he's thrown up the stairs by the force. He bangs against me, and then drops. In the centre of his back a black and ragged hole is burning. Flame bullet.

The dogs were howling from the top of the stairs, and when I turned I saw Das Uberdog pulling the knife out of his torn face. He peeled his gums back, away from the long teeth, displaying his wound.

I stepped over the body of Doordog, and joined Mandy at the bottom. She was standing with legs apart, my gun in both hands, just like she'd done, no doubt, in countless Bloodvurts. At the top of the stairs I could see the dogs scuffling about in panic, banging into the walls, their half-cut brains struggling with the messages. Behind them Bridget and Twinkle were standing. Twinkle had Karli by her side. Robodog looked okay, a bit wobbly, some blood on its fur.

'You hurt, Uber?' called Bridget, from the landing.

He didn't answer, didn't even look around, just put one paw down on the next step.

Mandy had the gun well aimed, but I could see her shaking some.

Uber brought another paw down, another step, holding the knife in his right hand. It had his blood on it, and more of the stuff was flowing down from his ragged lips.

'One more step, dogbreath,' said Mandy, 'and it's the big kennel.'

Uber raised his paw, staring her straight in the eye. He could see the sweat on her face, and the shake in her arms.

He started to bring down the paw.

'She'll do it, Uber,' shouted Bridget. 'I know her.' And then, more slowly, 'These are my friends.'

He stopped then, looked back up the stairs towards his lover, his fine and sleepy-eyed shadowgirl lover. And I wonder what thoughts she had found there, inside that dog man?

'Uber . . . that's enough.' Bridget speaking. No. Not speaking. Just thinking. I was tuned into them, the woman and the dog, and all the things that had gone on between them.

I think she was the purest thing he'd ever known.

And when he turned back to us, you could see that something had changed, something had clouded over in those deep eyes that had run with the dogs, whilst also contemplating the works of John Donne.

He stepped back to a higher level.

I guess the poetry made it through, this time.

'You coming on down, Twinkle?' I shouted.

'Karli's hurt,' she cried.

'Karli's done good. She's a real Stash Rider. Just like you, kidder.'

Bridget nodded when Twinkle looked at her. So the young kid came down the stairs, followed by the robodog. And Das Uber stepped aside, to let her pass.

Just like a man should do.

Twinkle came into my arms. There were tears on her face. I wiped them with my filthy hands.

It was all I had.

I looked up the stairs, past Das Uber, to where Bridget was holding onto the dogs. The look in her eyes told me a story. You know that one, about giving up something good, for the sake of something else. And then finding no way back? And maybe you don't want to go back anyway?

Yeah, I guess so.

For what I've lost, and for what I've taken, a part of this story is for you, Bridget. Wherever you are.

I still didn't have a clue where the Beetle was, except that the lights were starting to fade again, but I suddenly thought; We're going to do this! We're getting away with it! 'You're going home, Big Thing,' I said, making Twinkle laugh.

Mandy tucked the gun into the back of her jeans and then opened the front door. She went through, taking Twinkle with her, and the Karli Dog. I followed, the Thing on my back. He was squirming around on there, like he knew he was going home. Like he knew that we were going out there, into the dark of Claremont, to where the ice-cream van lay waiting.

But there was another car parked close by, a black and white job; another one just down the road. Cop cars. A beam of light came whirling into position, trapping us there. Shadowbeam! Full intensity. Inpho flickering over my face, searching for clues. Clues of fear.

Shecop Murdoch was waiting for us, over by a streetlamp, gun in hand. Takshaka Shadowcop was flooding out from the roof of one of the police cars, and he was smiling that smoky smile, as he transmitted.

DO NOT MOVE. YOU ARE UNDER ARREST.

'I guess we got you, Scribble?' Murdoch said.

Some other cops, real-life ones, four of them, stepped out of the cars.

'I guess so,' I answered.

F L A R E

'That's okay, officers. We've got this one.'

At Murdoch's word the four cops backed off a little, leaning against their cars, like this was some kind of easy squeeze.

I was standing in the doorway of the doghouse, my hands tight around Twinkle's shoulders and chest. Karli was snarling at the shadowcop, but keeping it under control. Mandy was in front of us, out in the rain some, so that I could see that her hair was getting a sheen on it. Behind me the Turdsville door was still open, but I couldn't chance a move, not with Takshaka beaming me. The deal was knife-edge.

'Shame about Tristan,' Murdoch said.

Her hair was drenched to the bone. She looked like a near-death drowning, and the intense look of purpose on her dog-ripped face was starting to tell me something.

'Is it?' I answered.

'Yeah. Died during custody.'

'I'll bet,' I said, but my heart was falling fast, into despair, and I felt the world slip to one side slightly, like maybe the rain was falling sideways.

'Found him this morning,' Murdoch was saying. 'Hung himself, from the window bars. I'm thinking that maybe he couldn't take it.'

'I think you're right.' I was stalling, keeping it going, waiting for a moment to come, some kind of loose moment.

Some things take a life to arrive, and a part of this story's for you, Tristan.

'Where's the tough guy, just now?' Murdoch asked.

Good fucking question!

'Who's that?' I replied.

Seeing colours . . .

'The Beetle?'

'You killed him, Murdoch. That Mandel finished him.'

'He got one of ours.'

Murdoch's voice was hard and cold when she spoke, and I was getting the story now, what was going down here, and why she was keeping the dumb cops back.

Shecop had gone into personal mode.

I think she was waiting for a move from us, a legit reason to blow.

Colours playing on the edge of my vision.

MURDOCH! I'M GETTING A GUN ON LINE. HE'S CARRYING!

His beams were playing over me, trying to find that lost gun. He seemed to be ill at ease in the night air, as though his real home was the Takskaka Vurt, and this was just rain-soaked boring life.

You just made a big mistake, Shadowfuck, leaving Mandy in the shade...

'You want to use it, Scribble?' Murdoch said.

...and not bothering about the house corner...

'I couldn't beat you, Murdoch,' I replied, playing it out. 'You're the best.'

...where the colours were playing.

I caught a glimpse of movement, as Mandy pulled the gun from the back of her jeans, keeping it hidden behind her back.

Be careful, soldier. Just one bullet left in there.

Murdoch smiled. And then somebody called her name.

'Murdoch!'

The Beetle's voice! Full of colours.

The shecop turned her head, just a fraction, *that's all it takes,* over towards the side of the building. We all turned then, to see the Beetle in his glory, walking out from the side alley, bathed in a rainbow.

Karli started howling.

The Beetle was naked. His body was a blaze of shapes, ever-changing. Beetle was no longer flesh. The fractals had taken pos-session, moving in swirls and arabesques through every part of him. He was the Shining Man, the walking firework. The darkness fused and popped all around as he moved, through a halo of fire, and the rain turned into sparks when it hit his skin. Best of all; the Beetle was walking with that loose-limbed Stash Rider cool that I never did master.

Flare. My man had flare.

'Murdoch!' he shouted again, the words coming in colours. 'Leave them alone!' The fleshcops made a clumsy move, away from their vehicles, reaching for gun comfort, shocked and blinded. One of them tried to grab Beetle. *Bad move, buddy!* Just one touch and that cop was sizzling. He went through all the colours before dropping to the pavement. Cop sure left a beautiful corpse. In the confusion I pulled Twinkle backwards, towards the open door. She had Karli by the lead, and that robodog wasn't keen on missing the action.

'Get in the house, kid,' I whispered, hard. 'I mean it!' I dragged her back, with the dog, getting myself between them and the trouble. I wanted Twinkle and the dog together, in case it all went wrong.

Murdoch saw the Beetle coming towards her and swung her gun around, shouting to the other cops; 'Keep it simple, people!' Only Shaka kept his beams aligned, moving from me to Mandy.

MURDOCH! IT'S NOT SCRIBBLE! HE'S NOT GOT THE GUN!

'What?' Now Murdoch was looking well nervous, not knowing where to look.

IT'S NOT SCRIBBLE! Takshaka going wild, firing his beams everywhere. One of those beams, a red-hot one, caught the Beetle in the chest. The shining man just took the heat on board, loving it, until his colours shone like snake-diamonds.

One of the other fleshcops got it together, lost it, went for panic mode, starting firing. The Beetle didn't even jerk from the impact. Pieces of his body flew apart from the force of the bullet, colours raging. Beetle just carried straight on . . .

Oh Bee.

. . . carried straight on, as more cops opened fire. He was almost on Murdoch now and she was firing at him as well. He caught the round full on, and his body was blown apart, splintering into a shower of fractals. And the colours were draining from my life. Into the spaces. The Beetle's voice coming through.

My name written in a cloud of sparks in the night air, in the Manchester night air. And then falling away to nowhere, where the angels live.

IT'S THE GIRL! Takshaka had focused on Mandy.

Murdoch started to turn again towards us, bringing the gun around, but Mandy was already out there, on the edge of nothing, watching the Beetle losing the race, and she was calling out Beetle's name as she . . .

Save something!

I stumbled backwards, heading for the doghouse door.

. . . as she pulled the gun around, activating.

Noise and flame.

A bullet tracing out a path of fire.

And as I was falling back, under the weight of the Thing, into the hallway, I saw Murdoch's body catch that flame bullet, full on, in the heart's place.

Suck on that, bitchcop!

Murdoch screaming, and then the explosion of gunfire, as the cops took Mandy. Her body was blown back, blood and flesh exploding, all across the walls, as she bounced against the bottom stairs, coming to rest at our feet. I had Twinkle and Karli pressed up tight against the wall. Twinkle was crying for Mandy, and the dog was yelping. The Thing was still fixed to my back, wriggling around, calling my name out loud. And then I was kicking the door shut, bullets punching back holes in the wood.

A rain of splinters, hard as glass.

I was hitting home the door bolt, but already the guns were letting up.

I was down flat on the floor by now, the Thing cushioning me, Twinkle alongside, and Karli. Mandy in my arms, getting crushed.

No use.

Still didn't bring her back.

For Mandy and the Beetle, Stash Riders, a part of this for you.

The firing stopped, and Shaka's transmission came through, loud and angry, almost human.

WE HAVE YOU. JUST COME OUT CLEAN. NO OTHER
WAY OUT.

Dogs howling from the stairs above.

Das Uberdog and Bridget were standing on the landing above,
surrounded by wailing halfdogs. The full pack had gathered, making a vicious gang. Bridget was calling me to come up.

'Is this where it ends, Mister Scribble?' Twinkle asked.

'Not yet,' I answered.

'We're the Stash Riders, is that right?'

I turned my eyes to that face of tears.

'That's right,' I said. 'Out on the edge, loving it.'

COME OUT CLEAN.

Or come out dirty.

THERE IS NO OTHER WAY. NO OTHER WAY.

Wanna bet?

They gave us maybe two seconds to consider, before putting
one single bullet through, high up on the door, like a warning.

Twinkle screamed out.

'Don't let it scare you, Twink,' I whispered.

'I'm not scared, Mister Scribble,' she answered. 'Don't you get
it yet?'

I looked her deep in those strong eyes.

'Keep screaming, kidder,' I said.

Twinkle screamed like a wounded child, like Cinders in a climax
love scene.

LET'S MAKE IT EASY.

'Let up, Shaka!' I shouted. 'We've got a young kid in here. That
cunt just wounded her!'

SORRY ABOUT THAT, SCRIBBLE. WE'VE GOT SOME SAD
COPS OUT HERE. JUST LOST ONE OF OUR BEST. GOT NO
PROBLEM WITH THE YOUNG GIRL. SEND HER OUT. WE
GET HER TO HOSPITAL. YOU WANT TO DO THAT?

'I can't trust you on that,' I shouted back.

WHY EVER NOT?

Because the world's on your side, not on mine.

I let him wait five seconds, before answering; 'Okay, Shaka! I'm sending the kid out. Go easy. No tricks.'

WE WILL. WE WILL.

'She's in a bad way.'

TAKE YOUR TIME.

That was all I needed.

I ran up the stairs, dragging the Twinkle along behind me. Past Das Uberdog, who had his charges in hand, waiting for the call up. Those mad dogs were howling at his fingertips, baying for blood.

Cop blood.

Worst enemy. Best meat.

'Take those cops out, Das!' Bridget shouted.

And as I passed, Das Uber was already leading the dogs down, towards the front door. Karli was looking at the pack, as they descended. Robodog had a yearning look in her eyes. 'You wanna go with them, Karli?' asked Twinkle.

Karli leapt for the chance, heading down the stairs after Das Uberdog.

Police were expecting a young kid to come out. But they were getting a pack of cop-eaters.

I wonder how they coped with that?

'You got another way out, Brid?'

She smiled at me. And then gave me the answer.

Shadowgirl didn't even have to open her mouth.

D E A T H   F O R   L I F E

We were running through a soft mud. Didn't even want to think about it; smelt like the world gone bad. Couldn't see too well, just pushing on, ankle deep, retching. The Twinkle in front. Pictures on the stone walls as we passed, painted in shit.

Just caught glimpses.

Dogs fucking women. Men fucking dogs. Half and half split babies being born, all wreathed in the foul miasma that rose from the mud.

Das Uberdog's face glowing in the darkness from the wall ahead.

Those painted eyes fixing me, demanding belief, so that I couldn't move. Dogshit leaking into my shoes, Twinkle turning around to urge me on. 'You like it down here, Mister Scribble?'

No! No, I don't!

'So stay here then!'

The young girl pushing on through the shit.

Oh my god!

'Wait for me, Twinkle!'

Bridget had led us to this cellar, down from a pantry door set in the kitchen's wall. 'They most probably got cops out the back, Scribble,' she'd said.

'We'll deal with that.'

Staying pure. Featherless. Through a hole in the wall, into this dog toilet.

And there *was* a cop waiting for us.

He was floating face down in the slow tide.

A cop in dogshit, drowning.

That's one I'll keep with me.

And sparks of colours coming from the fuse-box as we passed, Beetle's colours. *Did good, my man.*

I was wading after Twinkle, heading for the light ahead, the soft glow of streetlamps shining through the swung-back doors set in the cellar's roof. Following Twinkle up the steps, faint glints of the Beetle's colours shining from the doors' sprung locks. We emerged into a garden, overgrown with tall weeds. And a dump of maybe fifty-five full to the brim binbags waiting for collection.

I guess the Council gave up on this house years ago.

The smell was sweet and high, but beautiful, free from Turds-ville. From the front of the house I could hear the sound of dogs barking, people screaming.

I hope that you dogmen took some cops out that day, and that some of you are still running free.

An open gate in the back wall led onto a small street. Don't ask me its name. It's enough that we took it. There was a small road ahead of us, away from the trouble. It led onto Parkfield Street, and we were struggling down it, running with the pain. The Thing was weighing heavy on me. Twinkle racing ahead.

I knew these little back streets fairly well because they were clustered at the back of the Rusholme Gardens flat. We took a left, and then a right, onto Heald Place. Down that, out onto Platt Lane. The park just over the road from us. The streets were still full up of Asian kids, and there were lights and noise coming from the park, the deep rhythms of Bhangradog songs.

No cops.

We made it across the road alright, the Asians looking at me funny, but I was used to that. Into the Platt Fields. The trees were swaying in a slow winding dance to the beat, brushed by waves of noise from the sound systems up ahead. Even the rain was caught up in the pulse of Bhangra; it blew into my face until I was soaked and the Thing was taking in the moisture, until he felt like a thick lump of sponge on my back, weighted like a pig. I was almost collapsing under him but I kept it going, making for the dancing kids ahead. 'You alright, Big Thing?' I asked. He gave me some answer back, along some Vurt wave; all I caught here and there were scattered words; my name, my sister's name, mixed in with the gibberish. He was alive, that's all that matters.

I had the Thing. I had the yellow feather.

All I needed was a quiet and private space, and time enough to take them both. But first some distance, between ourselves and any stray cops. So I headed into the Bhangra crowd. It must have been getting on for midnight now, but those kids were still dancing. The system was draped under rain sheets, but the rain didn't put the dancers off; this was their night of the year. They were high on Eid, and young Asian life pulsed through them.

They let us pass.

They were laughing and pointing; the white guy with the strange lump on his back, the young kid racing ahead. I guess we looked like fun of some kind. That's alright. I can handle that. They let us through anyway, towards the paths that led down to the boating lake.

Almost there . . .

A shot of light ringing through the rain, bringing a breath of fire to my ear. I managed a painful twist back, over my shoulder, swinging the Thing around, out of the line of vision. Through the veil of rain I saw a cop coming up fast on us, his flame-gun blazing with inpho. And then the Asian kids were really cheering us on. Because the enemy of fun was after the madfuckers, aiming to screw us down. I guess that's how they saw it. Twinkle was well ahead of me now. The Thing was getting to me, pulling me down to a slow motion crawl. I was slipping on wet grass, fighting for a hold, pushing against the rain, which felt like pins of steel, cutting the skin. Everything was wet and hazy, all bleached out in the moonlight, a violet and green shadow playing on the grass in front of me.

Shakacop!

He was in full Takshaka Yellow mode, beaming down from the Platt Fields' aerial, filling the world with his snake of smoke, whipping the air above the Bhangra into the colours of old myths. The kids were responding for sure, but not in kind. Because the Takshaka was a Hindu, and these kids were Muslims, and that's a world of difference. The dreamsnake was coming down for me and I was failing myself, my own sweet dreams, and all who had believed in me. Slipping on black mud, dragging myself onwards, towards the glistening lake. But no chance of getting there.

No chance.

The first bullet hit. A hard push in the back. I felt its vile energies hitting me, pushing me down. I tumbled into the grass, face first, but then up again, finding the strength somehow, still believing.

'Keeping running, Twink!' I cried.

Second bullet hit. Shot from a cop gun, fired on a shadow tracer beam, it went in straight and pure, pitching me forward, so that my head was pressed flat against the mud and the grass, hard on it, right down, and I was just lying there waiting for the pain to come, waiting for my back to set on fire, and the life to go wandering away.

Should've cottoned it.

Pain didn't come.

Wasn't thinking too good.

The dreamsnake colours lighting up the field all around, Takshaka hovering above me. Another shot rang out, but there was no impact this time. I craned my head around some, looking back, to where these Asian lads had surrounded the cop. It looked like a crazy scrum. And then looking back to see Twinkle there, miles away it seemed, through the walls of rain, down by the lake. I tried to get up, but the Thing was a dead weight on my back. All I could manage was to roll over, onto the Thing, so that I was looking straight into Takshaka's wounded face, his split-ended tongue hissing like the rain, between the long fangs.

Then that snake whipped down, fast and true, a vicious blur. But he didn't go for my neck, which was the usual target, instead he sank those daggers into my ankle, piercing the skin, and the shadow smoke was all around my body and I was gone, a total shadowfuck, collapsing . . .

Into a world of numbers.

Falling . . .

A realm of mists, where green and violet inpho played on waves of shadows. The smell of jasmine enveloping me. I was falling through the clouds of yellow, and as I was falling I could still move around, twisting to the right.

Still falling.

Twisting over again, trying to face upwards. But still falling. Turning around in a full circle, but no matter the direction I faced,

I was still falling down, down towards the snake pit. And all these numbers floating by, pure and naked information, wrapping me up in mathematics. The records of all my crimes were being written in the saffron air. And all of the Stash Riders' crimes. Everything. All we had done, and lost, and killed. I was coming to it then, the story, where I was, with my hair still wet from the outside rain, inside this palace of numbers.

I was inside of Takshaka's head, Copvurt Yellow, where he played all his inpho, working it all out, all the crimes of the world. I was falling through this sea of maths, without any feelings of up or down, just travelling, until something whipped itself around my leg, low down, around the ankle, where the dreamsnake had bit. I was pulled back tight by the pressure, my spine jack-knifing, so that the Thing was pressed between my shoulder blades and the small of my back. Thing didn't make a sound, cushioning the blow for me. Then I was whipped back the other way, so that my head came up towards my stomach, pulling the Thing with me, until I was looking direct into the king of snakes.

Takshaka was floating in space, his tail wrapped around my ankle, his face inches from mine, so I could smell the shadow-breath, and see the orange cells of inpho moving around inside his eyes.

I'M THINKING I SHOULD JUST DROP YOU.

This isn't real!

YOU'VE BEEN A PAIN IN THE GUT, SCRIBBLE.

He was beaming direct into my skull, drilling through the bone with his words, pricking my soft brain until I got the message, each word a new pain.

THERE'S SOME BAD MOTHERS DOWN THERE. SOME REAL TASTY EQUATIONS. THEY CAN FRACTALIZE A MAN IN SECONDS. THIS IS A YELLOW VURT. THE COLOUR THAT KILLS. YOU WANT THAT?

He let my head fall back so that I was suspended over the space. Down below there were numbers and symbols clashing against each other. It looked like a set of jaws down there, opening and closing. And where the equations were being solved, broken numbers were being discarded, forming themselves into columns of jagged teeth.

SHAME ABOUT THE BEETLE. HE WENT OUT GOOD, DIDN'T HE? I LIKE THAT IN A MAN. COULD'VE FOUND A PLACE FOR HIM ON THE FORCE. WE NEED SOME DEMONS LIKE THAT. I'M TELLING YOU SCRIBBLE, THE STATE OF THE PURE COPS WE GET, WELL IT MAKES YOU WANT TO CRY.

He loosened his grip a little, so that I jerked down some two feet or so, before he caught me again, tightening.

WHOOPS! NEARLY LOST YOU THEN.

He brought his ravaged face down to my new level.

EXCEPT FOR MURDOCH, OF COURSE. SHE WAS GOOD AND FINE. SUPER PURE. AND OH SO VERY GOOD IN BED. WHOOPS! THERE YOU GO!

And I could feel his tail unravelling.

Then I was falling down, into the mouth of the numbersnakes, screaming.

'Aiiiiiiiiii!!!!!!!!!'

Down the world, accelerating, snakes hissing from the blur as I plummeted, my mind going blank, and dreaming, so that I landed in somebody's soft arms, and they were raising me up, and this soft voice calling to me, softly, from the dream's mouth.

'I've got you, Scribble,' the voice said to me. 'I've got you in my arms.'

I opened my eyes to see the Game Cat's crooked smile.

He was floating in the tunnel, holding me tight, one-handed, like I had no weight on me, like I didn't have a Thing on my back.

'Cat!' I called out, just the name, the one word. All I could manage.

'Never mind,' he said. 'Just watch this.'

The Cat raised up his free arm. There was a ball hammer in it, and I could see the snakeweed sap dribbling there, on the head.

Takshaka came down fast for him, hissing with anger and frustration.

So I guess the snake lost the edge, losing to anger.

Cat was super cool. He swung the hammer around, in a wave of heat. And then swung it back, inch-perfect, timed like a Vurtball player, going for the winning pitch.

Met that snakehead, full on.

There was a clang of light, then a hissing, burning sound. And the crunch of flesh against steel. Something went sliding past my head, and when I turned to look, I could see Takshaka tumbling over and over, tail whipping, screaming, blood pumping from his face. He fell into the jaws of numbers. The equations closed over the King Snake, biting shut, until only his cry was left. And then his long body was snapped in two. An explosion of orange sap, spraying all over. Me and the Cat covered in it.

Game Cat dropped the hammer after him. 'You think I do this for just anyone?' he whispered, snake juice dripping off his face. 'You think I'm doing this for you?'

'You killed him?'

The Cat took a yellow feather out of his pocket. 'You don't kill something like Takshaka. You just win the current game.'

'Thank you.'

He placed the feather in his mouth, working it. One by one the list of Stash Rider crimes deleted themselves from the air. Cat pulled out the Takshaka feather, placed it in my mouth.

'This isn't for you,' the Cat answered. 'This is for Tristan.'

Then I was gone, pitched out, jerked back, where no jerkout switch ever lived.

I must have passed out some few seconds there, on the field of mud, because when I opened my eyes there was this smiling face staring down at me.

'I don't know what you did, mate, but that snake just went woomph! It was great.'

I felt a strong hand clutching under my shoulder, and then lifting me up, until I was looking direct into this Asian face. The rain was dripping over his colour, like rain in the dusk. His black hair was wetted down all over his eyes, but I could see the life in them, the energy.

'Go for it, mate,' he said. 'Whatever it is.'

Then he was leading me over the grass, to where Twinkle was waiting. I was looking all around, expecting a snake to come hunting for me. But there was no sign, no colours, just the grey rain pock-marking the waters of the boating lake.

I fell into Twinkle's arms.

She reached up for my face to scrub some of the mud away. It felt good, her touch. I took the young man's hand in mine. He smiled. Over his shoulder I could make out the rest of the lads running wild, away from the lone cop. He was naked in the rain, the kids sprinting away with his clothes, and no doubt the gun. Cop sure looked lonely out there, in the drizzle, pink and shivering.

'You do good, now,' the Asian said, and then walked away, into the rain. Over on the playing fields they were shutting down the system; the lights going out, one by one, until darkness settled.

Midnight.

Twinkle took my hand. There was still some dogshit on me but the rain was taking care of that. But the Thing on my back was—

The dead weight of...

I was suddenly back on the field, feeling the bullets hit. But now seeing for real where those bullets had landed.

'They shot the Thing,' I said to Twinkle.

'Don't worry,' she said.

But I couldn't stop crying. 'Thing is dead.'

All I could say. All I could think about.

Because that was Desdemona gone.

'Keep going, Mister Scribble. Big Thing saved you.'

'What for?' I asked the girl. 'What for?'

Because you can't swap death for life.

Not even in the Vurt.

The boating lake shining with the last remnants of the day. The bag of dead flesh on my back. Me and that young girl, walking along the water's edge.

Heading for nowhere.

Shit cleansed in the rain.

DAY 24

'Tough shit.'

A N   E N D
T O   F A S T I N G

'You know where the Slithy Tove is?'

'Sure. It's just over the hill. We passed it.'

'That's where Barnie works. You remember Barnie?' Twinkle nodded. 'He'll help you. Go there. Through the trees. Keep to the darkest roads you can find.'

'Mister Scribble . . .'

Her young face was wet from the trip.

'You're on your own now, kid,' I said.

'What about you, Scribble? What are you going to do?'

'Some things.'

'Keep the faith.'

'That's right. Keep the faith. Go on now.'

Twinkle set off, into the dark morning, through the breath of trees. She looked back just the once.

'Keep going,' I called.

Keep going.

I pulled off one shoulder strap, and then the other, until the Thing was loose. I lowered him to the ground.

His dead eyes looking up at me.

I think they were his eyes.

Thing was dead, for sure. Two holes in his back where the bullets had lodged.

But that's not good enough. I had the Curious feather out of my pocket, and I was forcing it into his mouth, if that was his mouth? Any orifice would do. Pounding and pounding on his chest. 'Come on! Come on!' Working the feather some more, deep enough for Lazarus, so why not the Thing. Bringing my fists down on his chest . . . thinking about the Beetle and Mandy and how I'd lost them for nothing . . . bringing my fists . . . bringing my fists down . . . again and again . . .

Nothing.

It brings nothing.

His dead eyes.

I have lost you, my alien . . . and all that goes with you.

I pulled the feather out. Then picked his body up, carried it to the lake's edge.

I lowered him into the waters.

The Thing floated for a moment, until the water had soaked through to every vessel. Then he sank away. Beneath the waves.

It's over.

I looked back to where the Asian kids were packing up their gear. The rain was letting up some, and the road seemed miles away, like I was free and safe for a while.

Don't believe it. We're neither free nor safe, until we've earned it.

I walked over to a clump of trees, found the place there, amongst the flowers and the insects, where Desdemona and I used to lie down, hidden by the leaves, to take our pleasures. The lake glimpsed between shadows and branches; flickers of yellow coming off the feather.

Time to go.

But where? You've got nothing to give, Scribble, what's the point?

I put the feather to the very edge of my bottom lip.

Pulled it away again, trembling, unsure.

So long we have travelled for this.

Feather back in.

Deep this time.

Felt the glitters there; a curious shade of yellow.

Desdemona calling.

In my last moments of reality I pulled out the feather and placed it in my pocket. The Curious Yellow coming on . . .

Desdemona, somewhere . . .

An end to fasting.

A   C U R I O U S   H O U S E

My face bathed in a yellow light.

'Looking good, Stephen.'

'Cheers.'

'You've done well. You should feel proud.'

'I know that. But I can't help feeling down.'

'Don't say that. You got through.'

I moved the razor across my cheek, revealing an area of skin, and then wiped the foam onto a flannel.

'I've haven't got what she wanted. Don't you know how that feels?'

'Don't I just?'

I wet the razor in the sink. The water looked dirty.

'I really wanted to please her, you know?'

'I know.'

'She had her heart set on that bag.'

'It's doesn't matter, Stephen. Believe me. She'll have a good birthday anyway.'

'You know what Des is like.'

'Believe me. No one knows better.'

I looked deep into the eyes staring back at me. Yellow eyes.

'See what I mean?'

The neon tube above the mirror cast a yellow gloom over my face. The light seemed almost thick, and my hand had to push gently through the air, as I brought the razor back up. It was my father's open razor, the one sharpened on the leather strop hanging up beside the sink. He hated me using it. But what the hell? It wasn't every day that your sister gets to be sixteen. I was taking her out tonight. I wanted to look good. Especially because . . .

'I should've moved on that bag—'

'Stephen!'

I was talking to myself in the bathroom mirror. Calling myself by name.

'As soon as Des spotted it, I should've got the money out there and then. Oh no. Not me. I wanted to surprise her with it.'

'So you let that guy steal it off you. Big deal.'

'It's not just that—'

'You got her something nice instead?'

'No. I—'

'You didn't get her anything?'

'No. There's nothing else she would—shit!'

I'd taken a nick out of my face. Blood fell into the water, swirling. I reached for a tissue and when I looked into the mirror to stop the flow it was my father's face that I dabbed at—

Oh my god! I was . . .

'You know I forbid the use of that blade.'

I was . . . I was . . .

'It is a man's blade.'

'Father . . . I am sorry.'

What was this? Where was I? This feeling? What is it . . . think . . . think!

'Give me the blade, Stephen.'

'Please . . .'

This isn't real! Nobody calls me Stephen any more.

'Must I punish you again?'

'No . . .'

I'm getting the Haunting!

'Father!'

He was swinging the blade . . .

This isn't real. I'm in a Vurt. Jerk out!

The razor coming for my face.

Jesus Christ! Jerk out, you dumb fucking—

'Looking good, Stephen.'

'Cheers.'

'So you got Desdemona nothing, eh?'

'Don't remind me.'

I was looping my best tie into a Windsor knot. My father had shown me this, when I was seven years old.

'Wouldn't have done any good anyway. She'll never be yours.'

'Look—'

The knot was all wrong.

'Sorry, Stephen. My fault.'

'Yeah. Stop putting me off.'

I was standing in my bedroom, talking to myself in the wardrobe mirror. I pulled the knot loose to start again. There was a small shaving nick in my left cheek. The square of tissue paper—stuck to the cut by a film of dried blood—wasn't the best thing to have on your face, the day of your sister's birthday. But that's okay. It would be healed in a minute or so. I was waiting for Desdemona to get back from college. We were going out that night, celebrating, and I had my best suit on, all washed and pressed. Now I just had to get this knot right. And the weak lemony glow from the bedside lamp wasn't helping any. It made my eyes look kind of yellow.

'She's going to be real angry, Stephen.'

'I don't think that's—shit!'

The knot was all crooked. I pulled it loose again.

'Having trouble? Here let me—'

'I don't want help! And stop calling me Stephen!'

'It is the name I gave you, boy.'

'My name is—'

Wait . . .

'You will damned well use it.'

My father had taken the two ends of the tie in his big work-scarred hands.

'How many times must I teach you the Windsor?'

It wasn't me in the mirror! My father . . .

'Father . . .'

'It is a man's knot.'

He crossed the tie, wide end over narrow, through the loop, down, around and behind, up to the right. Wide end down through the loop, crossed at right angles over the narrow, pushed through the loop one last time and finished by slipping the wide end through the knot in front. He tightened the finished Windsor, pulling it gently, until the knot was right up against my throat.

This isn't real!

'There. Perfect. Simple. Elegant!'

He pulled the knot tight. Tight! Pulling down on each end of the tie until my throat was closing and the breath leaving me. My hands coming up, but so weak I—

The Haunting!

'Even a fool could manage it!'

All my air was used up. Bursts of light behind my eyes. Pain. The fierce glare in my father's eyes.

This is Vurt!

'But not my boy, evidently.'

Darkness, and the end of pain beckoning.

Jerk out! Come on! Work it!

The pain dying away as I lost the will to—

'Oh Christ!'

I was shivering amongst the trees, down by the lakeside. The leaves were rustling from the gathering wind. I couldn't stop shaking.

Made it.

Made a way out of there.

A shadow falling across the moon.

Christ, that was bad. And no sign of Desdemona.

Shaking, shaking . . .

Breathing in gulps of air. Again. Again. My lungs aching, and my throat, and a sharp pain on my cheek from the razor's edge.

And then letting out the air, in a long passage.

Something coming between the moon and the trees.

Found a way out somehow.

Except that you can't jerkout of a Yellow.

The leaves shaking as something moved amongst them.

So what was . . .

'I have found you, Stephen.'

My father pushing the branches aside, the glint of light on the razor in his hand.

I'm still in the Vurt!

'I won't have any child of mine out after ten.'

Father stepping forward, blocking the moon's light completely, until there was only darkness. And the blade . . .

Get out of here!

His hand around my neck—

'Looking good, Scribble.'

'Looking good yourself, birthday girl.'

'You taking me out tonight?'

'Bet on it, Des.'

'Where?'

'Platt Fields.'

'Platt Fields? I was maybe expecting a meal. Then a club. I feel like dancing.'

'I know. But there's a little clump of trees there, side of the lake. It's private and cosy, and we could . . . well, you know . . .'

'Scribble! You're disgusting!'

'It's you that makes me like this.'

She pushed me backwards, onto the bed. Then she jumped on top of me, and started to really tickle me, just where I can't stand it.

'Des!'

'I'm not going to some dingy park. I'm going dancing!'

'You've got to.'

'What do you mean, got to? Who says got to? Hey!—'

I manage to get a grip on her body, and then kind of throw her over, but gently, until I was on top of her, and she was smiling beneath me.

'We've got to go there, Des. Don't ask why. I just know we've got to go.'

'Why should I?'

'It's important.'

She went quiet then.

Her bedroom was a warm glow of yellow, the last rays of the sun coming through the drawn curtains. Her eyes were too much for me, too full of life.

I lowered myself down, until our bodies were touching all over, and my lips were on hers.

'Careful, Scribb.'

'Why?'

'You'll crease your best suit.'

'It's all for you, Desdemona. All for you.'

We kissed some more.

'You got me a present, Scribb?'

'I tried to.'

'Scribble!'

'I tried to get that bag you wanted. Well, I did get it. But...'

'Don't tell me, you lost it?'

'It was—'

'I hate you.'

'It was stolen, Des. This guy on the bus. I was bringing it back home. I was going to wrap it and everything. But this guy just snatched it away from me, ran down the stairs, jumped off just as the bus was moving from the stop. I didn't know what to do.'

'You know what this means?'

'I know.'

'It means we can't go to Platt Fields.'

'I know. Why is that?'

'I don't know. Crazy, isn't it?'

'I'm sorry, Des.'

'It doesn't matter. We'll just stay in tonight. We could—'

'That can't happen. Father...he...'

'Has he been hassling you again?'

'He went for me with the razor before. I was just shaving, you know.'

'I know.'

'And then . . . in my room . . . well, it was bad.'

'This is a curious house, isn't it, Scribb?'

'It's a bad house.'

Then I pulled her blouse free from her belt, to reveal the hard ridges of the scars on her lovely stomach. I put my lips to them, trying to kiss them away. Nothing would work.

'I'm going to kill that man, one day.'

'I don't think it's possible, Scribble. He's not real.'

I moved back up her body, to look at her eyes again, trying to work out what she meant. I don't think she knew. And neither did I. Just that it was true.

'Thanks for the card, Des.'

'What card?'

'My birthday card.'

'Don't be silly. It's my birthday, Scribb. Not yours.'

'No. I mean a few days ago. My twenty-first birthday.'

'Scribble, you're only eighteen!'

That stopped me. 'Oh god.'

'I know. I can remember sending it as well. What's happening, Scribble?'

'I got you a present anyway, Des.'

'Show me!'

I put my hand into my jacket pocket, feeling something fluttering there, not knowing what it was until I pulled it out. And then still not knowing.

'Oh Scribb! It's a feather!'

'Looks like it.'

'Look at the colours in it. All those yellows! They're just the same colour as the light in this house.

'Just the same. It's curious.'

'I keep getting this feeling, Scribble. Like I'm being haunted, or something. I can't work it out. Like there's another world out there, and I just can't get to it.'

'I'm getting the same. Can't explain it.'

'What does the feather do?'

'I think I'm meant to tickle you with it.'

'That's sounds right.'

She pulled up her blouse some more, offering me her stomach and breasts. I stroked the yellow feather gently over her body. Starting at the dragon tattoo, and then down, and across, and then up . . .

'Oh god. That feels good. It's making me see pictures.'

'What do you see?'

'Me and you walking away from this house. Growing old together. Keep stroking. That's it. That's good. We're living in a little house, miles from here. Miles away from father. Keep doing it, higher. That's it. On my neck. Feels lovely. Miles away from the pain. On my lips, please, Scribble. Yes! Miles away from the knife. In my mouth now. In my mouth!'

I had the feather poised on my sister's lips, and my whole being was telling me to push further, to let her take it in deep, and I didn't even know why. I just had to do it to her. Gently pushing . . .

'Scribble!'

'What?'

'Your eyes!'

'What about them?'

'Yellow! They're turning yellow!'

Oh shit!

'Take that feather away, Stephen.'

'Father . . .'

'It is a young boy's game.'

I was lying on top of my father, pushing a feather into his mouth. His hands were coming up to hug me. I tried to push the feather in, don't know why, just had to, but his bite clamped down hard on the flights, so that the feather was lodged solid between his teeth. Then his hands came down on my back and I felt the blade going in.

Felt like my back was fire. He stabbed again.

Christ!

The pain was unbearable. I was trying my best to pull away, but his strength was too much for me. I felt the razor tearing its way out of the small of my back, ready for another strike.

'Father, please . . .'

Wait . . .

'It is all that you deserve, wretched boy!'

But as he spoke the feather was loose in his mouth.

This isn't real!

He cursed me then. Called me a sister fucker.

This is Vurt! Jerk out!

The razor biting into me.

No! No, don't jerk out! I was getting the story. There is no jerkout. It just starts again. This is Curious Yellow. And that isn't my father under me. It's my sister. It's Desdemona! This is just a Vurt father. He's living inside Desdemona. There is no going back. No jerking out. You can only go forward.

The razor was cutting into my skin again.

The pain was terrible. Blood on my father's face. Must have been my blood.

Never mind that.

A sudden glimpse of Desdemona's eyes looking back at me from my father's face and her voice telling me to—

Push the feather in!

It took everything I had left, fighting against all the rage and madness, until I had the feather wedged up against the top of his mouth. He bit down hard again but I was too far gone by then, too full up of despair.

Shove it!

Deep to my father's throat. Which was Desdemona's throat. Where it belongs. Immediately his body starts to fall away. The razor slips free of my skin. I pull the Curious out of his mouth and take it into mine.

Please, God, I'm right on this one.

Where it belongs.

My father screaming somewhere...

And Desdemona's voice coming through clear...

But Scribble, we're already in Curious Yellow. How can we—

looking good stephen cheers looking good stephen cheers looking good stephen cheers cheers my face bathed in yellow light which is bathed in yellow light which is

!!!!!WARNING!!!!!

which is a man's blade the blade swinging for me in the mirror of the mirror of the mirror curiouser and curiouser the blade swinging a thousand times as it

Layers upon layers...

!!!!!WARNING!!!!!

each the reflection of the other as it

What was that voice?

one thousand times through the yellow air which is yellow upon yellow as it as it looking good stephen

!!!!!WARNING. YOU ARE NOW IN METAVURT!!!!!

cheers as it as it curiouser and curiouser as the blade swinging for desdemona

What is happening?!

one thousand knives reflected each one sharp as sharp as the mirror as they as they cut into my sister who was

WHAT THE HELL IS GOING ON?

who was clinging to me who was clinging to me covered in blood

That voice. I know that voice. It is the voice of...

her own age at last nineteen years old and in my arms as I saw the thousands cuts being made each cut being made twice the real and the image

YOU ARE SERIOUSLY FUCKING UP MY SYSTEMS!

desdemona sister

That voice! It was the voice of...

falling away from me in blood as I clung on tight to her one thousand times as I my father reflected in the mirror reflected in the mirror reflected in the mirror reflected as I as I saw the blades coming in again sister

PLEASE EXPLAIN YOURSELF!

It was the voice of Sniffing General.

OH IT'S YOU. I MIGHT HAVE KNOWN.

Sniffing General... can you...

I HOPE YOU REALISE...

blood all over

What's happening, General? Can you help me?'

... THE TROUBLE YOU'RE CAUSING ME.

Tell me!

YOU'VE GONE META. NOT JUST ANY OLD META.

sister screaming from the cuts

MIRROR META. YOU'RE DOING CURIOUS...

curiouser and curiouser

... INSIDE OF CURIOUS. NOBODY DOES THAT! NO-BODY!

Get me out. Get us both out!

THERE IS NO WAY. YOU'RE CAUGHT IN A LOOP.

our father digging his one thousand ways through desdemona as he cutting as he smiling

You've got to, General!

IT CAN'T BE DONE... I DON'T KNOW HOW... NO ONE'S EVER...

Blow that Choke out of your nose and do it!
    IT JUST CAN'T BE DONE! HOBART . . . SHE'LL . . .
sister falling apart
It just gets worse, General.
    WHAT DO YOU MEAN?
taking the silver feather reflected one thousand times out of
my pocket
    DON'T DO THAT!
sister reaching out for me as she as she reached out for me
bleeding and the bleeding was bleeding the wounds were
wounded
You think I have a choice, General?
    PLEASE!
I pushed the silver sniffing general feather in as I as I pushed
the silver feather in over the top of the curious yellow
    THAT'S ME YOU'RE PUSHING IN!
I need a door, General . . .
two feathers at once who's ever done that before?
    NOBODY DOES THAT . . . SCRIBBLE! SCRIBBLE! IT
    HURTS!
Tough shit.
the silver coming on the yellow which was yellow in the yellow silver in the yellow in the yellow the thousand mirrors cracking . . . as I . . .
father swinging the razor at my sister . . .
as I . . .
waiting for the menu to scroll . . .
    1. EDIT
    2. CLONE
    3. HELP . . .
menu stops . . .
as I stopped my father's hand . . .

WON'T LET YOU.

Shit! What number was the door? What number!

YOU'RE MAKING A FOOL OF ME, SCRIBBLE. I WON'T ALLOW IT.

that's enough, father . . .

as I . . .

What number was the door? What number?!

as I took the razor from his hand and then I . . .

HOBART WILL PUNISH ME!

Four for a door. Four for a door. That's it.

as I pushed the razor into my . . .

NO!!!!!

as I pushed the razor into my father's eye . . .

coming back to me now the feelings as I as I thought about the number four my father screaming with his hands coming up to his eyes as I got the menu up to my eyes . . .

1. BLUE

2. BLACK

3. I'M NOT GIVING YOU THE MENU.

That's okay, Sniffer. I don't need it any more.

as I thought about the number five

Five for alive.

a door opening up as the mirror broke and our father was putting red hands up to his eyes and the door opened in his eyes and I could see the trees of platt fields through the holes in his eyes

'Sniffing General . . .'

A new voice.

HOBART . . . MISS . . . I AM SORRY.

'What is the problem?'

I was pushing des towards the door in father's eyes

NOTHING I CAN'T HANDLE, MISS HOBART.

'I am trying to stay asleep, General. Please explain.'

desdemona won't go through she's clinging to me dragging me along as well

WE'VE GOT A MIRROR META IN CURIOUS YELLOW, WITH AN ILLEGAL LIFE-DOOR BREACH PLUS AN UNAUTHORIZED SWAPBACK ATTEMPT WITHOUT ADEQUATE EXCHANGE MATERIAL.

'Is that all.'

MISS HOBART . . .

Please, Scribble . . . come with me.

my sister talking to me . . .

It can't happen, Des. It just can't.

'Don't make me angry, general.'

MISS HOBART . . . PLEASE . . .

so I'm thinking about the number one whilst they argue number one for a blue world seeing the thousands of blue names scroll down thinking about P for pleasure

'Where are we, Scribble?'

My sister and I sitting on the park bench in Pleasureville, listening to the birds singing and watching the play of dappled light on the newly cut lawn. Kids are skipping. No sign of the postman. I had two, maybe three minutes before the General dragged me away from this sweet blue world. I had my sister with me, and she looked happy at last, just like I remembered her; that was Pleasureville Blue for you.

'We're inside a Vurt, Des.'

'It's lovely.'

'What do you remember?'

Her smile faded for a second as she searched through her memories. 'Nothing,' she said. 'Nothing at all, except that the world is beautiful and that you are my brother and that we should just stay here forever. Shall we do that, Scribble?'

'No.' Her eyes went blank for a moment, filled with a blue void. 'This isn't the real world, Des. The real world is not beautiful, but it's where you belong. No, don't try to understand. Just believe what I'm saying. I'm sending you back, Des. If I can.'

'You're coming with me, Scribble?'

'I don't belong there, sister. This is my place. This is what I am.'

'Scribble!'

'It can't happen, Des. It just can't. I love you too much. Or you don't love me enough.'

Which adds up to the same thing. The same pile of bones.

I looked deep into my sister's blue eyes, saw the truth there, and then looked away. Sister said nothing. A boy and a girl sitting on a park bench on a sunny day, the girl looking into the sun, the boy with his head in his hands.

THERE YOU ARE! I'VE BEEN LOOKING ALL OVER.

'Hobart's telling you to deal with it, General.'

YOU'RE ASKING THE IMPOSSIBLE, SIR.

'Send my sister back!

SHE HAS NOTHING TO EXCHANGE WITH. IT CANNOT BE—

'I'm staying here.'

OH . . .

'Scribble! What's happening?'

My sister's voice calling . . .

IN THAT CASE . . . JUST LET ME CHECK THE CONSTANT . . .

'Scribble. Please don't . . .'

She was holding tight to my hand, trying to pull me with her. But I was firmly rooted now, working the Vurt like I was born to it.

'You know the truth, Des. Keep the faith. Don't stop thinking about me.'

My father's eyes opening, blood-red in a blue Pleasureville sky.

'*Scribble!!!!!!*'

THERE. I HAVE IT NOW . . . THAT'S FINE, SIR.

'Just do it!'

and desdemona falling away the touch of her fingers the gift of her eyes falling falling into the eyes of our father and through to where I could catch glimpses of the shifting branches and the moon on the lake in the park where the world is good and the rain is tender . . .

I pull Curious Yellow out of my mouth, leaving the silver there. All the layers fall away until I'm seeing only darkness.

I SUPPOSE WE OUGHT TO DO SOMETHING ABOUT YOU?

'I guess so,' I answer.

The menu scrolls down.

   1. BLUE

   2. BLACK

   3. PINK

   4. SILVER

   5. LIFE

   6. CAT

   7. YELLOW

   8. HOBART

PLEASE SELECT YOUR DOOR OPTION. NOT THAT YOU'VE GOT MUCH CHOICE . . .

'Give me a six, please . . . General.'

Falling . . .

Sniffing General was sitting behind his desk, lining up three lines of Choke powder.

'By God I need this.'

I didn't say anything. Game Cat's door lay just beyond.

'I'm in trouble with Miss Hobart now.' He paused between

sniffs. 'It's all got to be accounted for, you know? She'll want a full report. That's a lot of work, and I blame you entirely. She almost woke up then. Do you know the consequences of Miss Hobart waking up? Before the right time? Do you? If she should stop dreaming? Why, it's unthinkable. We'd all be out of a job. Including you, Mr Scribble . . .'

He looked up at me. 'Sir . . . are you crying . . .?'

I don't know what I was doing. Only that my back was killing me. I felt weak, and the room was swaying slightly.

'Here . . . can I . . .' Sniffing General was rising from his desk, clutching a paper tissue. I don't know what I looked like but the General stopped in his tracks before he even got close.

'My god . . . you've been cut . . . let me . . .'

'That's alright, General. I'd like to see the Cat, please.'

'Straight away, sir.'

I started to collapse.

But the office door was open now.

The Game Cat waiting there to greet me.

DAY
FOREVER

'And sometimes, just

sometimes . . . '

A LIFE OF
SURPRISES

The fool's card is pinned to the wall in front of me. The silver feather replaced in the Cat's cabinet.

There are one thousand things in this room, and I am just one of them; living amongst objects and gifts. Writing all this up on an antique word processor; some desperate swap for some desperate feather.

The Cat's over in his armchair, drinking his wine, working on next week's issue. He likes to write with pen and ink; the future with the past.

I'm forty-one now. I feel about twenty-five or so. Look it, too. Living in Vurt really slows down the rate of change. God knows how old the Game Cat is. He looks a youthful fifty.

Twenty years.

Twenty years gone by, since Mandy first stepped out of that all-night Vurt-U-Want. Do they still have those places? I don't keep up with life.

Real life. Sure, the Cat tells me stories now and again. How Des and Twinkle share a house somewhere. With the kid. That's right. Des was pregnant when she came out of the Yellow. About five hours pregnant. Game Cat claims that the kid is mine, spawned halfway between Vurt and real; when Desdemona was inside Cinders that time, and we were making love, unprotected, on a Catholic bed. I don't know if that's possible. I don't know what is, and what isn't possible. The Cat says that it's a first; impregnating one woman, whilst making love to another. He reckons that's not bad going for some guy who wasn't very good with women.

I don't know.

Das Uber dog is getting old by now, as dogmen will; he's very high up in the music industry, in partnership with Dingo Tush. Bridget doesn't seem to feature. The Cat can find no traces. She's out there, somewhere, waiting to happen. Cinders and Barnie have split. I don't know where the chef is. Cinders would be too old now for starring in porno feathers, so I don't get to see her. Maybe I should find out where she is, what she's doing. The Cat took me down a few times, through door number five. We'd spend a few hours just wandering around, unseen, underhanded, looking for stories. The Cat loves it. I don't know ... it didn't appeal somehow, all those candid shots, made me feel like a ghost.

Sometimes I ask the Sniffing General for a door access; a blue or a black. There's this new actress just coming up. Her feather name is Blush. She's twenty years old, very good at what she does, full of Vurt. Blush is a natural. She looks a lot like Desdemona, a little like me. She's going to be famous.

I don't know. I just don't know.

I go through door three sometimes, to the Pink world. Just to get rid of some feelings. So does the Game Cat. He visits the ones involving boys and sailors. Maybe I should've realised years ago. He doesn't bother me. Treats me like a brother.

Maybe he knows by now; I'll always be waiting.

I wonder sometimes why he keeps me here. Sure, I help out with the mag, writing reviews sometimes, copying his style. I suppose he's teaching me something.

What else?

No clues about Karli Dog. I like to think that she roamed the streets for years, running with the pack, and then died in action. That's a good story.

And sometimes, just sometimes . . .

I find myself riding some blue or black door, and this woman comes up to me, riding the same feather. She has the most beautiful eyes, and a dragon tattoo on her left upper arm. We play for a while, working the game together like experts, always winning, never losing. She's thirty-nine years old. I'm twenty-five. It doesn't happen that often. I suppose it must get to her, the widening gap of age.

Cat tells me that she's got a new man now, down on the real world. That's okay. I can handle that.

Her wounds have healed; so have mine.

I guess I always loved Desdemona more than she loved me. That's why her staying here would have been a betrayal, a betrayal of life.

What else?

The Crash Riders feather got made eventually. It was a hard Yellow, and the money comes in useful, kind of, just to bribe the General now and again, into letting me pass through doorways I shouldn't.

It was the Cat who persuaded me to write down these memories. I don't know what to call it yet. Certainly not Crash Drivers. I might just call it after my name, or after what I am. What I have become.

Maybe you're reading it now.

Or maybe you're playing the feather.

Or maybe you're in the feather, thinking that you're reading the novel, with no way of knowing . . .

No matter.
The game is over soon.
Just one more moment...
And then it's gone.

...a young boy takes a feather out of his mouth.

DATE			